THE FALL

Bethany Griffin

Indigo

First published in Great Britain in 2014
by Indigo
This paperback edition first published in Great Britain in 2015
by Indigo
an imprint of Hachette Children's Group
a division of Hodder and Stoughton Ltd
Carmelite House,
50 Victoria Embankment, London EC4Y 0DZ
An Hachette UK company

1 3 5 7 9 10 8 6 4 2

A catalogue record for this book is available
from the British Library.

ISBN 978 1 78062 138 8

Printed in Great Britain by
CPI Group (UK) Ltd, Croydon, CR0 4YY

www.orionchildrensbooks.co.uk
www.bethanygriffin.com

Also by Bethany Griffin

The Masque of the Red Death
The Dance of the Red Death

To Noel, who loves creepy things, and who is nine right now,
like Madeline at the beginning of this story

1
MADELINE IS EIGHTEEN

The first thing I notice is that my blanket is gone. The last of my nightly rituals is to pull it all the way to my chin, and it never falls away, no matter what nightmares I wrestle before I wake.

But something else is wrong; I try to move, and though I don't seem to be paralyzed, my arms are pinned tightly to my sides. My brain is slow; the horror saturates me gradually. I struggle, twist to the left, and free one arm.

Reaching up, my trembling hand gets only a few inches before my fingers touch cool stone. I blink. My lashes spider-touch my cheeks, and then that touch is gone, so my eyes must be open. The dull, compressed darkness is so absolute that I cannot see my shaking hand, even as I bend my elbow and press my fingers against my right eye, and then my left—gently, very gently—to make certain both still rest in their sockets.

My eyes are intact. But the relief dissipates as I recognize the shape of my prison, the feel of the thin padding beneath me, the slope of the cool stone. The plush lining . . .

This darkness is the darkness of a coffin.

Not any coffin. A stone sarcophagus. Perhaps even one I've been in before, years ago, on a dare.

I've been buried, but I'm not dead. I'm not dead. I can't breathe. What is that sound? Is someone here? No, it's me, crying and using precious air . . .

Tremors shake my entire body, but the box I'm in does not shift at all.

I must be in the vault, held in place by solid stone. Beneath the house. The dead of my family press around me. We're entombed by marble shot through with a vein of pink, a rare and costly stone, thick enough to keep the waters of the tarn from seeping down into the crypt.

Panic claws at me. But I cannot succumb to it; I cannot fall into one of my fits. Not now.

The house is heavy and filled with hate. I slow my breath and relax my arms. The lace at my sleeve is rough against my wrist, and suddenly I realize what I'm wearing. A dress that I hid deep in the recesses of my wardrobe, praying never to see it again. The lace at the neck is stiff and scratchy. Tight. When I move my hand, the pearl buttons at the sleeves press into the sensitive skin of my inner arm, likely to bruise. I should have burned the dress. I would have, had I known that I would be buried in it. Buried.

Claustrophobia sets in. The not-so-gentle cousin of madness.

One of my arms is still pinned tightly down. The freed one rests, trembling, on the silk of the dress, which I know is white, though I can't see it. No part of me is not touching the accursed fabric. Tears wet my cheeks. I cannot breathe. I cannot breathe.

I claw at the collar. The box is so tight that my elbow hits the side each time I move.

The lace catches my fingernails and one of them breaks, the pain bitter and sharp.

Blood, trickles down from my fingertips and I am choking on bits of the desiccated dress and the coarse dry velvet of the coffin's lining with every inhale. This small space is so very hot. I cough as velvet particles line my throat.

Only the ring on my finger remains cool. The ring I always wear, given to me by my brother, Roderick, as a token of his love.

It's very heavy.

My hair has been pinned tightly against my head.

My eyes burn. I check once again to make sure that they are intact.

I hear panting and know that the sound, animalistic, desperate, is coming from me.

Who chose this dress?

Who put my hair up?

Was it done lovingly?

I throw back my head and scream. Somewhere in the house above, there is one who hears me. The one who buried me alive.

2
MADELINE IS NINE

Wind and rain, lightning and thunder, a storm throws itself against the House of Usher, rattling every window, including mine. Thunder pounds the earth and the house groans.

Carefully, I carry out my bedtime rituals. Without them, I would never sleep.

I pad across my room to the heavy wooden door. Through the floor I can feel the house breathing. I position a thick book to keep the door from swinging more than half open.

My candle flickers. I must have the door positioned correctly before it goes out.

Taking two steps back, I survey the room. The half-open door still feels . . . wrong. I adjust it, nudging the book with my foot. It creaks, louder than a door should when

moved so slightly. I rest my hand against the wood—too long, because feelings seep into me that are not my own.

The house wants me to open the door. To put the book back on the bureau, to straighten the rug. The house hates closed doors.

But completely open doors are as terrifying as being closed in with . . . whatever might find its way into my room. There are things, living and dead, creeping through these halls, and I'd rather they ignore me while I sleep, as they do during the day. The house will protect me, but I feel safer with the book holding the door in place.

Lightning flashes as I turn, illuminating the empty corridor, and my path back to my four-poster bed. Outside, the trees are lashed by wind and rain. I blow out the candle and pull the quilt to my chin.

And now, I listen. The clock in the hallway ticks away the minutes. It will chime, either at midnight, or upon the hour of its choosing. A sound patters in the hallway. *Pat pat pitter pat,* coming closer, ever closer, stopping before my doorway, and then *pat pat pat* over the threshold and into my room.

I don't dare breathe. I lie as still as possible, straining my eyes against the darkness. A slight shape approaches, slinking through the gloom. A flash of lightning reveals the solemn face of my brother. His silver-white hair gleams as the unnatural green-white light fades.

Thunder crashes, and we both jump.

Roderick crawls up into my bed; he is shaking.

"The storm?" I whisper.

"Yes," he whispers back.

Roderick is afraid of nearly everything.

I put my arms around him, trying to stop his trembling, but instead it infects me, and we sit there propped up among the pillows, shuddering together.

"Roderick, it's only a storm," I whisper.

His eyes accuse me of lying. Nothing here is just anything. This is not just a house. We have never been simply children. We are Ushers.

The storm makes my hair crackle. Lightning flashes again, tingeing the entire world green. The house is so huge around us, and we are so small. But we're together.

"The house is unsettled," I tell him.

He doesn't want to hear about the house. It frightens him more than anything else, and he likes to pretend he's brave. He can't tell, the way I can, that the house is protecting us, from the storm, from the ghosts. From everything.

"Tell me a story," Roderick begs, snuggling down into my blankets.

I close my eyes. The stories are part of this place; they flutter around me like moths, dark and bloated, the size of my father's hand. Some are like visions, the events unfolding as they might in a dream. Some are tales that I have heard and remember, the ones that Father tells sometimes. Which will the house give me tonight?

"Once on a windy night." I try the words out, testing them to see if they feel right. A gust of wind makes my windowpane shake. Roderick edges even closer. His thin, birdlike bones jut into my side. He nestles into my pillow, nudging me over, even though he knows I like to be in the exact center of the bed.

"There was a beautiful maiden with golden hair who was lovely as the sunrise." He reaches out and touches my hair, which is not golden; it's silver-gilt, like his. "But the maiden walked outside in the dead of winter and caught cold and died. In the nearby forest lived a hermit, who was old and ugly and gnarled as the root of a tree. He wanted to capture the maiden's ghost, which was said to linger, pining for her lost love, the brave knight Ethelred, who slept every night by her tomb.

"While brave Ethelred was sleeping, the hermit crept up and cut off a lock of the knight's hair to use as bait and placed it in an urn made of clay mixed with blood, and set the urn out on the cold sand where the sea pounded the shore."

I stop to take a breath, and to listen. The wind is hitting the house in a rhythmic manner, much like the sea in the story. Somehow the story, though dreamlike, insubstantial, is more real than this cold, dark bedroom.

"For nearly a year the hermit sat, night after night, on the beach, in the cold, waiting. Finally, he saw the ghostly form of the maiden. When she came near the urn, there was a flash of light." Outside lightning strikes, illuminating my brother's narrow, huge-eyed face. His frail body no longer trembles, and his fascination warms me. We are both immersed in this story, at one with the house.

"The ghostly maiden curled up like a wisp of smoke around the lock of hair. The hermit slammed the lid on the urn and took her to his hovel.

"Brave Ethelred came to the hermit's home and beat upon the door."

We hear a rapping sound, and Roderick shoots up in bed. His eyes are wild.

"The wind must have blown a shutter loose, and it is hitting the side of the house." I take his hand. He sinks slowly back down beside me.

"What happened next, Madeline?" he asks.

"The hermit would not let Ethelred in, so he lifted his mace and hit the door, and then stuck his gauntleted hand in through the hole and began to rip and tear all asunder, so that the noise echoed through the forest."

I pause, listening for the ripping of wood. Instead Roderick throws back his head, and he screams until I fear his throat will be torn apart.

I wrap my arms around him.

"Be still, Roderick, be still," I beg, but he keeps screaming. Desperate to calm him, I press the blankets up against his face to try to stifle his voice.

Our mother glides into the room. Her hair is long, pure white against her nightdress. She shines in the lightning as Roderick did, and is more graceful than even a ghost. I can't take my eyes from her.

When she reaches my bed, she slaps me hard enough that my head hits the headboard.

My eyes burn, but I don't say anything as she scoops my brother into her arms and carries him away. The house whispers to me, louder in my ears than the storm outside.

I lie in the center of my bed, listening to the crash of thunder, and to the splintering of wood, which comforts me. The house is caught up in the story too.

3
MADELINE IS FIFTEEN

On the lower level of the great Usher library, which spans three glorious tiers of disintegrating books, is a glass case holding a butterfly collection compiled years ago by my mother and her sisters. I often find myself here, drawn by the library but bewildered by my inability to unlock the knowledge in the books.

The butterflies are distorted by the rounded glass. I stand before the case, my fingers dislodging years' worth of dust, just looking, wondering. I was like these specimens, trapped by my mother's cruelty. Is there a pin through my middle? What words would be on the parchment identifying me?

A pocket watch rests heavy in my hand, hidden in the pocket of my dress. I toy with it, even as I stand transfixed by the brittle dead insects.

The words on the identifying parchment slips are in Latin. Could I learn to read them? Everything I try to read slithers about on the page, and I cannot make even the simplest words stay in place. A dead language may be easier for me to decipher.

But even staring too long at the labels makes me dizzy.

I steady myself on a table, knocking a sheaf of blank paper to the floor. Left behind, as though waiting for me, is a page filled with cramped handwriting and blurred ink, followed by other pages. A journal.

Like so many books in this house, the bindings have nearly crumbled away.

A crash from inside the butterfly case makes me jump . . . and then another crash. The velvet-covered boards that hold the preserved insects are collapsing inwards. Gossamer wings disintegrate before my eyes, and the library blurs around me for a moment.

I should go to my bedroom. In case of a fit, I'd rather not fall and hit my head on one of these tables.

The thought is not fully my own. So . . . the house wants me back in my room. As a child, I would have thought it was protecting me. I collapse into a leather armchair and lift the journal gingerly.

I do not want to die, but I must be very clever in order to survive. The answers are in the library. My guardian and I are sure of it.

I start as the watch in my pocket begins to tick.

Sometimes I twist the pin round and round while I'm thinking. A nervous habit. For a moment, everything seems clearer. I look back to the page.

The answers are in the library.

What answers? What is the house hiding?

4
FROM THE DIARY OF LISBETH USHER

My name is Lisbeth Usher. I am cursed by beauty, the delicate beauty of a dewdrop, which lasts for but a few moments. Three days ago I could leave the house without fear. Three days ago, I had a future.

Then my sister, Honoria, put on her best dress, the one she was supposed to wear on her wedding day, and went up to the widow's walk. No one was with her when she jumped. But I suspect that she did it solemnly. Honoria did everything solemnly. She rarely smiled. Now that the curse has passed to me, I understand why.

I will not succumb. I will not. Unlike Honoria, who passed the curse to me, I will protect our youngest sister. I will not die. The house has claimed my mother and my sister. But I will prevail. In the end I will laugh at all of them, wringing their hands and wailing about being consumed by the House of Usher.

5
MADELINE IS NINE

Placing one hand in front of the other, Roderick and I crawl forward through the accumulated dust of the library. Roderick points to a table, and I head toward it. In our carelessness, we overturn a stack of books. Roderick smears the dust on the leather cover and peers at the gold writing. I hold out my hands, and he gives it to me, but as I open it, the pages disintegrate and fall to the floor. I shrug; there are plenty of empty corners to investigate, and books that are in better condition than this one.

A chest sits halfway across the room, a thing of carved dark wood. I gesture toward it. Roderick grins.

The seeking game is our favorite game. We crouch under tables and lurk in dark corners, always together, always searching. We are intent on going through each room of the house, learning their shapes, textures, temperatures.

Tasting the melancholia of each space.

They are very important to me, these little explorations. The house is so huge, and sometimes the rooms seem changed when we enter them. If we don't explore, we could someday wander into a corridor we've never seen before, and we might not find our way back out. I'm more worried for Roderick than for myself. He doesn't pay attention.

The floor creaks outside the door, and we scurry under a table. A pair of soft velveteen house shoes, the hem of a dressing gown sweep by. Father. I sit, unable to hold my crouching position, as he pulls the heavy draperies shut. That means Mother will be joining him. I tell myself not to be afraid, but it is Mother, so of course I am.

Father sits at the table, right above us. Roderick puts a hand over his mouth, stifling a laugh. But I frown at him. I don't want to make Father angry. A servant brings him tea.

So this dismal room is in use. So few of the rooms are. Most are haunted rather than lived in.

And then Mother comes and settles herself on the faded blue fainting couch. She covers her eyes with a dark velvet cloth. Roderick makes his frightened sound, and I reach for his hand. Even Roderick, her beloved, cowers in fear when our mother has one of her spells.

There is a curse upon our family. We are cursed. My parents are ill and often in pain.

"Perhaps we shouldn't separate them," Father says. His tone tells me that he's resuming an ongoing conversation. "They are twins."

Roderick scoots away from me, toward the door. He's ready to run. If we go now, we probably won't even get in trouble, but I have to hear. What is Father talking about?

"Nonsense," Mother answers. "They have the rest of their lives to be together. Sending him away may delay the illness."

"You truly believe this?"

"The doctors have assured me."

Mother always believes the doctors. They live in our tower. Father says that they descended upon our family like white-coated vultures, hungry for bits and pieces of our ancient family. The local doctor won't visit the house; he says it is too far from the village and the main road. More likely he doesn't know what to do for us and is afraid of the house. Many of the locals are. With Mother so sick, we need a doctor here all the time, as much as we need a cook or a butler, or the flock of maids who dust the cabinetry. So we have Dr. Paul and Dr. Peridue.

"We have to give him the best possible chance of survival," Mother says. "To do anything less would be murder." Her voice rises, and Roderick pales.

Father's fingers tap against the table. It's a habit of his. He must be trying to write. The table above our heads wobbles. His hand is shaking, and that always agitates him. He throws down the quill, or perhaps knocks it off the table. It lands on the floor beside us. If he retrieves it, will he discover us? The feather is long and glossy and black. The ink soaks into the floor.

If Mother is getting one of her spells, soon she will be able to sense our breathing. Her hearing is exquisite. If you drop a pin, she screams with pain; her agony is also exquisite. It's fortunate that she has not sensed us yet.

"Perhaps you should go far away and take them both," Father says. "You say often enough that you wish you had never come here."

"Sending Roderick will be enough. There is something poisonous here, something that infects the children, turns them to monsters." Mother says these things all the time. It's because she's ill. Still, Father seems offended.

"I was a child in this house," Father says. "My sister and I were children here."

"I know. And so was I."

Silence. Father shuffles his papers, as though his tremors might stop and he might be able to actually write.

I grip Roderick's hand. They cannot take him away from me. We are inseparable. Without Roderick, I will be alone with Mother and her cruelty. Father? He has no time for us. Even when he is conscious, he is distracted. And so often he is insensible from his illness. I will be completely alone. The curtains rustle, and the floor creaks.

A scrap of paper drifts down. I pick it up and strain to see the writing through the gloom. Roderick peers over my shoulder.

I love you.

Was this what Father was writing? Does he know we are here? I touch the brownish ink. A bit flakes away from the intricate L. Too old to be freshly written. So who wrote it? Where did it come from? I peer beneath the tablecloth. Mother is staring toward Father.

"And will Roderick ever really return to Madeline?" Father asks.

She doesn't answer.

My chest is tight and tears run down, smearing the grime on my face. My hands press against the floor, which goes from warm to icy. Rage overwhelms me, followed by grief. I'm not sure which emotions are my own.

Roderick takes the scrap of paper from me. Is it . . . could it be a message from the house? He slides it between the pages of a disintegrating book. And then, very quietly, we slip out of the room. Our parents are too absorbed in their own pursuits to notice, or to call out to us if they do.

6
From the Diary of Lisbeth Usher

Things that confuse the house:

Music, particularly drums, repetitive music. Waltzing.

The tide.

Saying a poem repeatedly.

Patterns in paintings and wallpaper.

The ticking of a clock.

All of these can distract the house from what is happening within the walls. Be warned. They also make it querulous; pictures are likely to fall from the walls when it regains its awareness.

Or worse. Deaths. When angered, the house becomes more dangerous than ever. Unfocused. It might even strike out at an Usher.

7
MADELINE IS NINE

"Don't be frightened, Madeline," Roderick says.

We stand in front of a small wooden door that he discovered behind a wall hanging on the first floor. He pushes it open, and we look into the depths. Three stairs lead down to an indistinct darkness. The roof appears to be hard-packed dirt, tunneled directly into the earth.

"I want to see where it goes," he says. "I think it might lead to the crypt."

Our parents have forbidden us ever to go beneath the house. Because of the crypt. It is a sacred place, and dangerous.

I eye Roderick. Usually he is much more timid than this. Something is pushing him to be brave. It's easy to see how proud he is of this discovery. A hundred times we have walked past this door. Something of significance

must be behind it. Except, in this house, the secrets hide behind secrets, and tight places like this hole in the earth make my stomach clench with fear.

Roderick lifts the torch that he took from an alcove in a twisty corridor on the second floor.

"Do you know how to light this?"

When I touch it, my fingers come away slick with animal fat. We are not allowed to handle torches, so this is one more uncharacteristic act of rebellion.

The tunnel terrifies me, but Roderick is begging me with his eyes.

"I love you best of anyone, Madeline."

When he says this, he knows that I will do anything for him.

"Let's get this over with," I say. I am three minutes older than Roderick. Being older means I must be braver.

His smile is full of delight.

Squaring my shoulders, I take my beeswax candle and hold the tiny flame to the end of his torch. It bursts into fire, and we both jump back. My cheek feels tender, nearly scorched.

"Shall I hold it?" I ask.

"I'll keep it." He points down into the tunnel. "You go first."

He may be acting brave, but he's still scared of the dark. And he's sending me into the pit first with no light, and no guess as to what could be waiting below.

"Leave the door open." I sit and edge downward an inch or two. Looking up, the torch makes his face golden and his cheekbones frighteningly high. "I mean it, Roderick. I don't care if the servants come along and see what we're doing. I don't want to be closed in."

"I won't close the door."

I scoot a bit farther. The earth is slightly moist. I pat it with my hand. It feels unhealthy, as if the meanest plant wouldn't grow in this soil, even with sunlight.

Bits of earth rain down on me as Roderick wriggles back and forth above me. And then, with a sense of horror that is neither brave nor heroic, I hear the angry creak as the door slams.

8
MADELINE IS FIFTEEN

Moonlight shines blue through the window, bathing the parlor in clean, bright light. Roderick is home from school for four nights.

He strums a mandolin. He calls it a guitar, but I am sure it is a mandolin. It belonged to Father, and when he felt well enough, sometimes he sang lullabies to us while playing it. Or perhaps that was part of a story that I imagined. Father was kind, yet so often distracted—in pain.

The only sound is Roderick's intermittent strumming and the wind outside, but we don't need to speak to understand each other. We sit, comfortable, warm, complete.

We are alone. The servants have retired; they are afraid of the corridors and the corners of the house on nights when the moon is full and the wind is blowing the last leaves from the dead branches of the white trees that surround the house. At my feet, Cassandra snorts and watches us with her wise dog eyes.

The wind blows, and through the window I watch a decaying tree crash to the ground.

"It's good to be home," Roderick says, and I am overwhelmed with happiness. For once I'm not alone. We are together and content.

But the pleasure is not completely mine. The house wants him here. Wants him to stay, though I know that he won't.

The room goes even darker. I can barely make out the shape of my hand or of Roderick's. Only the silver arcs of his fingernails, glowing slightly.

"Madeline . . ."

Dark foreboding washes over me. My heart misses a beat. Roderick is here, but his time with me is so short.

I turn to face him. There are so many things that I must tell him. But my movement distracts him from whatever he was about to say, and he leaps to his feet, stalking across the room.

"Candles," he says. "There's no point in sitting in darkness."

He won't look at me now, and I can't look away from him. Cassandra rolls over and whines. I ignore her, captivated by Roderick's energy, and his willful ignorance. Since he's been away, I can see, it's become easier to pretend the things that frighten him aren't real. He'll never admit that at this moment, like the boy he used to be, he's afraid of the dark.

He lights one candle after another, lining them up across the table until the darkness is nothing more than a memory, and we are encapsulated in this room, where candle flame gleams in dark wood, and his hair glows silver-blond, the exact same shade as my own.

He takes paper from my desk, the same paper, embossed with a U for Usher, that I use when writing to him, nearly every week since he's been gone away to school.

He takes my ink and my quill without asking. He never needs to ask, but I know what he's doing. He's reminding himself of the wide world away from the House of Usher, and that he'll be returning to that world soon.

"I must write a letter," he says.

I shiver. My mood mirrors the mood of the house, and I am afraid to touch the woodwork, just inches from my head, afraid of the iciness that will meet my fingertips. Roderick, as always, is unaware. I am careful, very careful, about what I do, where I go, even what I think. But Roderick ignores our danger. If my love for my twin brother was selfless, I would prefer it when he's gone; he is safer then. But when he goes, the loneliness is overwhelming. He knows what I'm feeling. He's more sensitive to my emotions than to the undercurrents from the house.

"My friend," he says gently, "will be expecting to hear from me."

"You go back to school at the end of the week," I remind him. Cassandra hears the pain in my voice and thumps her tail. Roderick doesn't notice. He's engrossed in his letter.

The doctors will want to examine us tomorrow. They are always excited when they can see us together.

Roderick stares out the window, weighing the words before he writes them. Hunched over the desk, he's far away from me. Above his head, ghosts shimmer. As always, they remind me of bits of mist, silent. The dusty remnants of an old house.

School draws him away from the house, back into the world. There is a way to get him to stay. To make him forget the outside world.

Horror overwhelms me. This thought is not my own.

Curled on the settee, I struggle to ignore the house's urgings and rediscover my contentment from earlier.

9
MADELINE IS NINE

The secret tunnel door is firmly closed.

"I asked you to leave the door open!" My voice quivers, and I despise myself for showing my fear.

At least we have the torch. Though I am farther down the tunnel than Roderick, I can feel the warmth of it, and I can still see the flickering above me.

"I didn't close it," he insists. I believe him. "And Madeline? It won't open."

I crawl up next to him, and we both push with all our strength. It doesn't budge. I sigh. "We have to follow the tunnel."

It is what the house wants. And despite my horror of closed-in places, I am curious. Who . . . or what . . . scratched this passage out of the hard-packed earth and stone? Father had warned us about dangers in the cellars

and cavernous places under the house. On Roderick's dare, I tried to steal the keys once, when Father was in bed with one of his fits, but he caught me before I reached the door of his bedchamber. It was the only time Father ever screamed at me. But this time the house is obviously watching, and it won't let us come to harm.

As we creep along, the earthen ceiling presses down so that I have to lie on my back, twisting my body back and forth.

Roderick's shoe touches my face.

"Slow down," I warn him. My skirts bunch up around me, slowing my progress.

The air is very still. My hands are dusted with particles of dry earth, and I imagine they are clogging my throat. I choke.

Pebbles rain down on me.

"Sorry," Roderick calls. "I was trying to get a hand-hold, to keep from slipping down on your head. The dirt is crumbly."

This tunnel could cave in on us at any moment.

If Roderick and I are buried beneath the house, at least our parents won't be able to send him to school. That's probably why he's being so brave, pretending not to be afraid of the only place he's ever known, because he's about to be sent to a new place.

I twist, dislodging my skirts, and scoot forward. Within

a few feet, the tunnel opens to empty space. I fall, landing on my feet with a painful thud.

"Roderick," I call to warn him, but he's already sliding down, so I dive to the side. Not fast enough. He mostly lands on top of me. At least he holds up the torch with both hands, protecting us and our only source of light.

As it is, the light from the torch barely dissipates the murkiness of this space. Roderick walks around the perimeter of the room, running his hands over the walls. I stand in the same place where I fell and watch him. The walls here are made of overlapping metal plates, and in the center of the room is a large, square stone.

As Roderick moves, the torchlight shifts, illuminating the openings of other tunnels, all around us. For a second I see red eyes staring in, but when I blink, they are gone.

"Roderick?" I move closer to him, and to the light.

"The air feels different in this spot." The oppressive atmosphere of the chamber makes his voice thin and reedy. "I see a door."

Roderick holds up the torch, examining an iron door set in the stone wall. When he pushes, it screeches forward a few inches. He turns sideways to slide through, and I do the same.

Now we are truly in the vault—where dead Ushers are observed, and then put to rest, deep under the house. Entombed in solid stone.

I put out my hand to touch a stone sarcophagus, but my fingers are covered with greenish dirt. I pull back, hiding my hand in my skirts—as if there is anyone here to care about touching sacred objects with filthy hands.

"I dare you to get in one," Roderick whispers.

All day, he has had more bravado than me. Being the brave twin is my only claim to any sort of importance in this house, where Mother loves Roderick best and Father spends most of his waking hours wandering through the rooms staring at nothing, ignoring us both.

"That one." Roderick points at a grim-looking box that sits up on a trestle. Made of some sort of ceramic, the surface is cool to touch. Before I can lose my nerve, I take a deep breath and climb in. Sliding my legs beneath the half-open lid is the hardest part, until I feel the pillow touch my hair. The entire coffin is lined with velvet, and a moldy scent rises around me.

Ignoring the smell, I soak in the horror of lying in a coffin. Roderick steps back, and the darkness startles me. But I savor the power. If I can be strong enough to control my fear, then I can do anything.

"Let me try, Madeline." He wants to have strength too, and how can I blame him? Fear is a hateful thing.

I climb out and take the torch.

"Look." Roderick lets out a little laugh. "I'm dead. I'm a dead Usher, lying in my coffin." He folds his hands over

his chest and lies back. Seeing him in that position terrifies me in a way that lying in the coffin myself did not.

"Shut the lid," he commands. I shake my head. We are good at sensing each other's feelings, so he will know how much the thought scares me. But he looks at me with his liquid eyes, smiling, proving that he is far from dead. The lid makes a loud grating sound as I slide it forward and he disappears.

"Madeline?" He calls out almost instantly, his voice muffled. "That's enough, let me out." And I feel his fear.

I grip the lid with my free hand, but it won't budge.

10
MADELINE IS FIFTEEN

My feet make no sound as I slip from my bedroom into the corridor. Cassandra follows. I thought I heard Roderick in the corridor, but he is very obviously in his room. Even from here, I can hear the sounds of his breathing. Roderick's door isn't fully closed. Though he ignores the power of the house, he knows instinctively not to be trapped inside any of the rooms. I brush my hand against his door as I pass, pulling away quickly so the house can't urge me to go in.

The moon shines through the window at the end of the hallway, nebulous and green. Forgetting to be watchful, forgetting fear, I approach it. The windows here at the front of the house overlook the roiling waters of the tarn. I lean on the ledge below the arched window.

A black curtain billows into my face. Silk slides against

steel as the curtain unravels from the rod, pushing me to the thick carpet that muffled my footsteps moments ago. The cloth molds to my face, pressing into my mouth as I gasp, trying to draw enough air to scream. I tear at the fabric, but it wraps around my hands until they too are caught up in it.

I can't move, I can't breathe.

A growl reverberates through the hallway, and the cloth pulls away from my face. Cassandra's paws are pressed against my rib cage, and she's tearing the curtain away with her teeth. She's saved me. From the house.

The house knows that I was prepared to confide my fears, my discoveries, to Roderick. That I'm no longer eager to please it, that I know its true nature. That I'm learning more every day.

I sob, wiping my mouth with my sleeve. I spit the last bits of fabric onto the floor. Unconcerned, my dog licks my chin. Laughing, cruel faces of my ancestors watch us from the dismal works of art that line the wall.

Cursed Ushers. Did they manage to keep the house happy? Or did they live their lives in fear? The house rewards cruelty. It loves darkness and despair and death.

And I am its favorite.

Shuddering, I put my hands over my face. The house is angry. Roderick tends to provoke it, with his disbelief, his constant departures. But this attack was directed at me.

Was it yet another warning, or was Roderick supposed to rush out of his room and save me? Would that have happened if I had managed to scream? And what would have happened then?

He is here for three more nights. Only three nights. Somehow, I must keep both of us safe.

I put my arms around Cassandra and let her pull me back to the safety of my bedchamber.

11
MADELINE IS NINE

Roderick screams from inside the coffin. "Madeline, Madeline, Madeline!"

Terrified, I prop the torch on a pile of stones and rush back to the sarcophagus, to Roderick's muffled panic. Using both hands, I try to pull the lid back, but it still won't move.

"Madeline!" He calls my name again and again. Tears blur my vision, making it even harder to see in the murk of the crypt. I reposition myself and heave with all my strength, but nothing happens. Desperately, I run my hands over the lid, trying to find a latch or a handle.

"I'm going to get you out," I promise. "I'll save you."

The torch sputters.

The ceiling creaks.

I try not to let Roderick's fear overwhelm me. The

house led us here. Surely it won't let us die here.

Behind me, the iron gate slides open with a loud grating sound. I grab the torch and spin. Father stands on the threshold. His hair is wild and his eyes unfocused. Maniacal. Is he in the middle of one of his fits?

"Father?" My voice wavers.

He is holding his own torch, which he hands to me, and then he leans over the sarcophagus.

"Roderick is inside?" It isn't really a question. If he can hear anything, he can hear Roderick screaming, but I answer anyway.

"Yes. Please get him out, please."

"There's a latch on the side." Father is feeling the stone, searching with his delicate musician's fingers. "I know it's here." He finds it. The lid makes a terrible sound as it slides back.

Roderick throws himself forward, eyes wide and frightened. I lean in to embrace him and help him out, but I have a torch in each hand. So I have to watch as Father pulls Roderick into his arms and attempts to soothe him. Jealousy twists inside me. I should have been the one to save Roderick. But then I hear the house murmuring. It knows that I was brave. That I am stronger than Roderick. The house loves me.

12
Madeline Is Fifteen

Seated in an armchair before a brick fireplace, in the tower occupied by the doctors, I ignore the fire crackling behind me, except to vaguely appreciate the warmth.

Roderick fumbles with the buttons on his white shirt. Our eyes meet, and he freezes, his fingers on the last shiny button. I drop my gaze to my lap, and after a noticeable pause, his shirt falls to the floor. He's teasing the doctors. He'll let them examine him, but he won't act as if any of this is more than a silly joke designed to waste his time.

"Good, good," Dr. Peridue says, writing something in his ledger. Father invited him first, years ago, to study, and perhaps cure, Mother's illness. Dr. Paul came later, repeating Peridue's original promises, but then Father got sick. Neither of them could be saved, despite the doctor's assurances.

Dr. Peridue appealed to Father's pride in the Usher

lineage, saying how he wanted to study us, to learn all he can about our ancient aristocratic diseases. But the doctors stayed because of Mother's desperation for some way to escape the curse.

"Your father was extremely healthy in his youth," Dr. Paul remarks.

With sudden vividness I remember Father convulsing on the floor, foaming at the mouth, when Roderick and I were very young.

"Perhaps you will be lucky, like your father," he tells Roderick, then the doctors' eyes shift over to me. Not so lucky. Not so healthy.

Roderick puts out his arm, and both doctors hover, preparing the silver needle, greedy for his blood. He is not usually so compliant; there are shadows under his eyes.

"Didn't you sleep well?" My voice startles everyone, even me.

"No," he says. "I dreamed unsavory dreams. I dreamed of suffocation."

Dr. Paul hands Roderick his shirt. "No reason to fear suffocation. Your lungs are as healthy as the rest of you."

So far, Roderick's mind seems unaffected too. At least most of the time. Mother was right, all those years ago. Sending Roderick away has staved off the illness.

"Let's walk outside," Roderick says, ignoring the doctors. "I'm chilled."

I doubt it will be warmer outside, but maybe we can stroll far enough away that the house can't hear us. Maybe . . .

"I want to see your garden," Roderick says. "It's the only thing, besides you, that I really miss when I'm away."

We slip through the dark corridors and out a side door.

"Hold still, Madeline," Roderick says. "What are these?" He's brushed some dark fibers out of my hair. From the curtains.

I sweep them away. Hoping he can't read me right now. If I tell him what happened, he'll assume I had a fit. He'll think I'm a danger to myself and shouldn't be allowed to carry candles through the hallway. He refuses to see the real danger.

"Oh, look." I step forward. Before us is a gnarled elm tree holding a swing, placed here for some long-ago Usher child. It's dangled bravely there for years and years.

"I always hated this thing," Roderick says.

I turn toward him, surprised.

"I could never swing high enough. Not like you."

Arranging my skirts, I sit on the twisted wooden seat.

"Father showed me how to swing. He used to push us, remember?"

"Yes, but you'd lose yourself, entranced in one of your stories. Smiling to yourself, though nothing I could see was amusing. . . ."

I start to laugh, but he stops me.

"You were still as a statue, and yet you went higher than me. As if someone I couldn't see was pushing you. It scared me, Madeline."

A shivery feeling travels from my carefully laced boots all the way up the back of my neck. I do remember swinging and laughing with the joy of it. Wasn't it Father who used to push me? It was so long ago. . . . Cassandra nudges a fallen tree curiously. I stand. I will not swing today, even though I love the way the wind tussles my hair.

Roderick laughs, giving the swing a disdainful nudge. "I had quite an imagination, didn't I? Always afraid."

As we walk away, the swing glides through the air, much higher than should have been possible with his push.

I do not point it out to Roderick.

He's horrified by this place, by the things he cannot explain.

And yet he leaves me here.

At this thought, he turns, his eyes wide and surprised. He's sensed my resentment, through the bond we share, but he won't acknowledge it. He can't, not when he's already thinking of leaving. He pretends he can't hear my thoughts, feel my feelings.

I push the hurt away. I am the one the house speaks to, the one the house flirted with, the one the house won't let go. Father once told me that the house needs me most of all, and this pleased me. I was happy to be loved. Father was hunched over, we were pressed in the alcove by the grandfather clock, and he whispered, forcing out the words. He meant for me to be terrified; his fingers, when he brushed my hair from my eyes, were clammy with sweat. Foolishly, I was not afraid.

No matter how hard I try, I can't recall his exact words. Just the intensity of his gaze. The house wants Roderick, but it wants me more. Most of all, it wants us here, together.

The garden wall is crumbling.

For the first time in my life I don't just *want* to go with Roderick; I think I have to get away.

Roderick paces back and forth. He reaches up to touch the leaves that cling to decaying branches. One of them falls to the ground. It might have dangled there, suspended between life and death, for longer than we've been alive.

Roderick is in a strange mood. This is not the time to tell him about my growing fears. He will return soon. Our birthday is only a few weeks away, in March, that odd time between true winter and the green burst of spring. I will read further, learn the secrets of the house. Find proof, so that he doesn't think I'm being silly and superstitious. If that doesn't work, I will try to be logical, try to convince him that even if he does not believe the house is watching us, that things here are amiss.

Roderick laughs as the wind blows old autumn leaves down from the overhanging eaves of the house, and they scatter about us like dismal confetti.

13
MADELINE IS NINE

Mother plaits my hair into two long, shining braids. Roderick is gone—the coach took him two weeks ago— but I am living with my loneliness.

"I want to walk in the garden," I tell her. One of her black curtains has been swept aside, and the sun is shining through the window.

"You shouldn't speak of such things," she says in a low voice, pulling my hair.

I shrink away from her voice and her hands. I don't ask why. Either she will tell me, or she won't. Asking won't have any effect. She stops braiding and stares toward the window, lost someplace between memory and madness.

"You will make the house jealous," she hisses. "With your silly talk of sunshine and gardens."

The house shouldn't be jealous. I love it and will always

return to it. She ties my left braid with a ribbon to match my rose-colored dress. We are reflected in her mirror, mother and daughter, so very alike.

I shiver.

A vase of delicate white lilies stands beside her bed. A gift from Father, they certainly did not come from our grounds. But I know I can find flowers of my own in the overgrowth of weeds that surrounds the house.

"I'm going to walk in the garden." I sound defiant, and I like that.

Mother pushes me away. "Your voice makes my head throb. Go somewhere else to play." She puts her hand up to her forehead and closes her eyes. She is so beautiful I can't help admiring her, hoping that she will love me someday.

"Close the curtains before you go."

I jump to obey, smoothing the fabric over the window, and then tiptoe out of the darkened room, still determined to spend this glorious autumn morning outside.

Skipping down the hallway, I enjoy the sound of my shoes against the wood floor. When I get outside, the wind will be ruffling the dead leaves, and I will hunt for flowers. I step down the dark stairway.

Thud.

A heavy battle-ax is buried in the wall beside me. My cheek stings where it grazed my face. I twist to face the

suit of armor at the top of the stairs. Its gauntleted hand opens and closes, empty.

If I had taken one more step, if I had skipped any faster, the steel blade would be buried in my head instead of paneling. Ghosts rush up and down the hall, so dense that for a moment I cannot see.

I press my hands against the wall. It is cold to the touch, as chilly as the floor of my bedroom in January. Cold means anger. The house *is* jealous. Without meaning to, I put my hand to my cheek.

I imagine that I am a statue, concentrating on my breathing. I blink over and over, holding back tears. My fingers come away from my cheek stained with blood. The house hurt me. My legs give out, and I collapse to the floor in a heap of skirts and anxiety.

The planks of the floor grow unnaturally warm. I place my hands in my lap. I should have listened to Mother. The house was not trying to hurt me. No. It's so big, it lacks finesse. It wants me to stay close, so it can protect me. I sit completely still, showing the house that I do not plan to leave it, not now, not ever. The blade of the ax quivers back and forth. I do not move. I sit, watching the axe. Letting the house know that I trust it.

14
From the Journal of Lisbeth Usher

My young sister is in the garden, swinging on the garden swing. I will be strong. If I let this curse have the best of me, then it will fall to her. When I have my fits, she kisses my forehead. I don't tell her that even the touch of her lips is horrifying to me, everything is horrifying. I just close my eyes and wish the days of my life away.

Hyperesthetic fits. I fall, as if dead, in a trance, though I'm unbearably aware of everything that happens around me. My hearing becomes sharper. Light burns my eyes. The touch of a blanket is torture.

When the fits last more than a few hours, I lose consciousness. It's a mercy to be freed from the agony.

But coming out of the fit is an agony on its own. Slow, and ponderous. First my awareness returns. Then, perhaps, I might be able to move one finger. Eventually my hand can curl into a fist, and I might be able to bend my elbow, with intense concentration.

Sometimes when I wake, I'm filled with rage and hate that I do not believe is my own. In stories, curses aren't like this. Princes are turned into frogs or beasts. Princesses are trapped in towers.

The princess is never the monster.

I worry about what I am becoming. In a fit, I can't protect my sister. It's just the two of us now. Our guardian, Mr. Usher, has gone to town for a few days. He isn't really a part of our family. He doesn't love us. It is up to me to make sure that we love each other. Otherwise she may grow strange, and starved for love, here in this dreadful old house.

15
MADELINE IS TEN

It is evening, and I sit alone before the chess set, the one with little knights in armor that clank when you move them. I'm under the table in one of the parlors, because this is where Roderick and I last played. Being here makes me feel close to him.

There is no one to play chess with me. The ghosts don't know how. They can't concentrate long enough to care.

Father drifts into the room. He is wearing shoes and trousers. It's been weeks since I've seen him in anything besides his silk dressing gown and velvet slippers.

And he isn't shuffling. Sometimes he drags his left leg just a little, a memory of some old injury, he says. From under the table, with the threadbare tablecloth partially in the way, he looks to be putting one foot in front of the other masterfully, a man with a goal.

"Madeline," he says. I peer up at him through the table-cloth. He puts out his hand, beckoning to me.

I push the game board aside, careful that the pieces remain upright, and crawl out. I brush the cobwebs off my dress, like Mother always tells me to do, and take the hand that he offers. Holding his hand feels safe.

We walk through the hall with portraits of silvery-haired men and women, all wearing black dresses, all so starkly young. Some of the portraits are completely obscured by cobwebs, layers and layers of heavy white curtains. But I know what's there. Ushers.

Ushers who married Ushers and had baby Ushers. The corridor's paneling is rotting, and in some places it has fallen completely away, revealing cracks like arteries in the stone.

"The house is grand," Father says in the singsong voice he uses for lullabies and nursery rhymes. "No one else has a house quite like it."

Following him, I consider the carved woodwork and the portraits through his eyes and try to appreciate their beauty. A feeling of safety flows into me when I put my free hand on the balustrade. Father is flattering the house, and it is pleased.

Father squeezes my hand. I smile up at him, and he smiles back. Like the men in the portraits, he is handsome.

At the top of the last set of stairs, we come to a place

where Father can touch the ceiling. This is not unusual. In this house some doors lead to walls, and half staircases go nowhere. These stairs lead directly to a dark tiled ceiling. Father releases my hand and pushes. Through the trapdoor, more stairs lead up onto one of the roofs.

Oddly, there is no wind. The night is so clear and still that it makes me want to weep. There is a walkway, and a railing that comes to my waist. It seems a very low railing.

"It's a widow's walk," Father says.

"What is a widow's walk?" I ask.

"A place where women used to come and pace and look out to sea."

"But we aren't near the sea."

"No. Not now," he says. "It's been a long time. Too bad—the smell of the sea would cover the stench of the tarn, wouldn't it? This house has been away from the sea for far too long."

I don't know what he means, so I don't say anything.

"You miss your brother."

The loneliness is like a cloak that covers me from head to toe. Madeline the lonely, Madeline alone. I know they will not bring Roderick home. Mother won that battle, and there is no going back. Roderick spends his nights cowering in his bed and crying into his pillow, but still they will not bring him home.

"You miss your brother," Father repeats in exactly the

51

same way, as if he doesn't remember saying it the first time.

His eyes have gone wild, and I pray he doesn't have one of his fits here on the roof. If he does, I don't know how I would keep him from falling over the railing.

"You must promise me something, Madeline."

"What?" I touch the skirt of my dress, where the lace has deteriorated. Something about a hole in lace asks to be touched and expanded. Like a half-healed wound.

"Promise that you will never think of jumping."

We have come to the end of the walkway. When I lean forward, I can see flagstones in the courtyard, far below. To fall from here, or to jump, would mean certain death. My body feels heavy. It would be easy to fall. The world wavers. I cannot tell whether it is from my distress, or if the atmosphere has thickened since we've been standing here.

"I would never jump."

"You say that now, but you don't understand." He stares over the edge, seeing something that I can't.

But I do understand. I'm his daughter, an Usher. And I am completely alone, even here with him. Still, I do not want to die. Not today.

"This is a good place to go for a little cleansing air," he says. And we stand, looking out over the decaying trees of the old forest, where clumps of moss hang from white trunks that lean insanely against one another, twisted, rotting, but still attempting to grow.

I look past the allure of the flagstones, across the hills and valleys of the roof, past a place where the black slate tiles meet and overlap. To the left is the forest, the trees ravaged, scorched by lightning, white as ghosts.

They will not bring Roderick home, but I have another request, since Father is considering me with compassion. It's such a small thing.

"A stray cat had kittens in one of the outbuildings," I say quickly. It wouldn't replace Roderick, but it might alleviate some of the loneliness at night.

Father turns his wild eyes on me. "Madeline, you must never bring a pet into this house." He is holding the rail so tightly that his knuckles have gone from their normal pallid white to the purple of fresh bruises. "Do you hear me?"

I nod, and he struggles to control his agitation.

"Mother said that I should be strong."

"Before you and Roderick were born, I gave your mother a puppy. It adored her, but she didn't reciprocate. The puppy disappeared. There are some things, Madeline, that the house can't protect us from. Things that it's better not to even be aware of."

I want to know everything, even if it's horrible. Even if it hurts. That's the way we learn, isn't it?

My attention is caught by the gardener's shed at the edge of the grounds. My mother loves flowers, but it is difficult to find them, here on the grounds. Father has them brought in at great cost, on the coach. Still, perhaps I could make something grow. Flowers, or some tenacious little vines. If I can't have my brother, who looks to me for bravery in the face of danger and distraction from his fear . . . if I can't have a kitten . . . at least I can care for something. I won't just walk in the gardens, searching among the overgrowth for flowers that might please Mother. I'll make my own. I'll ask for seeds.

16
MADELINE IS FIFTEEN

Pain builds behind my eyes, and Roderick blurs. I tell myself that I can wait, that I must wait. If I collapse now, he will think that I am trying to keep him from going back to school, and that must not be the reason he decides to remain with me. Not pity.

He stands beside his horse with the wind ruffling his hair. I put my hand against Cassandra. She is tall enough that I can lean on her. She presses against my legs, giving me the support I need. If it weren't for Cassandra, I would beg Roderick to take me away right now. I would admit that I cannot bear to be left alone. But Cassandra is a full-grown wolfhound, and how could I take her . . . where would we go? Not yet, I tell myself. Not yet. Even if Cassandra was sent by the house, to keep me here—as I've come to suspect—I cannot abandon her.

"I'll be back soon," he says. "For our birthday."

But time moves slowly when you are alone in this house. Sometimes I suspect it doesn't move at all; I could be reliving the same monotonous days over and over, and I would never know.

Sunlight trickles through the clouds, but I refuse to shade my eyes. The light burns.

"I have something for you." Roderick reaches into his vest pocket. Eager as a child, I hold out my hand, willing it not to shake, pleased that I can hide my weakness from him.

"I saw it in a store window and thought of you. I meant to save it for our birthday, but you seem so sad . . ." His gift falls, small and cool, into the palm of my hand. The sunlight glints off it, and the pain shooting through my head is agonizing.

Forcing a smile onto my face, I look up into his eyes.

He puts his hands on my shoulders. "Soon," he says, and kisses my forehead. Then he turns away, as though if he doesn't leave me now, he won't be able to go.

"Take care of yourself, Madeline," he says. And while I'm blinking from the bright sunlight, he gets on his horse and he leaves. I stand at the edge of the causeway, because he expects me to be visible as he rides away, but I don't watch. If he turns to wave, I don't see.

The trinket is cold against my skin. I open my hand,

curious, despite the waves of pain engulfing me, to see what it is. But I am losing control. Cassandra whines, and I cling to her, desperate for balance, and the golden thing falls from my grip.

The echo, as it hits the stone tiles that line the courtyard, shakes my entire body.

My senses are overtaxed. I'm losing vision, but my hearing is acute and painful. Cassandra nudges me toward the house. But I've dropped . . . I fall to my hands and knees, searching, running my hands frantically across the cool, smooth stones. For a moment, I think I hear a faint ticking. Feeling along the stones, I find the trinket. A pocket watch? It's a tiny version with exposed clockwork, strung from a piece of black velvet. I close my fist around it. There are never enough pocket watches in the house. The one I'm carrying is the third that I've found, or stolen. I doubt there are any left in the house for me to swipe. Has Roderick noticed that I carry one in my pocket? Could my brother be more aware of the house, of its weaknesses, than he wants me to believe?

I try to make sense of his gift, but thinking is so difficult, and everything goes dark as I fall.

17
MADELINE IS TEN

Sitting on the floor of Mother's sitting room, I wait for a doctor to arrive. Mother started one of her fits just a few moments ago. Dr. Paul, always ready to examine Mother, enters, places his satchel on the floor, and takes off his tweed jacket.

"You sent for me?" His voice has gone all high-pitched and wobbly. He probably hopes that she will need to be bled. He has a special little knife he uses for cutting, and a basin for catching the blood.

The bed creaks as he sits down beside her and places a hand on her forehead. "You have a fever." His voice is gentle. Dr. Paul is always gentle with Mother. She is the reason he stays. Dr. Peridue stays because he wants to publish his book. Dr. Paul stays because of his admiration for my mother.

I slide my hand into the pocket of his coat, and find a rabbit's foot. Does the doctor have bad luck? I replace it and slip my hand into the other pocket. This one is empty.

Mother laughs at something Dr. Paul has said, and I jump. My surprise makes me drop the jacket, and it hits the floor with a quiet thump.

I catch my breath. The thud was not from that rabbit's foot, but from something far heavier.

I crouch beside the doctor's bag and wait. When no one comes to investigate, I run my fingers over the lining of his jacket until I find an inside pocket.

A gold pocket watch. It is heavy in my hand, and I can feel the ticking. This is exactly what I need. There is also a small packet of pills. As an afterthought, I rip the seams of the pocket and take the pills as well. He will think that it all fell out somewhere. Maybe he'll search the house, but I am good at hiding things. He will never find it.

I hold the rabbit's foot for several moments. But it was in a different pocket, so taking it may raise his suspicions. Finally I put the mangled paw back into the coat. Dr. Paul is examining my mother. He will need all the luck he can muster.

From Mother's sitting room, I could go straight downstairs, through the kitchen and out a forgotten side door to reach my garden. Sometimes I stop to examine some oddity, to look into unused rooms. But always, the house compels me to keep moving. To explore, but not to stop and think about what I'm seeing. Perhaps it is trying to protect me from the spells that plague Mother whenever she thinks too hard. Today, instead of going to the garden, I find myself back in my bedroom.

I hold the watch in my hands. I know already that it has to be wound every day. There is an inscription inside the watch: TO OUR BELOVED SON, WE ARE SO PROUD OF YOU. I press my fingertip against the gold, wondering if I could scour the words away. Dr. Paul is never getting this back.

I put the packet of pills in the back of my desk; I'm not sure whose pain they were meant to ease.

18
MADELINE IS FIFTEEN

Waking is slow. I'm not surprised to see my own ceiling above me. This isn't the first time the servants have carried me, unconscious, to my room. Someone even removed my boots. At first I can only move my fingers and toes, but eventually the ability to move returns, and I'm able to rearrange the covers, pulling the blanket to my chin. Roderick is gone, but something nags at me, a faint memory. A need? Curiosity presses at me.

Cassandra thumps her tail on the floor, happy that I'm awake.

From the alcove beside the bed, I remove a tattered sheaf of papers. Lisbeth never dated her entries, and with the bindings gone, it is impossible to be sure which ones were written first. It makes the narrative difficult to piece together, when reading at all is a chore, especially so soon after a fit.

I should ring for some soup, something bracing. Instead, I rewind my pocket watch, set it beside my pillow, and begin to read.

19
FROM THE DIARY OF LISBETH USHER

The Usher curse. It falls upon the house's favorite. And his intended. Rarely, the house focuses its love upon a female child, but the girls, as mates, are often the most afflicted by the curse.

Years ago, Mother invited a preacher from a nearby village to sanctify the house while Mr. Usher was away. He was one of those ministers who stand on street corners and yell at people. A swaggering man, full of beliefs and bravado.

His face turned gray when he entered the house.

"There is something here," he said, and his voice faded away. "You have invited evil into your midst!"

We watched him from the corners. He shuffled up and down the hallways, refused to spend the night beneath the Usher roof. Mother gave him a charitable donation, and he left.

How I wish he could have done something. Mr. Usher is distracted. Less and less likely to read with me. Less likely to *assure me that the curse can be broken.*

He has promised, while he's away, to visit a doctor in the city and discuss my symptoms. To bring me medication. Perhaps one of the city doctors will even pay a visit.

20
Madeline Is Ten

I wake and sit up in bed. Somewhere, in a narrow bed, in a stone building that I recognize from other visions as his school, Roderick stares out an arched window.

The curtains of my own larger window are in shreds. I'll have to ask one of the servants to sew new ones. Again. I go to it and peer through the ghostly green phosphorescence.

Roderick is lonely and afraid. Emotions I know well. Sometimes, when I am lonely, I like this connection between us, but more often it is terrible, being aware of his fears and my own. Together we have more fear than a person should be able to live with.

Repositioning the door to my chamber so that it can't swing all the way shut, I climb back into bed, careful not to step too close to the base of the bed; I have a horror, a half-forgotten memory from some long-ago Usher, of something grabbing my ankles from underneath. I know it's only a story, one of the dreamlike ones that float through the house like moths. But it was so real. . . .

I lie awake for a long time. The clock in the hallway strikes erratically, and shadows whisper their way through the halls.

When I do sleep, finally, I dream of places I have never been and people I have never met. In particular, I keep coming back to the image of a boy, but when I wake I cannot remember his face.

21
FROM THE DIARY OF LISBETH USHER

It was midday when we came to the House of Usher for the first time. Or, more accurately, it would have been midday anyplace else in the world. There, or here, as I should say, for I am writing this from inside the house, it is always near dark and gray.

We traveled from the city, with all of our trunks and boxes of belongings.

"This is going to be marvelous," Mother assured us. "So much bigger than our old house. So stately. People will know." She nodded. "They'll know that we are someone. It will make us important, staying in a house such as this."

The months since Father died had been a great trial to Mother. She was treated poorly by Father's creditors.

"We will never have to fear anything again," she said, rubbing her hands together. It seemed a greedy gesture, but since Father's death, our house in the city had been cold, and perhaps

she was just trying to warm herself.

The house was bigger than I expected, even from Mother's rapt descriptions of its grandeur. The road curved, and I saw it for the first time. It was horrible.

I considered running away, even if I had to jump from the carriage, but Mother expects me to behave like a young lady. And so, even in the grip of terror I felt at my first glimpse of the House of Usher, I did not shame her.

She tried to maintain her optimism, but as we approached the house her face lost its rosy color, and her hand fluttered at the collar of her dress.

"The house appears to have fallen into some disrepair." Her voice was little more than a whisper.

"It's looking at us," my younger sister said. "I think it wants to eat us." This might've been amusing; many of the things she says are.

But Mother fainted dead away, and nothing we could do would revive her.

22
MADELINE IS FIFTEEN

It is time to leave the house and explore. Not my gardens, but the front of the house, the grand entrance. Lisbeth described it, but for the life of me, I cannot remember looking upon it. A coldness sweeps over me. Cassandra barks once, and then pads after me. Her presence calms me, though my hands are shaking.

"I am going outside." The housekeeper makes a sign against evil as I walk past. She doesn't say anything. I wasn't expecting her to.

Lisbeth's description made me want to look upon the entrance. The house is waiting, as it so often does. I need to see what Lisbeth saw, to help make sense of her horror as she came to the House of Usher. The outside air is so cold that I can see my breath.

A walkway runs along the side of the house, around the

tarn. Cassandra falls into step behind me.

I proceed to the front of the house and look up. It's a glance, really, and then I'm staring at my boots. I can't look directly at the front of the house. My head is driven down, as if someone is behind me, pushing me. I try to raise my eyes, but they burn and begin to water.

I have to piece the thing together in my head like a jigsaw puzzle. It is dark, a sort of gray color, faded stone. There is a great front door, and a causeway that has been built to replace the drawbridge. There are the windows, the roofs, each one taller than the last, a stone gargoyle.

My eyes are forced away.

Mother told me once that no matter how brave you think you are, how sure you are of your faith or your convictions or of the rules of science and nature, you can barely glance at the House of Usher. Your eyes won't let you take it in.

She was right. And when my weak eyes slide to the ground, they are assaulted by the stinking, rotting tarn, black and lurid. Some long-ago Usher tried to drain it. He drowned and is buried below the house, not in the vault with the rest of the Ushers, but in a sort of coffin that was sunk into the water. At least that's what someone wrote in a ledger in the library. I do not disbelieve it.

Did I ever think that the house was benevolent? That it was warm?

Its windows are like eyes. A sort of electricity buzzes in the air, moving across my skin. What does it want? Why have I been pushed to come here? Does it expect me to be frightened? Amazed? I am, but maybe not in the way that the house intends.

Looking up again, I see a face, achingly familiar, through an attic window. A ghost?

The stones are crumbling, though none have fallen. The house is so stark, so massive and unnatural against this landscape. Not so in the back. Over the years I've nurtured plants from the very stones, have used the crumbling stones and the many cracks and crevices to support vines. Perhaps it is time to start on the front of the house. I hum softly, a habit when I think thoughts that might anger the house.

Cassandra puts her nose into my hand and breaks my concentration. I find that I have moved forward. The toes of my boots are nearly touching the fetid water.

23
FROM THE DIARY OF LISBETH USHER

I've come to believe that everything is a distraction. I realize that I must find answers, but then a fit comes upon me and I am unable to read. I find an interesting passage in the library, something that might relate to the curse or the history of the house, and my sister shows up, with two servants and a tea set. She says she wants to play at being grand ladies. I know she's bored here. Mother says she is too old for a governess, and yet she is still very young. Too old for games, not ready to decide what to do with her life.

The same things about the house that horrify me fascinate her. The ancient weapons that line the entranceway, the morbid oil paintings, the crypt.

Sometimes she cocks her head as if she is listening to voices or seeing something in the corners, beyond heavy dust that shimmers in the air.

Even Mr. Usher is a distraction, with his white smile, the slight *half-formed dimple that makes him seem dashing, somehow. He's sworn to help me, but he loses focus, begins pacing and reading, tracing the family's lineage on great sheets of paper that cover the tables in all of the parlors.*

What is it that I'm not supposed to find, and will I recognize it when I find it?

24
MADELINE IS TEN

"Your husband is ill," Dr. Peridue tells Mother.

I crouch outside her sitting room, listening.

"He hasn't opened his eyes for three days." Dr. Peridue sounds angry, as if Father's illness is an affront to him.

"His trances can last for weeks." Mother is calm.

"And his arm is broken."

An audible intake of breath tells me that Mother is surprised.

"His arm is broken?"

"Was he doing something strenuous? Lifting something?" Dr. Paul asks.

"He was helping Madeline with her reading and writing," Mother says. "It is difficult for her, but he has so much patience. For her." Her voice drips bitterness. Over the last months, since Roderick left, Father has roused himself from his apathy. He has been spending a few hours with me in the evenings.

Dr. Paul's ledger creaks as he opens it, probably realizing he should be recording the conversation, particularly if Father *is* dying. Which I don't believe. The house won't let it happen.

"He wouldn't have broken his arm teaching her how to write," he says.

Mother gives him a wry smile. She and I both know that the house was showing its displeasure. Because when we practice writing, he tells me secrets. He writes down the things that he cannot say, because of his illness. And if I try, sometimes I can read Father's messages.

I love that he pays attention to me, but I'm not sure I can believe the secrets he shares. He whispers that the house will harm me, but how could my house hurt me? It loves me like a parent . . . more, because it's always with me. It wouldn't hurt Father if he would listen to it.

The doctor shuts the ledger and leaves, and Mother turns her irritation on me.

"Your father is sick to dying and your brother doesn't love you. Not enough."

Mother's teeth are sharp and glittery in the light of the slender white candles she prefers.

I press my thumbnails into the flesh of my palms and try not to cry.

"Look!" Mother holds up Roderick's latest letter. She is so angry; she is shaking. "If he loved you, Madeline, he would come home for the holidays instead of visiting the home of a friend. Why should he need a friend when he has you?" In a lower voice she says, "I need him well, but he must return eventually. He can't stay away too long. He is an Usher."

Mother wants to protect Roderick for as long as she can, but in the end, he's still an Usher, and he must have ties to the house, whatever that means. Ties to me . . .

I am too afraid to respond. Staring into my lap, I study the needlepoint I was supposed to be practicing before the doctors interrupted. I was supposed to be stitching the black tailfeathers of an ominous-looking bird. I wish Father could come and protect me, but Mother is right. He's injured, and it's my fault.

Ghosts shimmer around Mother, feeding on her vicious-ness. They are translucent, like strands of mist. Mother isn't aware of them. If she breathed them in, would she choke? And would choking keep her from saying such things to me?

As I think this terrible thing, she coughs. Once, twice, nearly choking, just as I wished. Her eyes bulge and her face flushes. It gives me courage. The ghosts never really do anything, but at least they aren't on Mother's side.

"You sent Roderick away," I say. She spins toward me,

faster than I thought she could move, and rakes her fingernails down the side of my face. I cry out, but now that I've found my courage, I don't stop. "You wanted him to go to meet other young men. Aren't you glad that he has made friends?"

She steps back, surprised that I've stood up to her.

"Friends aren't important. Your father *chose* me. I had sisters, but he chose me. Roderick must return to this house of his own free will. I don't think that will happen.

You and Roderick don't have the luxury of choice. If he doesn't return, you will fade away, here among all these ghosts and dusty corners, all alone, Madeline Usher, faded away to nothing. What will we do when we can see the wallpaper through you? How will we even find you?"

She glides away, and I glare after her.

"I won't fade away," I whisper.

Because Roderick is my brother, and I know he will come back to me.

25
MADELINE IS FIFTEEN

The house is unsettled. A new doctor has arrived. As though we need another; we are already overrun with physicians. I must write to Roderick, no matter how difficult putting pen to paper is for me.

Opening a drawer in my desk to retrieve my ink bottle, I find a bit of parchment. *I need you,* it says. I wad it up, careful not to touch the clotted brown words, and let it fall to the floor. Beneath where it lay is a collection of tiny bones. A mouse . . . a mouse died within my desk. The bones are dry and crumbling. It must have happened a long time ago, and as I peer closer, I find something else—a dried human finger. It looks delicate, slightly bent at the joint, and so white that it glows in the semidarkness.

I scoot back from the desk, still considering it. I wrote a letter to Roderick last week. I write to him every week.

How then, did a mouse decompose in my desk drawer? And fingers don't just appear. . . . The house is not just whispering in my mind. It's warning me, only I don't understand. My fear is a deep thing, like a cough that lingers, the symptom of an illness that you know you will live with until you die.

"Miss Madeline?"

I slam the drawer closed, concealing the bones as if they are some treasure. Perhaps they are. Regardless, I don't want the servants to remove them until I've examined them further.

"The doctors are waiting," the maid says. She's new. Maids don't last long, only the older servants like the housekeeper, Miss Billingsly, and her sister the cook, gnarled by age. Neither of them ever leave the house. Like me, except I won't ever get to be old.

The doctors are always waiting. But today is different. Today I'll meet the new doctor. He's quite young, an apprentice studying under the other doctors.

I caught a glimpse of him as he carried in his belongings. I tell Cassandra to stay and then carefully close the door, forcing her to remain in my room.

"Watch your step," the maid warns, but I trip over the rug anyway, distracted by the empty spaces on the wall.

"Where did the pictures go?"

"Pictures, miss?"

"The oil paintings that were on this wall."

"I'm not sure, miss."

She is new. Perhaps she doesn't know. I try to remember the subject of the paintings, but can only call up somber dark hues and a fine layer of dust.

The memories tug at me and then disappear, leaving only frustration.

At least, as we climb the stairs, some paintings remain. I study each of them, determined to remember these, at least, in case they ever disappear. Bowls of apples, a pear on an ornate platter, vases filled with sickly flowers, white flowers, red flowers, a plate of fruit that surely rotted long years ago . . . then, amid the still lifes is a painting I've not seen before. A dead girl. She is lying with her hands folded, as if in prayer. Or perhaps she is not dead. Her cheeks are very pink, and her hair is long and fair. Like mine.

I lean closer, to be sure the painting is of some other Usher, not me, but the maid taps her foot. The doctors are waiting.

I tell myself that there is nothing to be afraid of, that the house is not threatening me with that painting. The girl's hair was not the exact same color as mine, the exact same length. I should have brought Cassandra with me, but she hates the tower and the doctors. One more stair-case, one more set of stairs. Exactly twenty-seven more steps. The maid pushes the door open.

Inside, the new doctor stands just across the threshold, smiling. He is young, with curly hair. Thanking the maid, who blushes and curtsies low, he gestures for me to enter the room.

The doctors sit comfortably in chairs, in a semicircle, wearing their spotless white coats, but they leave me standing.

"Dr. Winston has come specifically to study you and your condition," Dr. Paul says. "Isn't that wonderful? We may let him stay, since he's so eager to work with you."

"Why aren't you disrobing?" Dr. Peridue shakes his head, annoyed. "Why did you make us wait for you? We shouldn't have to send one of the maids."

They've been here since I was a child, but they show me no fondness, and I've never expected it from them. I ignore Dr. Peridue's querulousness and unbutton my dress with fumbling fingers. Stepping away from my clothing, I try not to let them see that I'm chilled and frightened.

The endless clanking and clicking of their machines in the next room makes me nervous, but I know from experience that when you are in the tower long enough, you stop hearing them.

The new doctor stares at me, and then looks at the floor, at the dress I was wearing just moments ago. It is surely still warm.

"I didn't expect her to be beautiful," he says.

The wallpaper in this room is curling away from the walls. I don't know what color it was originally, but it has faded to the shade of dried blood. I look at it, rather than at him.

While I am used to being talked about as if I am not here, I hoped he would be different. He is not so much older than me, and he is handsome.

"Her delicacy is a symptom of the malady. Look at her pale skin. Translucent, as if she had been eating laudanum. Which, I assure you, she has not. We rarely medicate her. We tried morphine on her mother, but it didn't work."

"I expected from your description that she would be skeletal, and that her hair would stand out around her head like cobwebs. She is . . . ," he falters.

I watch him watching me. He can't look away. I see his struggle. He is trying to pull his gaze from me, but he is mesmerized. And there's something in his eyes I have never seen before. Something warm and attentive.

"You are making a fool of yourself, Dr. Winston. It's as easy to take blood from a pretty girl as it is from a homely one." Doctor Paul's voice is low; he's annoyed.

My mouth curves up into a tiny little half smile. I may not like being talked about this way, but I am not impervious to flattery and attention, and the doctor is so very young. Would he like to kiss me? Is that what I see in his eyes? I am very curious about kissing.

"I beg your pardon, but if the symptoms progress as you have indicated, it will be hard to watch her, this beautiful creature . . . her fading will be a tragedy."

My smile freezes and I narrow my eyes, still looking directly into his face. Forget staring demurely at the wall-paper; let him see that I am real. Our eyes meet. His cheeks flush, and I allow myself to imagine kissing him. Though his pity leaves me cold, his lips might be warm.

26
MADELINE IS ELEVEN

Thrusting my hands deep into the recently tilled soil, I dig out a hole, put in the bulb, cover it with earth, and pat down the soil to keep it secure. One of the gardeners gave me these bulbs. He warned me that they were poisonous, as though I might take a bite. I imagine sinking my teeth into one, simply to see what might happen. Would Mother be upset if I died?

Would the doctors rush down from their tower, and hook me to their machines?

I once saw Dr. Peridue drinking a vial that looked full of blood. When he noticed me watching him, he went back to measuring vials and mixing potions. But his mouth was stained red.

I continue my planning, hoping that these bulbs will grow into something beautiful. I want to see that

something strong can grow with its roots in this house. I collect water in an urn, dark with age, that I took from a corner in one of the front rooms. There were ashes in the bottom, but I shook them out and discarded them. I carefully pour a splash of water onto the places where I planted each of my bulbs. Standing, I brush the dirt from my skirts.

At the edge of the garden, one of the doctors is watching me. It's Dr. Peridue with his notebook. He writes constantly. He says that he will record everything, that he's chronicling his own account of the accursed Ushers. If there was ever any kindness in him, it was lost long ago.

"Your mother would like to speak to you," he says.

I follow him. Mother's rooms are in the oldest part of the house. She and Father require complete and absolute silence. I know how to walk without making a sound. But sometimes the house itself won't let you; it groans as if the placement of our feet causes it pain. To keep us from creeping about. To make us notice the house itself—it does not like to be ignored. So Mother had Roderick and I moved to another floor, and now that he's gone, I'm alone.

"You are very lucky," the doctor tells me. "Your mother tells me the malady struck when she was very young. You are eleven, and as yet have shown no signs of it." His voice is disappointed. He composes himself as we pause at the threshold of Mother's room. "Here we are," he says.

I tiptoe inside. There is a painting of a pale-haired child beside her bed. Only one. Roderick. Beside the painting is an abandoned book. Sometimes she likes me to read to her, to prove that I still can. The Usher malady makes reading difficult.

"Madeline," she says. "What were you doing?"

"Planting my garden."

She laughs.

"Poor child," she says. "Poor lonely little girl."

Her window is open. Usually she surrounds herself with heavy lengths of velvet. The servants make curtains and wall hangings and rugs so that all she has to touch is her beloved black cloth, so soft I can barely tolerate the way it feels against my skin. But today it is spring, and the air is balmy, and even Mother wants to let it in. A good day for planting a garden.

I picture the flowers growing in the light, in the fresh air, covered by butterflies. I can almost hear the humming of bees.

A butterfly flutters down to the window; it drifts, barely moving its wings.

"Kill it," my mother demands in a low voice. "Smash it with your fist."

"Mama," I say, trying to distract her. "Would you like me to read to you?"

She ignores my question, a slight smile on her lips.

"I wasn't born here, you know," she says. "But my mother was an Usher, from generations back. We came for a visit, and the house was so grand, so mysterious . . . you sense the mystery of it, don't you, Madeline?"

I nod, eyes still on the butterfly, wishing that I was so free of care that I could glide away.

"Gardening is for servants," she says. "You should be reading, or painting. Those are appropriate pursuits. Our family has long been a patron of the arts. Your father used to paint. I found it charming."

Will she forbid me to go outside? She must have seen me through the window. Any sort of happiness fills Mother with a slow, burning anger, because she's here, trapped and sick.

"Our holiday lasted on and on," she continues, "and I was glad. I wanted to live here in the big house and be a great lady. Now I sit here with you, and I look forward to dying. Smash it, Madeline."

I don't know what madness overtakes me. Perhaps it is her use of my name. She rarely uses it, and though her tone is cold, hearing it upon her lips warms me. Her eyes are upon me. She has the ash-blond hair that distinguishes Ushers, but she did not inherit our lavender eyes. Roderick and I got them from Father. The brown of her eyes is deceptively kind.

I bring my fist down and feel the butterfly's wing rip.

The tiny twiglike appendages snap as my hand smears them into the pitted stone of the windowsill. The intact wing flutters once.

Mother laughs, and I feel a thrill. It's the house, feeding on her cruelty, and now mine. In the corner, the ghost of a stately gentleman smiles and then evaporates.

"You are as cursed as I am," she says.

I look at my fingers. They are stained, not with blood, but with the colors of the butterfly, orange and yellow.

"You shouldn't cry," she says. "You should never cry. Sometimes it brings on the spells."

She's smiling. The house watches and listens. I glance at the bedside table. Surely it isn't watching us through my brother's portrait. But something flickers in the painted eyes. I look back to Mother, somehow expecting her casual cruelty to have diminished her beauty. But she is as lovely as ever.

I wipe my tears with my sleeve. If the house approves of Mother's actions, then can it truly be on my side?

Can it truly love me, if she doesn't?

27
MADELINE IS FIFTEEN

The young doctor has been with us for a week. From outside, I see his slender shadow pacing in front of one of the tower windows.

In a thicket on the west side of the house I find a bit of statue, the torso of a girl holding a pitcher. A long time ago, it might have been the base of a fountain. The interior of the pitcher is worn smooth, as if by running water. Though it is heavy, I pry the statue from the earth and use a small cart from the gardener's shed to bring it to my garden.

Working here, I can forget for a little while my illness, the curse, my fears. I'm not Madeline Usher now; I'm just a gardener.

Standing, I look over the area. Bits of statues have been grown over with vines. Part of a stone bench is exposed

beside a wild rosebush that I've been able to coax into growing.

"Good morning."

I turn to see Dr. Winston, the apprentice doctor.

"Good morning," I answer. A sickly sort of sun is shining down through the clouds, gleaming against his dark hair.

"This is beautiful." He gestures to my garden. "I'm surprised you can get anything to grow here."

Cassandra raises her head and bares her teeth at him, but I smile. His approval warms me.

"I search for plants that thrive in the shadow of the house."

"You've done beautifully." He sits down on the cracked bench. "Where did you find this?" He holds up the urn that I use for watering my plants.

"Inside, in the dusty corner of one of the unused rooms."

I'm shoring up the dirt around a delicate little vine, encouraging it to join its fellows climbing the side of the house.

"I think it is a burial urn." He runs his hands over its surface. "I saw one like this in a museum. Look how the ceramic glitters. It's quite lovely."

I stare up at him. Unlike the other doctors, who always look so out of place . . . as he stares up at the massive walls of the house, his eyes adoring, the sun brings out a few fair strands in his dark hair, and he seems like he could belong to the House of Usher.

28
FROM THE DIARY OF LISBETH USHER

The locals think that we are Usher bastards, that the current Mr. Usher's father was our father as well. Though we look like Mr. Usher—our hair is the same odd shade—Mother only met him last year, when she was invited to visit the ancestral home. She returned to the city enamored with the house and the ancient family to whom she had discovered we are related. Mr. Usher invited her to come for an extended stay, and she was thrilled, but her excitement has soured.

"He will, surely, do some renovations," she said in her breathless way, when we complained that there was a hole large enough for a person to disappear through the floor of one of the bedrooms, and the carpet was threadbare, and that there was a water stain on the wall of Honoria's room.

Mother is less happy every day that we are here. To try to appease her, Mr. Usher bought us new dresses, and there are dozens *of servants. In the city, we only had a cook and a boy who ran errands. Mother says that the more servants a person has, the more important they are.*

But we hear terrible noises in the night, and Mr. Usher says odd things.

He is much younger than I expected, since I imagined that the master of such an ancient house should be elderly himself, and he is very interested in Honoria. She never smiles at him, but then, she never smiles at anyone.

Mr. Usher has a mad sister. They keep her locked up so that she doesn't do herself damage.

I wish to see her, but Mother says that it is out of the question and has forbidden me to go up to the attics. We are guests here until Mr. Usher proposes marriage to Honoria. Then we will have a home.

I'm not sure that Mother is quite enthused with this plan now that we have arrived, but we have no other place to go.

My youngest sister frets, even as I comfort her. At thirteen years old, she is easily frightened, though old enough to know better. The servants in the city said she was touched in the head, but she isn't simple. Just odd. Our mother is too distracted, too lost in her dreams, so I will be the mother that my youngest sister needs. She is the only beautiful thing in this terribly bleak house.

29
MADELINE IS TWELVE

Hesitating beside the kitchen door, I try to gauge the mood of the house. It is oddly subdued, as if it isn't aware of me at all. Good. I've discovered that if I show no excitement about going outside, the house will generally allow me to walk through the doors and stand on the grounds. Since Father tried to steal me away, the house is especially wary, so I must be careful.

Mother says it stormed every day, from the moment Father took me to the day that we were caught. Then she laughed her cruel laugh. "You didn't make it far, did you?" She claims Father hid me in one of the outbuildings. But why, then, do I remember hearing the sea? The entire thing seems like a dream, like one of the stories that float through the house, and I'm not even sure it was real. I've barely seen Father in the weeks since I woke up, back in my bedroom.

Sometimes, in the spring, the tarn, the stinking lake in the front of the house, overflows, and noxious water floods the grounds. I can see the unflooded part of my garden from my window.

Once again, all of my fragile happiness is encapsulated by my garden. It is all I've found to nurture. It is mine.

I created this seed of hope in the depths of a lonely winter, certain that if my flowers bloomed, it would prove that I am not cursed, that I might have life to look forward to instead of death. I've been building it in my mind, as important as any of my other rituals.

All around my clearing, there are rank black blooms, which seem to have burst from the vines overnight. The vines themselves are covered with rot, slimy to the touch. I pull them from the earth and discard them. In my flower garden is one lone dandelion, standing defiant against the army of roses. It is not one of my flowers; my bulbs and seeds lie dormant, lifeless, underground.

I kneel, clearing back the vines that grow over everything.

30
MADELINE IS ELEVEN

Father leans toward me. Before him is a canvas. He's sketched out the Usher crest in meticulous detail and is mixing red and yellow paint for the dragons. He stirs the paint round and round, the colors of sunset encapsulated in a ceramic bowl.

He calls this room his studio. It has wide windows that let in a little light for painting, and beside us sits a grand piano with a metronome that clicks back and forth, one two, one two, over and over.

"The house is seductive," Father says. "It reads our deepest desires."

But if that's true, then why was Roderick sent away?

Father laughs softly, still mixing the paint. "It doesn't always *give* us our desires, Madeline," he says, as though I asked the question aloud. Did I?

Bethany Griffin

"And sometimes . . ." He glances at the doorway. Mother is resting across the hall. "What we desired so much doesn't turn out to truly fulfill us." Is that why he's speaking so low? Because he's insulting Mother? "You must learn to question," he continues. "I know you are young, but you must not accept anything at face value."

The paint in his bowl is the color of rust. Like the hinges on the doors and shutters of the gardener's cottage.

Does he mean that I should question everything? Including what he's saying right now? He must see the confusion on my face.

"Not what I say," he clarifies. "You must be ready to trust me. On a moment's notice. Any moment."

I'm distracted from his words by a movement at the corner of my eye. A ghost.

Father laughs. "They aren't important. Long-dead Ushers, they have no effect on the world around them. The house brings them back. It never shows us the ghosts of our dead loved ones. Perhaps because it doesn't wish to drive us completely mad." He blinks, refocuses. "The ghosts aren't important. What is important is that you trust me, and are ready to go."

"Father, were you reading my mind?"

"Of course not," he says too quickly, as he splatters paint across the canvas, completely obscuring his intricate drawings in a blob of rusty near-red.

96

31
MADELINE IS FIFTEEN

In her journal, Lisbeth Usher claims that her beloved Mr. Usher kept his mad sister in the attics. I have never truly explored the attics where the nurseries are. Mother was afraid we would catch the maladies of former generations of Usher children and never allowed us up here. Though Roderick and I disobeyed her and crept up a few brief times.

The house was built over generations, with additions from various Ushers. The nurseries are nearly the highest part of the house. The doctors occupy the adjacent tower.

When Dr. Peridue offered to live in the house, Father agreed, so the doctor would always be available for Mother. The house is big enough for an army of doctors. I tiptoe up one of the staircases, avoiding their quarters.

The machine they keep going at all times, day and

night, pumps endlessly, audible even from the stairs.

I pass the last of the doctors' rooms and step into the nurseries. There are wide windows that face south, and big open rooms filled with dolls missing hair and other broken bits of childhood. A wooden rocking horse with a mane made of white thread stands in the corner. It only has one eye.

Low ceilings give the huge rooms a cavernous feel, full of shadows with open doorways through which you can see more rooms, and more still, like a house of mirrors, except instead of reflections, it's some warped version of reality, more rooms than could possibly exist, even in a house this huge.

I step over a headless doll. Blocks are strewn across the floor, as if a child might be returning to finish his castle. A broken toy drum lies in the corner; a drumstick has been thrust through the leather membrane.

A spider the size of my hand scurries across the room and into the mouth of a doll with blue eyes and gold ringlets. The Usher children of the past had an abundance of dolls. Mother never bought me any, though I had a stuffed pink rabbit that was unbelievably soft.

I walk slowly through tea sets waiting for a party that will never happen, step over faded chalkboards. *Abigail Usher,* one of them says. I keep walking.

Heavy ropes have been hung from the rafters. They are

decorated with paper flowers. I stand on tiptoe to peer at them. There are meticulously detailed cutouts of stars and moons, roses and tulips, created, perhaps, by some child who grew up long ago. Why would such coarse rope be used to hang these delicate papers? They all flutter as I pass.

In one of the dormers, a low area where the ceiling matches the slope of the roof above, I find a mattress and ugly manacles, black with age. Two pairs. One on each wall, directly across from each other. One manacle is mis-shapen, twisted to make it much smaller than the others.

Otherwise, the room is empty. There is an opening in the floor at the far corner of the room.

I touch the restraint, and the chill of this place settles over me. The house groans, and footsteps creak toward me, a lilting, dragging step that is oddly familiar. I whirl, but the room is empty. It's impossible to tell where the footsteps are coming from in this deceptive and endless maze of doorways.

I listen closely, my heart pounding. Still the steps creak steadily nearer. One of the servants? Or has the house sent something terrible to punish me for coming up here? Anything—anyone—could be hiding in these attics. The opening in the corner leads to a staircase that spirals downward from this room, a thing of wrought iron, with a flowing design of roses and barbs. I don't wait for the footsteps to reach me. I run, across the room, stepping once on the mattress. A noxious smell blooms from it, thick as a cloud. I don't inhale, just grab the banister, iron thorns piercing my palm, and bound downstairs.

From one floor to the next, the staircase changes color. First black, then a dark green, then a flaking white that comes off on my hands. Three floors down, it ends with a stone floor. I rush through one arched doorway, and then another.

A voice calls "Hello?" and then, warmly, "Oh. Hello, Madeline."

It is Dr. Winston. I've stumbled into the doctor's quarters. He is lying sprawled across a couch, reading. Seeing him like that feels intimate, somehow. Already unnerved, I try not to stare. His dark hair is tousled, and his clothes are rumpled, casual.

He lets the book fall to the floor.

"I heard someone, upstairs. . . ." I try to catch my breath.

"It's just the wind. It makes this old place creak. I hear a sound like footsteps limping back and forth nearly every night."

He watches me intently. I don't understand the look in his eyes.

"I'm surprised to see you running," he says. "With color in your cheeks, you almost look healthy." Of course, the intense look is that of a doctor examining a patient. "I have theories," he continues. "Ideas for a cure. We can't allow a beautiful girl like you to fade away."

His compliment takes me by surprise. I hope he thinks the flush on my cheeks is from running.

"What are you reading?" I ask, gesturing to the dropped book. But even then he doesn't take his eyes off me.

"*The Belphegor*. I found it in your library."

"I hope you are enjoying it."

"Oh, I am." He leans forward, smiling. "Madeline . . ."

Like the servants, he is supposed to call me Miss Usher. His familiarity is not as inappropriate as the way he's watching me. He straightens his shirt, but his hair is still such a mess.

"I was hoping you would walk with me in your garden. Perhaps tomorrow afternoon?"

The thought of sharing my garden fills me with excitement. I feel myself lighting up from within, and I smile; he returns it.

Perhaps he mistakes my smile, because he reaches out, as if to touch me. I step back, but I don't run. Maybe just a bit of the smile is for him, rather than the garden.

"I'm sorry," he begins, but I never hear what he's sorry for, because a familiar voice calls for me from downstairs. Roderick.

32
MADELINE IS FIFTEEN

Dr. Winston and I race to the entrance hall, where we are caught up in the commotion of Roderick's arrival. The servants line up to greet him, but he barely notices. The school sent him home unexpectedly; he is ill.

He staggers up the stairs.

"Madeline," he says. "I'm so glad to see you, so glad to be home." Mother once said that Roderick wouldn't return to me. That I would fade away. But here he is. Ill, but when you are ill, there is no place you'd rather be than your own home. Or so I've heard. I've only been away once, with Father, and I did, quite desperately, wish to return home when my fits overwhelmed me. Dr. Winston joins the other doctors in hurrying Roderick to his room.

"You must stay away from him," Dr. Peridue admonishes as I try to follow my brother. "He may be contagious."

I wait until I hear them leave, muttering about whether it is safe to bring up Roderick's belongings that were left downstairs. Then I slip into his room and sit beside the bed to watch over him. He has a tendency to kick off his blankets during the night, and I don't want him to be chilled. Sleeping Roderick reminds me of childhood, of warmth and security.

When morning comes, I'm still beside his bed, ready to coax him to drink some tea. He holds my wrist as if he's afraid that I will leave him, even though he is the one who always leaves.

"I'm missing my exams," he says. I can't tell if he's happy or sad about this.

"What are exams?" I ask, trying to imagine the great mystery that is school.

"Tests of your knowledge." It is Dr. Winston who answers, not Roderick. He's standing in the doorway with his doctor's bag.

"Who are you?" Roderick asks. His voice is not friendly.

"I'm Dr. Winston. Dr. Peridue asked me to come see how you are feeling today. If you could remove your shirt . . ."

Roderick sits up, but he doesn't take off his shirt. He studies the doctor as he approaches the bed.

"Have we met before?"

I wait for Dr. Winston to say no; this is the first time

Roderick has been home since he arrived. But then, perhaps Roderick has seen him through my eyes, the way I've seen his school friend.

"Yes," Dr. Winston says, toying with his stethoscope. "We have met before."

33
MADELINE IS ELEVEN

Father sits at one end of the table, and Mother at the other. They are far from us, and from each other, but Roderick and I are near the center of the table, close enough to whisper together. Close enough to giggle, though nothing is really funny. The servants bring course after course to the table, but none of us eats more than a few spoonfuls.

Before us is a lovely centerpiece—Mother's favorite poisonous flowers, holly, poinsettia, and something else with large red blossoms.

Mother smiles at Roderick. "Your new jacket looks very nice," she says. He beams back, and when I look to the other end of the table, Father is also smiling.

Usher ancestors watch us with serious faces, hands placed menacingly inside dinner jackets that are not so unlike the new one Roderick is wearing.

"Go on," Father tells the servants. "Go to the kitchens and have something to make you merry. We can serve our own soup."

Mother frowns slightly at that. I almost don't see it, but Roderick kicks me beneath the table. He's about to truly start giggling, and his mirth is infectious. We rarely eat in the dining room, except on special occasions.

34
MADELINE IS FIFTEEN

The servants are in a tizzy. The doctors gather in corners, and even Roderick, though he can barely get out of bed, is oddly thrilled.

The body of a madman has been discovered in the attics. He was in the nursery, caught and strangled in the rope covered with fluttering paper flowers, decorations devised by some long-dead, long-forgotten Usher children. It wasn't the house settling when I heard those footsteps in the attic. Running away from them was wise, but my face flushes when I remember rushing into Dr. Winston's chamber.

The madman must have crept through one of the side doors and lived up there. Perhaps he had been there for years. My explorations may have disturbed him, and somehow he strangled himself, in that place where generations of Usher children were hidden away.

The servants are spooked, though this is obviously their fault for leaving doors unlocked. Miss Billingsly, the housekeeper, has given notice. She says her heart can't handle this job for another day.

They brought the man's body downstairs and put him in the parlor. No one knows what to do with him. I imagine that there are still stars and moons twined around his throat.

"I want to see him," I tell Roderick. We are in the parlor, and despite being sick, he's playing lord of the manor.

When I explored the attics, this lunatic must have been watching me. Following me. I want to look upon his face, but Roderick doesn't think it's a good idea.

He's still recovering from his illness and is very frail. A heavy blanket rests across his lap to protect him from the slightest chill. I'm not sure how he's managing to appear to be overbearing. I put my hands on my hips and narrow my eyes.

"Let the servants take care of it, Madeline. That's what they're here for."

"But I want to see him. How often do you get to look at a dead man?"

He shakes his head. A boy from his school died of fever last month, which is why Roderick was sent home to recuperate from his own fever. For a moment I feel bad, as if my curiosity is morbid, unladylike.

"But this is extraordinary and strange," I say, thinking of the books he's always reading. "It's something of an adventure."

"It isn't an adventure. It's petrifying, and such happenings fuel your superstitions. I would fire all of the servants for allowing this to happen, if I thought I could find new ones."

Roderick reaches up to touch my face.

"You could've been in danger."

I wonder, suddenly, how they knew the man was mad, when he was dead before they found the body.

"Yes. But not from some madman." My voice quivers. I lean down to whisper to Roderick. "I am in danger every day that I'm in this house."

"The house." His voice is flat, annoyed. "Madeline, stop. You're becoming as obsessed as Mother was."

"It's more dangerous than some madman." Whose lilting footsteps sounded so oddly familiar.

35
MADELINE IS ELEVEN

Though the ground is frozen and dusted lightly with snow, Roderick and I pull on ugly woolen coats that the servants have found somewhere, and go outside.

Roderick stops at the wall that surrounds the herb garden and scrapes together enough snow to make a ball, and then he throws it directly at me.

I gasp as the cold hits my face, some of it sliding into the recesses of the shapeless coat.

"I'm sorry," he says. "I suppose that's the sort of thing one does to a schoolmate, not a sister—" But I've scraped together my own snowball, and lob it at him. He throws up his hands in mock surrender, and I chase him, uncaring that the servants are watching through the kitchen window and that Mother would find fault with our lack of dignity. We run until we are both doubled over, laughing.

Our breath fills the air with wisps of condensation, like ghosts, except outside.

The house casts a long shadow over everything, but the light through the windows is warm. I see Father limping past the parlor window. Pulling the curtains so Mother can rest, and I'm glad to be away from the house, even for a few moments.

"I thought you were going to cry, when I first hit you with that snowball," Roderick admits.

"Iceball, you mean," I put my hand to my cheek, which is most certainly bruised. "Don't forget, I'm the oldest," I say. And the bravest. I don't say that part aloud, because I don't have to. I'm the one who stayed home.

"I wish you could come to school with me," Roderick says. "You're more fun than any of the others. Even though you are a girl."

"Come with me," I say, and pull him along to a wide-open space where bits of grass peek up through the fine layer of snow.

"This is where I'm going to plant my garden," I tell him. "It's all mine."

I lie down, solemnly moving my arms and legs in unison, to create a snow angel. Roderick throws himself down beside me.

"I could help you," Roderick says. "When I am home for the summer."

Part of me wants to say no, that the garden is mine, and mine alone, but instead I watch him climb to his feet and dust the snow from his jacket, and then I reach out my hand. He helps me to my feet, and we step away, looking back to the snow angels. Side by side, identical.

36
MADELINE IS SIXTEEN

Today is March fifteenth. Our birthday. Roderick is still home, sad because his illness keeps his school friend from inviting him for a visit. He's so disappointed that I am almost sorry for him, even though I'm thrilled that he's been allowed to stay through our birthday. We celebrate quietly. The servants only remember when Roderick arrives with fanfare, announcing that it is our birthday.

This year there is no cake with candles. I'm glad. Growing older is ominous when you are an Usher. The house is more determined than ever to control us. Live through us. Is this what happened to our parents when they were coming of age?

We are sitting alone, in the chapel.

"Roderick, what happened to Father?" I ask, considering a crack in the stained-glass window. He waits so long to speak that I turn back to him.

He raises his eyebrows. They are so pale that you almost can't see them. Mine are darker.

"I don't remember him dying. He was here, and then he was gone. . . ." I falter.

"You don't remember the funeral?"

I shake my head. Ashamed.

"There were red roses all throughout the lower floors, and it was unbearably hot here in the chapel. You were holding my hand. An organist came and played the old pipe organ. It was beautiful, but then one of the pipes fell. . . ."

"Roderick . . ." My voice fades, frozen by sudden fear. "That was Mother's funeral."

"No . . ." His brow furrows.

"When the pipe fell, it knocked over the roses. Hundreds of them, remember?"

Mother once said that the reason the Usher family donates so much money to charity is so that someone will send flowers when they die. We are silent for a long time, considering Mother's funeral.

"At Mother's funeral, there was a poem. . . ."

"Yes, one of the doctors read it. Dr. Paul, I think. He liked Mother."

Dr. Paul stayed because of Mother. Since she died, he only smiles when he is taking blood.

"As I remember, there was the funeral with the poem, and all the flowers, and another one with the pipe organ, and flowers. . . ."

"They were the same, Roderick. A long ceremony. And we were by ourselves, remember?"

We sit in the chapel and watch the sun dissolve, red as blood, on the stones of our ancient home.

"One day maybe I will disappear," I say softly, but Roderick doesn't hear me.

37
MADELINE IS TEN

While most of the ghosts in the house are misty and ephemeral, sometimes you can see a waistcoat, or a petticoat, and sometimes you can make out facial expressions. In the red parlor, I often spot the ghost of a child wearing a dilapidated sailor suit.

I haven't spoken to anyone, not Mother, or Father, or any of the servants, in days, so maybe it isn't odd that the little spirit is so appealing. I've brought the chessboard with me, in some sort of optimistic hope that the boy might be able to do what his compatriots can't, and move the pieces around.

"Hello," I say, smiling. I reach out my hand slowly, and then, as he turns his face toward me, freeze. His attention chills me, but still I press on.

"I'm Madeline," I say. "I suppose you are an Usher."

His hair is particularly pale. The same color as mine. I hold out the checkered board, an invitation. He shakes his head and then flashes out of existence. No evaporating fog, no wispy bits, just suddenly gone.

The wooden board falls from my hands, crashing to the floor, and at the same time chess pieces pour in through the doorways on opposite sides of the room, the cracks in the walls. Some are heavy marble in green and gold. Others are faded ivory, or perhaps bone. Shaped metal, gold and copper and age-darkened silver. They stream through the doors in a relentless tide, covering the ebony floor, the rug, the tip of my own slipper. A wealth of game pieces, and no one to play with.

What will the servants think of this, when they come to dust this room tomorrow?

I sit for a long time, wondering at the house, at what I've done wrong. From now on, I'll ignore the ghosts, as they ignore me.

38
MADELINE IS SIXTEEN

"Stay with me," I beg Roderick. "Don't go back to school." But I don't mean it as much as I did before. With Roderick here, I've barely caught a glimpse of the young doctor in days.

We are in the dining room. I am at one end of the table, and he is at the other. Just like Mother and Father used to sit.

"You know I can't. I promised Mother that I would finish. It's only two more years."

We sit in cold silence. I didn't think he would stay, but his refusal still hurts.

"When I'm away from here, I'm always telling my friend about you."

His friend.

"He is fascinated by you. I tell him how beautiful you

are, how imaginative. He's jealous that I have such a wonderful sister."

I have an odd sinking sensation, a combination of nausea
and happiness.

"Mr. Usher?"

I feel Roderick's start of surprise at this unexpected
and unwelcome intrusion.

Dr. Winston is peering through the gloom of the hallway into the gloom of the dining room.

"What?"

"Dr. Peridue has suggested that while you're home, I
might do a quick examination. He wants me to look specifically for signs of the family illness."

"No," Roderick says.

"It should be helpful to you, to work with doctors who
are aware of your family history. . . ." He trails off as
Roderick's face turns purplish red.

"I said no. Absolutely not. I do not have the family
illness."

"Of course not."

Dr. Winston turns away but doesn't leave.

"I remember you," Roderick says. "From somewhere."

Dr. Winston gives a little smile. "I'm the apprentice
doctor."

"Yes, but I know you from someplace else."

"We have passed before, at a country house. But I don't

believe we had ever spoken. I would remember if we had. Can I get you some water, sir?" Dr. Winston steps into the hall and returns with a glass of water.

Roderick's eyes are narrowed to slits. "You've been here for months. When will you finish your apprenticeship and become a real doctor?"

"Oh, I won't leave when I finish my apprenticeship."

My young doctor turns toward me and smiles.

"Unlike you, Mr. Usher, I want to be here."

39
MADELINE IS TWELVE

"Miss Madeline?"

I look up from my planting to see Mother's maid, Agatha. Her face is shiny with sweat, though the day is cool.

"Yes?"

"The physicians sent me to tell you that your mother is dead."

I am kneeling with my hands in the earth while an emotionless servant tells me that my mother is dead. I will never have a chance to make her love me. She will never again braid my hair, or tell me stories of when she was a girl.

I touch the slimy petal of one of the flowers. If the stems weren't covered with a creeping fungus, I would gather them for her. She loved flowers.

"Go upstairs and put on one of your black dresses," the maid says.

I don't remember walking to my room. On my bedside table, there is a sheaf of writing paper. I had begun to write a letter to my brother but had given up in frustration when the words kept dancing around the page. As of last night, there had been nothing interesting to say. And now I won't have to finish it, because Roderick will be coming home. He must. Our mother is dead.

Pressure builds at my temples, growing until light explodes behind my eyelids. I scream. Before I'm done, my ears are ringing. I take a step forward. The sound of my footstep echoes, and the light, the light in the room has become unbearable. I roll myself in a blanket and hide underneath my bed, sure that, like Mother, I am dying.

I cry from pain rather than sadness.

40
MADELINE IS SIXTEEN

Tonight is Roderick's last night home. We sit together in an alcove of the library. His eyes are closed, as if he's half asleep, while I flip through a book. A headache threatens, and with the headache, perhaps a fit. I fight it down and hand the book to Roderick.

Cassandra lies in front of the door. She has been lethargic for the last few days. I walk over and rub her head. She gazes up at me lovingly. I want to lie down and put my head on her back, like a child. But Lisbeth Usher claims the library holds the answers that I need, so when I can, I search.

"Look, Madeline." Roderick is pointing at an illustration in the ancient tome. "This is our house," he whispers. "But it isn't."

The House of Usher? Surely not, for the house in the

drawing sits on a dark cliff, and waves pound the sand below. But what did Father say the night he took me to the widow's walk, about being away from the sea?

Roderick drops the book to the floor. I kneel down to retrieve it, hoping, as I look up into his eyes, that there is something here, something that will make him believe, but he is already shaking his head, retreating to his precious logic.

"Roderick, it even says it is the House of Usher." I point down at the words.

THE LEGENDARY HOUSE OF USHER. It shows the family crest. In spite of myself, I feel a brief bit of pride. This house is so astonishingly old, and our family line, so ancient.

The scions of Usher picked up the very stones of the ancient mansion and removed them from the sacred land, taking them to the new world, even the dungeon and all of the instruments therein. The only thing that was lost was the goblet, and without the goblet, they could not mitigate the curse.

My eyes blur.

"Perhaps they moved it," Roderick insists. "Maybe that's why it's so creaky and all the angles seem wrong, as if it might be ready to collapse. But it isn't haunted."

What will it take to make him believe?

41
MADELINE IS TWELVE

As soon as the light and sound of the house grew bearable again, the doctors sent for me. It's only been a few days since Mother died.

"You've come to your heritage," Dr. Peridue says. Paunchy and bald, he is the oldest of the doctors. In his voice I hear happiness; he is pleased to have a new specimen to study. Before I came into my "heritage," he had little interest in me, but now that I've had my first fit, his eyes sparkle and he watches my every move, ready to capture me and add me to his horrible book.

"What will happen to me?" My voice echoes, and I feel small. This room has vaulted ceilings and three dank fireplaces.

"It won't be so bad."

He is lying.

Dr. Paul stares at me from across the room. His eyes

are red from crying. He caresses a syringe.

"Your brother will be staying home for the duration of the summer, won't he? That will be nice for you," Dr. Peridue says. "You've missed your brother." Then, to Dr. Paul, as if I can't hear him, "Remember how we thought she might come into the family illness when she was separated from her twin? Instead it was caused by her mother's death."

"Odd," Dr. Paul says. "I thought it would affect the male specimen first."

Dr. Peridue laughs. "It should have." He stares into his book, blinking. "The pattern has been broken. I believe that the house has chosen the female twin as heir."

Dr. Paul gives him a look. Either he doesn't believe what Dr. Peridue just said, or he doesn't believe in the curse.

"What is going to happen?" I repeat in a louder, stronger voice. "Will I go mad?"

Dr. Peridue smiles. He is enjoying this. "Like your mother, you will suffer fits. During these spells, your senses will become morbidly acute. The most insipid food will be unendurable, your clothing will be painful to your skin, and the quietest of sounds will inspire you with terror. You will have headaches, and you will lose consciousness."

"I don't believe you," I say, trying to be like Roderick when he is pretending to be brave.

But I do believe him. I believe every word.

42
MADELINE IS SIXTEEN

Up in his room, finally recovered from his illness, Roderick is packing, preparing to catch the coach, which passes the property once a day. He will leave, once again, determined not to listen to my worries about the house and the curse.

I sit in the chapel where Mother's funeral was held. And perhaps Father's. The light coming through the stained glass dances over the stonework. The windows are tall, peaked at the top, framed in old wood that has become silverish with age.

Sitting here, I can feel the majesty of the house. It is so old. Looming over and around me. How can I stand up to it all alone? When I become too determined, I fall into longer trances, sometimes for days at a time. And I forget things. Or do I remember things I never knew? Like the stories of long-ago Ushers that play behind my eyes when I'm trying to sleep . . .

Cassandra pads into the room. She eyes the window suspiciously, and then pounces on something. I can't tell what until she pounces again. The weak sunlight is moving across the floor, sparkling through the window, and the silly dog is trying to catch it.

This unexpected foolishness from a dog that usually looks so wise startles a laugh from me. And somehow the darkness in the house retreats.

43
MADELINE IS TWELVE

"What happened to the chess set?" Roderick asks, home from school for the summer.

He doesn't really care about the chess set. I don't tell him how it was buried by game pieces. How the servants left the pieces piled up in the parlor for weeks, and then one day it was just gone.

He does want to know more about the stories I have always told him. Where do I find them? I didn't know that everyone couldn't see them. They are like the ghosts that float about the corners of the house, ephemeral unless you reach out to them. And even after I see a story, live it in my head, I still don't know if it's real or fiction.

Are there other things that only I can do? I tested the servants, and it seemed that all of them could hear and speak. Even the gardeners, who were mostly silent, could speak when they had to. Can everyone hear whispers of thought? Can everyone feel the touch of something or someone lingering on their skin? Next I must learn if they see the ghosts.

The stories are not unlike fireflies. In the summer evenings, fireflies swarm around the tarn, making something hateful almost beautiful.

Father once said they were the memories of ghosts, lingering about. Maybe. But I'm not sure.

Grasping them requires living them, even if the story is long, and terrible.

So I mostly avoid them, unless Roderick asks for one. I want my own memories, my own stories.

44
MADELINE IS SIXTEEN

Dressed in his traveling best, Roderick waits for me in the corridor. We stroll through the lower galleries, stopping to admire the Usher coat of arms. The walls are lined with ancient weapons. This room makes Roderick proud of the house, proud to be an Usher. But I can't pretend I'm not distressed. The madman's body was removed from the parlor, but I can't stop thinking of Father.

"It's like the house swallowed him whole," I whisper.

But I have a sinking, unspeakable suspicion about what truly happened to him.

My words provoke Roderick's temper. "I'm going to prove to you that this house is not watching us," he says. "Once and for all, and then I'll never have to hear you talking about what the house likes, what the house wants, again."

"Do you hate to hear me speak so very much?" I retort, for what else do I have to talk to him about? I haven't visited important cities or read thick books. I have the garden and the house. I would think, since he doesn't believe it is haunted, that he would be proud to be the master of such an ancient and stately home.

We reach the wall of mounted weapons, and in a movement so fast I cannot follow it, Roderick takes a knife from the wall and holds it to my throat. The blade is cold, and shaking because his hand is trembling.

"What are you doing?" My voice is choked and slightly high-pitched. Roderick would never hurt me, but the knife is cold . . . colder than it should be. Poisoned?

"I'm trying to show you. The house cannot protect you. The house doesn't know you or care about you."

"It does, Roderick," I say, because I believe it, and because I'm not going to let him think that I'm afraid.

He presses the knife harder against my flesh. There's a look in his eyes that reminds me of Father, when Father was mad.

But he will not scare me into abandoning the truth.

"Roderick . . ."

"Houses cannot feel things. It is not a malignant beast; it's an old house that needs repair."

"And if I don't agree, will you kill me?"

He drags me in front of him, keeping the knife pressed

to my throat and the other arm around my waist. He's over a head taller than me now. We are close together. I am acutely aware of the blood pumping through my veins, and aware that I am no longer afraid. We are two halves of a whole. He would never hurt me.

In a blur, everything changes.

The wood floor shifts under our feet and we fall, both of us. The knife clatters against the flagstones, and blood drips after it.

"Madeline." Roderick looks stricken as I put a hand to my neck. He pulls me onto his lap and examines the cut. "I'm sorry, so sorry, you know I would never hurt you. I tripped," he whispers.

I'm lying in Roderick's arms. The knife is on the floor, and I see blood on his white shirt, but I feel nothing. The house wanted this, but I don't know why.

"The house isn't haunted," he says. "But I am."

45
MADELINE IS TWELVE

Shadows swirl around me and Roderick, as if my room were full of candles, all of them casting light and shadow on the wall. But we have no candles. Roderick pulls my blankets to his chin.

"Tell me a story," he whispers.

I reach out into the atmosphere and grab the first one that I can. It isn't pretty.

"Once there were three ancient families who lived on an inlet. All were noble families with castles, and they became rich by stopping ships and making them pay a toll. But eventually other shipping routes opened, and the families were forced to gain sustenance from the land.

"The land was barren and rocky, and could not provide for three families.

"So one lord of the straits, Archibald Usher, invited the

others to a feast, and as they sat at his table, he slaughtered them, one by one. He gave them poison that immobilized them. Then he caught a drop of blood from each of them, in a great gold goblet, and drank it, like the lords did in those days, tying his health to the prosperity of the land.

"But before he reached the last of his former friends, she used her final moments to curse him. She cursed him with a short tragic life, with a line that would never enjoy the spoils of his crimes, and with never being able to leave his castle for any extended time, so that he would never enjoy the homes of his slaughtered friends.

"In the end, he drank her blood, as well as the blood of her children, and he sealed his fate."

Roderick and I consider each other from our opposite sides of the bed.

"Was that true?" Roderick asks.

"I don't know." This simple, small question, this suggestion that he might be willing to believe, is enough to make me happy. And the fearfulness of the tale lifts for a few minutes, until I fall asleep and dream of murdered children.

46
Madeline Is Sixteen

The knife *was* poisoned. Not by Roderick, but by some long-ago Usher, or the enemy of some long-ago Usher. Around me, the house tremors and convulses, shaking so violently that I'm afraid the ancient stones are going to crumble. As I lie in bed, the house overwhelms me, its emotions different than they have been since I was a child—bolstering, supportive. Despite the attacks and my growing fears, it doesn't want to lose me. And I don't want to die, so we are in agreement.

Several of the maids give notice. Madmen in the attics followed by earthquakes are too much for the faint of heart. It was best for Roderick to go, both because of his fears and because the house is wroth with him. And perhaps because I'm too afraid to test our bond. What if I had asked him to stay, after he nearly killed me, and he still walked away?

Dr. Winston sits beside my bed every day. He holds my hand while the doctors cleanse my blood by pumping out the old and purifying it and then putting it back into me. It goes in cold, making me shudder.

"You can return to your garden soon," Dr. Winston tells me. Spring is passing quickly. Cassandra thumps her tail on the floor, and I resolve to get out of bed soon. To be strong for her, and for myself.

47
FROM THE DIARY OF LISBETH USHER

I knew this day would come. Mr. Usher has proposed marriage to me. He isn't young, being several years older than Honoria was at her death, maybe twenty-five, but many girls marry men who are older.

I'm afraid because if I marry him, I attach myself to this place and this curse forever. But we have agreed to help each other break the curse. We sit in the library, reading and reading. Accounts of the history of the family and the house. Snippets of information about horrible ancestors, murderers, plague, and of course, the curse. Most upsetting is the story of Archibald Usher, who built the house, and whose battle-ax hangs over the entranceway. According to the legend, he used a great gold goblet to catch the blood of his victims.

We search the dusty shelves of the library. Together. He touches my shoulder sometimes, touches my hand as I turn the pages of the book. He is gentle and kind.

If we were married, then perhaps I would not be so frightened at night, when the house seems more powerful and the curse wraps itself around me and caresses me before it strangles me.

I distract myself with stories of the past. Sneaking down to the secret places below the house. Mr. Usher does not approve. He wants to avoid the darkest places, but I know we can't ignore the crypt. The curse originated on those very foundation stones. Our ancestors walked here. When I go into the vault, all the history of the House of Usher presses down on me, filling me with power to face the future.

48
MADELINE IS SIXTEEN

"Madeline," Dr. Winston says, pressing a packet of crushed herbs into my hand. I'm supposed to empty the packet into my tea to help me sleep. "Meet me in the hall of portraits. In an hour. When I'm done mixing and measuring medicines for the other doctors."

His voice is much warmer than when he talks to the older doctors. With them he is cold and detached. With me, he is . . . attentive.

I wait in the hallway, so I don't lose track of time. Some hours, like the ones in the middle of the night, seem to last forever, while others flow so quickly there seems to be no interval between meals, no time between sunrise and sunset.

How will the house react to meeting him here, away

from the doctors' tower and all of their clicking, clanking machinery? In my bedchamber, he won't allow his eyes to linger on me like he did when he asked me to meet him.

49
MADELINE IS FOURTEEN

"It's daytime, isn't it?" I ask the housekeeper, peering out the door into the semidarkness. Cassandra pulls me toward the door and whines.

I know it is midmorning, but there is no evidence that the sun still exists, and the landscape is mottled with clumps of fog. I look to the housekeeper, seeking her advice. Should I let Cassandra go out into this midday twilight?

"When the fog is this thick, you can get lost in it, and wander into another world," she warns.

Would another world be better or worse than this one?

Then she is back to her duties, ignoring me. None of the servants wish to hear me speak, but the housekeeper is particularly superstitious. I've heard the whispers. She believes I am ill luck incarnate, which is why she won't meet my eyes. The servants think the curse revolves around me, not the house. They fear my misfortune will somehow rub off on them, that my very presence in the same room could destroy whatever good fortune they've got left. And if they live here, they aren't very fortunate.

Gathering my nerve, I pull the door open, and Cassandra bounds outside. I named her after a doomed prophetess that Roderick told me about, an ignored twin, left behind, who could see the future.

Cassandra's been pent up inside for too long, and she leaps into a run, bypassing the garden. I take a few tentative steps away from the house. For a moment she's ambling along, and then she's gone, through a patch of mist . . . to nothing. I cry out and follow, but the cold hits me in the face. It's cold even for February, and as I try to catch my breath, I catch sight of a shape in the mist. I step forward, straining my eyes, and then I see a creature, partially obscured by the fog. I can't tell what it is; the mist is too thick.

At a bark from behind me, I turn, relieved to see Cassandra bounding toward me.

The housekeeper is standing in the doorway, holding a lantern up above her head. The lantern is losing its battle with this unnatural darkness, but it illuminates the harsh stone of the house above her, smooth except for one great fissure.

A wide crack starts at the kitchen doorway and goes upward, but it's impossible to guess how far in this gloom. A fit of trembling overtakes me. My breath comes short and pained, as if this damage to the house is my own injury.

Cassandra whines, and I look at her. She ambles toward me, and something about her is different. Her eyes have changed. They are no longer puppy eyes, but instead golden and wolflike.

I step back. I don't know how I know, but Cassandra is part of this place. Then she puts her nose into my hand and makes a snuffling sound. It's something she has always done, and I kneel so that I can put my arms around her. Still, I don't look directly into her eyes, because I'm afraid of what I might see.

We walk into the kitchen. The housekeeper is back at work. The lantern, still lit, sits on the table.

"Should've gotten yourself a cat," she says. "Not an oversized devil dog."

50
MADELINE IS SIXTEEN

I pace the portrait hallway, tired of waiting for Dr. Winston to join me.

"Madeline!" He bounds down the stairs. "I thought you could take me on a tour of the house."

I return his smile. The house is oddly silent, no creaking or groaning. I can't tell what it thinks of this idea.

"It's all so fascinating isn't it?" He gestures to the portraits lining the hall. "It must be amazing to be part of such an old family, so much history. . . ."

Some silly part of me wishes that he would look at me with the same attention he is giving to these Ushers, long dead and gone.

"I've heard the servants speak of the vault," he says. "Do you think we could go there?"

"I don't have the keys," I say, which is not a lie. The keys are in Roderick's room. I'm not supposed to use them. And the vault is only for family. I still shudder remembering how Roderick closed himself into the coffin and Father had to let him out. I would prefer to take Dr. Winston to the library or one of the formal parlors.

From off in my bedroom, Cassandra howls. She's probably scratching at the door, frightening the servants.

"I should go get her before she breaks something," I say.

Dr. Winston falls into step beside me. "Such a large dog," he says. "And an unusual breed. Wherever did you find her?"

I smile to myself and say nothing. He wouldn't believe me, even if I told him.

51
MADELINE IS THIRTEEN

Today is Christmas Day, and I am utterly and completely alone. Mother and Father are gone. Roderick is visiting the home of his school friend. He writes that he will come home before the new year, and we can celebrate together. The servants hung mistletoe in the main hall. It withered and died before morning. They replaced it a few times and then gave up. It is an unusually cold winter.

My eyes are dry; there is no point in pitying myself. I am alive; there is hope.

Dr. Paul came to my room to take some blood before he and Dr. Peridue left for the city, where they will visit pubs and make merry.

Even though it makes me feel more alone, I am glad that they are gone.

I sit in the study where my father used to try to write

letters. Stirring the last embers of the fire, I hear something through the wall. A muffled snuffling.

I go still, trying to contain all of my own sounds, even my breath. What could it be? I slip to the door. Should I summon a servant? I know the sounds of the house, even the terribly strange ones, but this is unfamiliar. Cowering in the doorway, I prepare to run.

Laughter floats up from downstairs. The servants are drinking wine from the wine cellar. There is no one to stop them. No deterrent except their own fear. Last year one of them went down for a cask of something and was locked in. No one realized he was gone for nearly a week. Since then, they've been terrified of the cellars. As they should be. Though not enough to keep them from their holiday merriment, it seems.

A low cry raises the hairs at the nape of my neck. It's a harsh sound, like something frightened, something in pain. I step gingerly back into the room, running my hands over the wall. The scratching from within is only growing louder. I hurry back to the hallway and enter the next room, thinking perhaps someone is on the other side of the wall, playing some trick on me.

It is empty. But the scratching and snuffling and crying from within the wall is getting more insistent.

I pick up the poker that lies before the fireplace, and hold it, balancing the weight of it across my hands.

Another cry. I prod the wall with the poker. It is paneled, but like most of the wood in the house, it is rotting. I punch a hole in the wall, and then another. There is a sharp yelp.

Pulling at the paneling, I'm careful not to put my hand completely inside. If the sounds are coming from a mouse or a rat, I don't want to inadvertently touch it. But a rat would not make those sounds, ones that make my heart contract with fear that an animal might be in pain.

I pull the wood away, wincing as a sliver slides under my fingernail. The house doesn't appreciate being attacked with a brass poker. But whatever is behind the wall, the house must have sent it.

The air from inside the wall feels heavier than the air of the room, and it pushes against me like something solid. I fall back, the poker, my only weapon, clattering to the floor as something big leaps out of the wall and pins me to the floor.

I let out a little squawk, though I don't have the air to scream. My heart stops. Everything goes still and so silent that I can hear the pulse pounding in my throat. Then the animal whimpers, and everything comes back into focus.

I'm lying on the floor all tangled in my skirts. A puppy licks my face.

Her tongue is wet, and her fur is incredibly soft. Despite

my surprise, my fear evaporates. When I lift my hand, she lets out a piteous whine. She's a large puppy. One that will grow into a big dog. I've never held a pup before, and I'm not quite sure what to do, so I just sit for a long time and hold her, until she starts to wiggle. Then I take her back to the sitting room.

I offer her a helping of roast beef from the plate one of the servants delivered an hour ago. She takes the food gently, careful of my fingers, but then gulps it down. Her ribs are showing. There is a sprig of holly on the plate, some servant's acknowledgment of the season. I set it aside, and as the puppy still looks hungry, I give her the pudding that was supposed to be my dessert. She eats it in one gulp.

She wags her tail and puts her enormous paws on my knees. I sit and look at her.

I expected to spend this Christmas alone. The dog curls up, right on top of my feet, and goes to sleep, and I sit, as content as I have been in a long time.

52
MADELINE IS SIXTEEN

I stop in front of a rather dismal oil painting and raise my candle to scrutinize the shadowy image, hoping absently that Dr. Winston will join me in the hallway again. In the weeks since he's been here, he's shown a great interest in the portrait gallery. What Usher commissioned an artist to paint this tiny, dark portrait of the house? I stare at it, squinting. I recognize the front of the house, but it seems unfamiliar. Has it changed, or have I? I lift my fingers to touch the painting but quickly pull them back. The texture makes me imagine that my fingertips might sink through the canvas.

Here is the turret of the tower where the doctors live, and there are the windows. I suppose those are the ones I look through every day. Are they really so sinister? My eyes burn, and I feel mildly ill.

I step away and consider the next painting. Equally dreary, it is a rear view of the house. I study it. The fissure, the great crack that originates above the kitchen door, is in the painting, but smaller. Did the earthquake lengthen the crack? I should check. Perhaps Dr. Winston will join me in the garden.

I look even closer. Now I see my flower garden. A verdant clearing, and at its center, a lone dandelion. My own garden at the beginning of spring. The picture has changed to encompass the small changes I've made.

Hope surges within me. I can shape the future, if I want to badly enough.

53
MADELINE IS THIRTEEN

It is three days after Christmas, and I cuddle my puppy, Cassandra, determined to keep her safe.

Roderick has finally arrived, looking handsome, and taller than before. He tells me about school pranks and stern teachers.

"My favorite classes are mathematics and logic," he says. He hands me a parcel of books. I admire the new and undeteriorated paper, touch the soft leather bindings. I run my hands over them, admiring these gifts that I will never be able to read. "This is an adventure story that I thought you would enjoy."

I have nothing for him, but he doesn't seem to mind.

He is wearing a medallion on his shirt, an ornate star upon a ribbon.

"It was a gift from a friend," he says. I narrow my

eyes. Mother made it clear that I should be jealous of his friends, though I'm not sure why. "The house seems different, and so do you, Madeline."

I have no words for the changes in him. He is wearing spectacles like Father used to wear. His hair is cut neatly, and is not as bright as last time he came home.

Roderick tells me about cities with buildings crowded together and of harbors full of ships. I try to imagine such things.

"Perhaps I could come and visit you," I suggest. "I would love to see your school, your friends."

His eyes dart to the hem of my dress. It is tattered, muddy from walking the grounds, planning where I will begin my spring planting when the ground thaws a bit. All of my dresses are threadbare and dark, out of fashion, ugly.

"I would love to have you visit, but it is impossible."

I put my hands in my lap. His distaste shames me, even with Cassandra at my feet.

An enormous spider drops down over Roderick's head, dangling from a web more tattered than my dresses. I point up, too aghast to speak. Roderick follows my finger, then lunges from his chair, throwing himself over me as if to protect me.

Cassandra whines. She was lying across my feet, and now he is pinning us both into the armchair.

"Madeline?" he says into my hair. "Other people don't live as we do. Other people don't . . ."

The spider swings closer, but Roderick appears to have forgotten about it.

He seems comforted by being so near me; we are twins, after all. But tomorrow he will be gone and there will be no one to care about me.

Cassandra gives a sharp bark at the same time that the spider brushes the back of Roderick's neck. He jerks away, but I am all tangled in his arms, and so as one person, we fall to the floor.

The spider lands beside us with a thump. Cassandra nudges it with her nose. Roderick pulls me away, across the floor, while Cassandra pushes it the other way.

"Tell me again, about finding her?"

This isn't the first time he's asked. He wants to know all about Cassandra.

I tell him. It's nice to have a story to relate, though I'm not sure that he, or anyone else, believes me.

She puts her big puppy paw on the spider, and then, while I watch, she bites into it. Two spider legs jerk back and forth as Cassandra chews and chews.

"One of the servants must have lost track of her," Roderick guesses. "The house is falling apart. It's no surprise she got trapped in a wall."

He raises himself with one arm and looks down at me.

"Roderick . . ."

With his other hand, he's stroking my hair, but I pull away from him.

"You don't believe anything."

"I do!"

"About the house."

He kisses my forehead.

"The house is angry with you," I warn him. A year ago, these words would have terrorized him.

His eyes are sad.

"Don't tell me you still believe the stories we told each other about the house watching us. Surely you must have outgrown those notions." Cassandra turns her head toward us as she spits the remains of the spider onto the rug. "Use logic, Madeline. Logic tells us that a house cannot be alive. Therefore it is not." Logic. He did say that was his favorite study at school.

I watch him sadly. Logic has no place in my life. We no longer speak the same language.

"Father said that I must not ever have a pet, that it would make the house jealous." Our parents may have been mad, but they knew things about the house.

Roderick half frowns, and I can tell he's frustrated with me, his provincial sister with dark superstitions.

"You say the dog came from inside the house," he says, though of course he didn't believe my story. "So the house must want you to have the dog. You can stop worrying about that."

When I don't say anything, he changes the subject. "I did ask the doctors if, in the future, you could come for a visit to my school. They said that you were not well enough, but maybe next year. Try to keep yourself well and ignore all these superstitions, and maybe you can visit me in the future. Would you like that?"

I wait for the house to do something, to prove to Roderick that it hears him and cares, but nothing happens. Cassandra pads back to us and sits down on the floor, waiting.

"Good dog," I say. She has the face of some sort of old forest gnome, homely and bearded.

"She's a wolfhound, I think," Roderick says as he leans forward to pet her. "We'll know better when she's fully grown."

"I adore her," I tell him.

"She is altogether unsuitable, you know," he says. "She's going to be huge."

"I don't care. She's perfect," I answer.

"So are you," he says. He is looking at me strangely. The house is holding its breath in anticipation, and the emotion that flows into me, when I touch the woodwork, is somewhere between happiness and awe. Is this the moment when I am supposed to convince him to stay with me? I sense that he might be open to the suggestion. But he is happy at school, and if he refuses to believe in superstition, then he will not be safe here.

Roderick climbs to his feet, and the moment passes.

54
MADELINE IS SIXTEEN

Slipping up the stairs to the doctors' tower, I hope that if anyone notices me, if I find myself in an awkward chance encounter, it will be with Dr. Winston. I'm not supposed to have an exam today, so it would be odd for me to turn up here, but the hours stretch away endlessly, and I wish for someone to talk to. If I run into him, I can ask about some new symptom I'm having, ask him to walk with me, perhaps.

Dr. Paul is away, so only Dr. Winston and Dr. Peridue are in the house. Dr. Winston checks in on me every night to make sure I'm not walking in my sleep, but I haven't seen much of him—at least, not as much as I would like.

Dr. Peridue rarely leaves the house, not to visit family, or to go to the city. I suspect he has nowhere to go.

As I reach the third floor, an odd noise comes from the

room overlooking the west side of the house. I tiptoe over to the door and press my ear against it. It sounds like some enormous beast is sleeping inside. I put my hand on the doorknob.

Should I?

I turn the door handle, carefully, quietly. Intent on not waking whatever is inside. The room glows green. Phantasmagoric, thick air spills out the door and surrounds me.

One entire wall has been redesigned. It is now some sort of . . . machine.

I have seen their machines before. They spend hours constructing them. But nothing on this scale.

I take a step closer. There are tubes and vials. Something is being pumped around and around, through what appear to be copper pipes, to lead pipes, and into big glass vials that look like hourglasses, but instead of sand, there is red liquid within. A great bellows, acting as the heart, pumps and pumps, and every few moments, a burst of steam comes out of the top.

I step backward.

It is ingenious. No matter what it does, all the noise keeps the house from looking into this room. They have confounded the house. In this room, they could do anything. Their power—the power to defy the house— terrifies me. How can these doctors, these strangers, be so much more clever than any Usher who has ever lived here? How can I use this discovery?

I scurry back, careful to shut the door, leaving no evidence that I was here.

55
MADELINE IS SIXTEEN

Leaving me in the examination room, Dr. Peridue has stepped into the room with the machines, mixing some medicines together to make a concoction that won't make any noticeable difference to my condition. Dr. Winston leans close, watching the door for Peridue's return. As if he's about to say something that's secret and wrong.

"I've been hearing things. Feeling things, emotions that are not my own. The house . . . ," he whispers.

He can only speak this way because the machines keep the house distracted. And if the other doctors knew he was suggesting such a thing, I'm sure they wouldn't let him stay.

He takes another furtive look at the door, afraid of Dr. Peridue returning. Louder, he says, "Step up on the scale. You're down a pound from last week. Are you eating?"

I sit down on one of the uncomfortable chairs. Our doctors scorn basic comfort like cushions and pillows.

"There's something in the darkness here," he says under his breath. "All the history in this house, something that calls to me. And won't let me go."

His eyes shift, right to left.

I watch him carefully.

I know exactly what he means about the darkness.

Still, his intensity melts my fear, melts the reticence that took over me when he started talking about the house with admiration verging on love. Like the house, I react to strong emotions. I put out my hand to touch his arm.

"Meet me here later, tonight," he says, just as Dr. Paul comes in from the hallway, using the door Dr. Winston wasn't watching. Dr. Paul's eyebrows go up, and he looks back and forth between us. Dr. Winston busies himself among the medical instruments, humming softly.

"The servants say you aren't eating," Dr. Paul says.

My stomach rebels at the thought of food.

"Have you fallen into any trances this week?" Dr. Paul asks.

The doctors have been distracted lately. Dr. Peridue has had a series of toothaches. They have had to remove several of his teeth. The servants whisper that he keeps them in a bloody box under his bed.

"If I had been in a trance, the servants would have told

you," I say. The servants love making reports of my ill-
nesses and odd behaviors. And they would also report if
they had seen me creeping up to the tower in the middle
of the night, wouldn't they?

56
From the Diary of Lisbeth Usher

I am married. It was like a dream, something that happened to long-ago Ushers. The house became a palace, filled with flowers imported from who knows where, even though it is the dead of winter. We approached the front door in a sleigh. Mr. Usher tucked furs all around us, and then he led me inside, through scores of white lilies in crystal vases that mirrored the ice outside.

Mother was ecstatic, her hand over her mouth and tears running down her face.

My sister, who is almost grown, wore her own white gown. I enjoyed her amazement, but beneath it was envy, and that I did not enjoy. What is happening to her? All of her sweetness and innocence seems to have slipped away.

Mr. Usher had promised me a trip to the city, where we might find books that could shed light on the curse, on my illness, but instead he circled the property in the sleigh, calling softly to the horses.

"Now that it's time, I don't really want to leave," he said, and I agreed, because the way he was looking at me, full of admiration and longing, the rest of the world seemed unimportant, even finding a way to fight off the illness. I have not had a spell in ages. Perhaps marriage was the cure. Or love. Beneath my feet, the house seems to be singing a low, happy rumble of a song. Today was the best day of my life.

57
MADELINE IS SIXTEEN

I skip the third stair, the one that creaks, only to discover
that the fourth stair creaks now. Every single stair groans
with each of my light footsteps.

Walking through the examination room at night makes
me shiver, but the room with the huge machine is worse.
I stare up at the valves, the pumping mechanisms. What
is it?

I feel Dr. Winston behind me, even before his hands
touch my shoulders.

"Madeline," he murmurs. "Madeline Usher." I turn so
that we are facing each other. I want to see his face.

"I'm here," I say, raising my chin to look him in the eye.

"I can't believe it," he says. "Six months I've been here,
waiting for this moment."

He has been waiting; I've seen it in his demeanor. I

understand waiting. But what he's been waiting for isn't me. He's falling in love with the house.

"I wish you'd come before," I say. When I still trusted the house. Because I can never trust it now, and while he's in its thrall, I can never trust him. Does that matter? How important is trust? At this moment, I am not alone, and the house isn't watching, and Dr. Winston's eyes gleam.

"I'm here now." He drops one hand from my shoulder to my waist. He doesn't know that this can never be.

I have been alone for so long.

His closeness is intoxicating.

"The house will never let us be together," I say.

"We're safe here." He glances to the machine.

I laugh. "The House of Usher is far more devious than that. It only allows this thing to work because it doesn't truly care what the doctors are doing. If it sees me going into this room repeatedly, if it sees me going in with you . . ."

"You are the chosen of the house," he says reverently.

A splash of cold water? A slap in the face? This is why he wants me. He leans closer. "If the house is aware . . . we must make every moment count."

I put up my hand to stop him, even as he bends in for a kiss. He wants the house's love, not mine. But he takes my hand, pressing his lips to my palm. "You are so delicate." He traces the veins, his fingers caressing down my wrist. Every moment we spend here is a dangerous act of rebellion.

Right now he can deny the inclinations of the house. But for how long?

58
Madeline Is Thirteen

Cassandra paces in front of my door. It is propped, as always, with a book, but less open than it used to be; I can't have Cassandra roaming the halls at night. She knocked over a candelabra, spilled hot wax across the floor of one corridor, and singed one of the rugs.

She could've burned down the house. At least that's what Miss Billingsly said, full of housekeeperly indignation. As if the house could so easily be destroyed.

Curious, I edge my candle closer to the curtain. A gentle breath of air extinguishes it. No, the house cannot be burned down.

Fear of accidents isn't the real reason I keep Cassandra confined. Since the day outside when she seemed to change, when she ran through the ghostly mist creatures and returned to me with gold eyes, I've been afraid. Of

my own dog. I lie in bed, and the house whispers that I must be cautious.

And so she paces, and I wonder if I should reach out to her. The house murmurs. Care for the dog but never forget the house. Is Cassandra simply a distraction? Is she somehow in league with the house?

She gives a little low growl in her throat. A ghost floats by the doorway, pausing for half a second, then drifting down the hall.

If only I could be certain who to trust. My instincts aren't enough.

59
MADELINE IS SIXTEEN

Cassandra is missing.

The door to my room is closed tightly, but she is not inside. I woke up last night in Roderick's bed. I must have walked in my sleep. Usually Cassandra stops me, puts herself between me and anything dangerous, licks my face to wake me. But she didn't wake me, and when I return to my room, she isn't there.

A maid passes, bringing up my tray.

"You aren't supposed to skip meals, miss," she calls after me. "The doctors say it isn't good for you."

I ignore her and call for Cassandra, hating the fear in my voice. Surely if someone has seen her, they will tell me.

Dr. Winston is standing in the hallway, talking to one of the serving girls.

"Madeline," he calls, even though he is supposed to call

me Miss Usher. I put my hand on his arm, and he turns so quickly that we are standing closer than I meant, too close. The maid looks upset. Jealous? I don't care.

"It's Cassandra. I can't find her."

"I'll help you look," he says at once.

"Outside," I say, though I'm not sure why.

I hurry toward my garden. Cassandra and I have spent countless hours there. To the left of my garden, there is a small clearing, and a great crack in the earth, a sort of fissure.

And Cassandra is lodged half in and half out of the crack.

When she sees me, she whimpers and fights harder to dig her way out, shaking her head from side to side, then lets out one fierce bark. She's lodged so tightly that she can barely move. The earth has fallen in around her.

I scream, and dive forward, working to dig her out with my hands.

"I don't know if this is a good idea," Dr. Winston is saying. "There is something unnatural about that fissure. I don't think you should make it bigger."

"I don't have any choice. Help me."

He is right about the fissure. I'm troubled by the fact that the fur around Cassandra's face is now white rather than gray. But that doesn't mean that I will leave her trapped here a second longer than I have to.

I turn toward him, and he sighs. Then he shrugs and thrusts his own hands into the dry earth to help me dig.

The sun is not bright, but still, I'm sweating by the time we've widened the crack so that she can squirm her way out. She gives herself a shake, and bits of debris rain down on us. Then she sits and looks at me, wagging her tail. For once she does not bare her teeth at Dr. Winston. Maybe she is getting used to him.

60
From the Diary of Lisbeth Usher

The anniversary of Honoria's death approaches, and I find myself missing her. I am no longer the child I was when I entered the House of Usher. I sit with Mr. Usher's mad sister. I don't know what I want. Mother told me I wanted Mr. Usher.

Now Mother is gone.

It all happened so quickly. She came down with a fever, and then they were burying her. Gone.

I feel so alone.

It is worse for my younger sister. She adored Mother, of course, and even Honoria was nice to her.

And now that the wedding is over, I realize how cursed I am. It is worse than I ever imagined. I went to Mr. Usher and demanded answers.

"Tell me everything you know about the curse," I begged him.

"You are too young," he replied.

"*Too young to fall victim to a curse, or too young to hear the details of the curse? What is happening to me?*"

He looked sad.

"*Sit down,*" *he said. He put his quill on the table, where it lay ignored, with black ink bleeding from the tip.*

"*There is a plague on this house, a malady.*"

"*What will happen if I die?*" *I asked him.*

"*Then the curse will pass to your sister, as Honoria passed it to you.*" *I knew this, but hearing it confirmed made my heart heavy with foreboding.*

Why did Mother bring us to this place?

61
MADELINE IS SIXTEEN

We're in the room with the machine. A second meeting, furtive and exciting. Dr. Winston's eyes are all alight.

"It is my life's work to care for you," he says. "Your symptoms have slowed, you are nearly healthy! You look beautiful, radiant. There is a place, only a few days from here, a spa, with restorative waters. I could do the same for you. My own mother used to go there, when she was ill. She said the mineral waters were lovely."

"Where is your mother now?" I ask.

"Dead," he says, "but that has nothing to do with us."

It doesn't give me much hope in the benefits of the waters, though.

He keeps talking. I like to listen to him talk of curing me. Yet when Dr. Winston turns his attention to me, I

imagine that I could be like other girls, enthralled by a man. It's dangerous to pretend—I could start to believe— but I can't seem to stop.

Even Lisbeth Usher was happy and got her fairy-tale wedding, in the end.

62
MADELINE IS SIXTEEN

Roderick is home for the holidays. He's been here for one day, and we've already managed to fight. He didn't like the way Dr. Winston was whispering to me. Didn't like that Dr. Winston sits by my bed as I'm going to sleep.

"He's protecting me from the house," I tell Roderick.

"Is that what he tells you? He feeds on your superstitions? How can you listen, how can you believe . . ." It's the same old litany. Only I've changed in the months since he poisoned me. I am stronger now.

"You don't believe anything!" I find myself screaming in Roderick's face. "Do you think I'm a liar? Do you think I'm crazy?"

He shakes his head, as if my outburst has only saddened him. I don't know how to make him see, and I'm so exhausted by trying. Filled with the energy of my anger, I

storm away. Let him sit alone and laugh to himself about my superstitions. He leaves soon, and I don't care. At least Dr. Winston knows that the house is watching. Roderick is as oblivious as a child.

"Madeline?"

Roderick is following me.

I stomp down the hallway, feeling great satisfaction in the sound my feet make, the way my footsteps reverberate through the house. I turn the corner and see a familiar suit of armor. Everything goes slow and fuzzy. How could I have been so stupid as to walk this way, to revisit this place?

My brother is right behind me.

I see the gauntlet open; this time it is clear. The hand releases; the battle-ax falls. I feel the cold of the blade grazing my cheek.

But before it can bite into me, I fall backward, as Cassandra leaps over me. The handle of the battle-ax is in her mouth. She twists her body, desperately trying to avoid flying down the stairs, but then she is gone, tumbling, falling.

63
Madeline Is Sixteen

Cassandra is broken. The old doctor shakes his head; he is secretly happy. Dr. Paul puts his hands on her fur. I almost push them away. I don't like him touching her.

"She has a broken rib," he says.

Cassandra whines and stares up into my face, searching for something. She is so good and so loyal.

"Give her this for the pain," Dr. Paul continues, handing me a vial. "And keep her still. She's going to be fine."

Dr. Peridue frowns. Is it because Dr. Paul is helping me—or is he giving me a vial of poison, planning to rid them of the annoyance that Cassandra causes?

They leave together. They hate being summoned

from their tower. When I come to them, they have the power. Cassandra lets out a little yelp. They still have the power.

I consider the vial. Will it relieve her pain, or will it kill her? Trust or mistrust? I don't know what to do.

64
From the Journal of Lisbeth Usher

Today I stood on the widow's walk, thinking of Honoria and how she never showed any emotion, and how she stood up here and jumped. Did she know something that I don't know? Even with the horrors of the cures, why was death more appealing than life?

I didn't care for Honoria. Now I wonder if the house had something to do with this. It sets us against one another. I see it happening.

My younger sister wants Mr. Usher.

So I went to him and told him, if she is the one you want, then lift this curse from me and let me go.

But he said he would not. He said that the curse always visits the house's heir, but it falls harder on his intended. Because we are married, I'll go mad first. He smiled when he said it. I asked about his sister. Was her madness some other sort? But as always, he ignored the question. He will not speak of his sister. Or mine.

65
MADELINE IS THIRTEEN

I came across a creature in the woods today. And a grave-stone. The grave was covered with dead leaves and other debris from the forest.

I was farther from the house than usual, collecting gardening implements. We used to have a gardener, but his cottage has been abandoned, and the very walls are falling away. A shed stands near the old cottage, with some useful gardening implements inside. I don't feel it is wrong for me to take them. To use them.

On my way back from it, distracted by my plans for the garden, I wasn't watching where I stepped, and I rammed right into the hidden gravestone.

I cried out and fell forward, holding my bruised shin. Something slithered through the dead leaves toward me.

Cassandra growled deep in her throat and leaped in front of me.

I grabbed a stick and scrambled back. The creature was larger than any snake I'd ever seen, even in the long grass that borders the woods.

I held the stick before me, unsure if I should prod at it, or if I should run. My leg was trembling, and a trickle of blood ran down it. The doctors say I bruise and bleed easily.

The forest blurred, and I could feel a hyperesthetic spell beginning. Suddenly I could see through Roderick's eyes, feel what he was feeling, which was not unusual. What was unusual was that I couldn't separate my emotions from his, couldn't bring my consciousness back to the forest. I heard Cassandra bark once, and that was all. I was strolling as Roderick through the city streets, talking with his school friend, laughing, as all the while I struggled to separate myself. To return to being Madeline.

When I woke, my head was resting on Cassandra's back in a patch of green. No dead leaves were in sight; it was as if a strong wind had blown them away. There was no place for a creature to hide. Nothing to crunch underfoot as I struggled to my feet and staggered back to the house.

Cassandra pranced beside me, proud of herself, and I knew, beyond a doubt, that I could trust her. Whether or not she had come from the house, her heart was mine.

66
Madeline Is Sixteen

Doctor Winston stands in my doorway holding a box.

"It is a gift," he says. "It came by courier, from your brother."

I do not know why I feel disappointed. Did I really think that Dr. Winston had gone to the trouble to bring me a present for my birthday?

The box is wrapped with a thick gold cord.

I take it with trembling hands, praying that this note won't say Roderick isn't coming home tomorrow. He must be here for our birthday.

"Let me help you," Dr. Winston says, putting his hands over mine. His nails are clean, but broken from digging Cassandra out of the hillside, and that makes me like him even more than I did before.

It doesn't seem to appease Cassandra, though. She

growls as he pushes himself close to me, whatever warmth she felt toward him forgotten.

The string unravels, leaving the box exposed and ready to be opened, but he doesn't step back or take his hands from mine.

"I stay here for you, not the house," he says. "I know what you're thinking. I know you fear that since I can hear the house, I must be your enemy. But I'm not."

When I first met him, I desperately wanted to kiss him. That feeling returns. He's close enough, and I don't think he would object.

Unlike Roderick, he believes the house is sentient, though he seems half in love with it, and that is dangerous. Unless he comes to see the evil intentions, as I have.

I lift the lid from the box. Inside is a ruby necklace, heavy and ornate. Dr. Winston lifts it to my throat. I don't know what Roderick was thinking. It's far *too* heavy and ornate; it makes my neck look too thin, too fragile.

In the mirror, the rubies are a red gash against my throat.

"It suits you," the doctor says. He hooks the necklace and puts his hands on my shoulders.

Cassandra growls, deep in her throat, and she brushes against me as she stands, but before I can turn to admonish her for being a rude dog, Dr. Winston kisses me.

For a moment, all my anxiety is swept away by the

feeling of his mouth against mine. I twine my hand into his hair, surprised that it's rough and a little coarse.

He presses against me, and I allow him to maneuver me toward my bed. Perhaps he did not fasten it properly, or perhaps the clasp was broken, but as we move, the heavy necklace crashes to the floor. We break apart, both bending to retrieve it.

Dr. Winston's face is wide open and earnest.

"There are so many things I want to tell you. No one else knows, or believes. I wasn't sure if I could trust you, but now . . . ," he's saying.

There is a slip of paper on the floor. It must have fallen from the gift box.

I love you, it says. *R.*

I pick it up.

Dr. Winston seems fascinated by the movement.

I fold the note and put it on the table beside my bed. He puts the necklace over it, like a jewel-encrusted paperweight.

Raising my face to his, I wait for him to kiss me again, my entire being focused. I don't want to hear about the house, not now. I want this moment to be between the two of us, only. With this kiss, maybe he could release me from the part of the curse that Roderick and I don't speak of.

But the kiss never comes.

When I open my eyes, I see shock written across his face. Between us, the wooden floor of my bedroom has split, in absolute silence, with a wide, jagged crack.

Dr. Winston backs away from me, his eyes filled with fear. I stare at the floor, testing it to see if it is stable. When Cassandra relaxes, I know he's gone, though the splintered rent in my floor remains.

The necklace lies abandoned on my bedside table.

67
Madeline Is Seventeen

Should I feel different today? Does anyone actually feel different on their birthday? I pace back and forth, waiting for Roderick. He should have arrived hours ago, and I am agitated and excited. I have a new dress. One that hasn't had time to fade to the sickly weathered gray of the others. It doesn't matter what color they were when they were placed in there—red, pink, yellow, they all fade within a fortnight.

But this one is different. It's midnight black, like a raven's wing, and it has not faded. I will wear it to dinner tonight, with my new necklace.

On the first night after Roderick comes home, the servants always lay out dinner, course after course, in the dining room, so that we can eat among the cobwebs and ghosts. Then, after that first unexplained evening, they

return to the habit of delivering our trays of food to the parlor, like they have since our parents died.

Tonight I will put up my hair like a lady and walk down the staircase with him. We will play make-believe. Tonight will be special.

The clock in the hallway chimes and startles me.

Roderick should be here already.

Cassandra follows me, swatting pieces of heavy mahogany furniture with her tail.

I tell myself there is no reason to worry. Roderick has probably set out late.

I lead Cassandra through the unused rooms at the front of the house to the arched entranceway. A ceiling beam is lying on the floor, splintered into a million pieces. Cassandra sniffs it and whines, nudging me forward.

Over the years, the causeway has shifted. It used to lead to the drawbridge, another affectation of the crazy Ushers. The rusting chains that held the door still hang, thicker than my arm, along with the remains of the pulleys. New stonework was put in, halfheartedly, to replace that larger door.

Roderick generally enters through a side door the servants use for bringing in food and supplies. But today is special, and his arrival should be grander.

I touch the ancient drawbridge. The planks stain my hands black. I force the door open, using my shoulder and all of my weight. Though smaller than the original, it is still twice as tall as me, and wide enough to allow multiple horses through. To my left is a stabling area where the black coach is housed, as well as Roderick's white horses. I have never been allowed to ride. It's too dangerous if a fit comes on.

The door opens with a hideous and painful screech, and Cassandra and I walk outside into late-afternoon sunlight. When the drawbridge was taken down, the causeway was extended.

The smell from the tarn hits me when I step outside, gagging me. It's only the smell of water, I tell myself. Fetid water, but still, it shouldn't affect me so strongly. Cassandra and I make our way across the causeway. Halfway across, the combination of bright sunlight and the smell forces me to my knees. With my hands pressed to my stomach, I close my eyes and try to stay calm. This is not a safe place for a fit.

I stare into the water, willing myself to be well. Either I will go back and wait for Roderick in the house, or I will cross the causeway and wait for him in the shade of the white trees. I cannot stay here.

The water is dark, tinged with gray. It reflects the sunlight rather than absorbing it. As I stare into it, I see something looking back at me. Eyes. Great empty eyes. It's something ancient and monstrous, something

I've never even dreamed of. I look away, pretending to have seen nothing. The water, that lusterless water that doesn't move even in the worst of storms, ripples once and then composes itself, once again a mirror reflecting the house.

Looking forward, I take in the blighted forest, a series of dead white trees, standing until the next storm knocks more down. It stretches for miles and miles surrounding our property.

The causeway is paved with flat stones, but the earth underneath has settled, and the walkway is uneven. I tread carefully. Cassandra follows me, her fur bristling.

As I walk, the path seems to extend and stretch forever. Longer than it was when I took my first step. The tarn remains unruffled at the surface, but I can hear, all around me, the sound of slithering.

A vision hits me harder than any hyperesthetic spell I've ever suffered. I've been pulled in to Roderick's mind. He's riding, and something has spooked his horse. I can feel the movement, feel Roderick frantically holding on. I hear his laughter, quick and high-pitched; he's enjoying this, and yet terrified. And then he's flying forward, and I, on my knees, am falling with him. I fall without even the presence of mind to stretch out my arms to catch myself. Not that I could catch myself, because I'm not going to land on solid earth.

I plunge into the tarn, and sink farther under water than I've ever been. I don't move, frozen by surprise and fear. I've lived here my entire life and never touched this fetid water. It burns my skin, acidic. It flows into my nostrils, seeks entrance to my mouth, pushing and pushing. It moves, oily, over me.

I twist my neck, looking in the direction that I think is up, and there is light coming through the gloom. I should be struggling, but my dress is so wet and so heavy, and I'm sinking deeper and deeper into a complacent bed of silt.

Images flash before my eyes: Roderick on horseback, approaching the house; the doctors, cursing the loss of my body as a specimen for their experiments; Cassandra, howling over and over, long, mournful cries as if her heart is breaking. Cassandra's grief finally shakes me from my apathy, and I thrash my arms.

Something wraps itself around my ankle. A seaweed or fungus, perhaps? It twines, silky smooth, up my leg, and as I attempt to propel myself, the hold tightens. The water shimmers around me as I fight my way to the surface, and my wet dress clings to my legs, so very heavy, but I ignore the weight; if I think about it, if I let the horror sink in, I'll never reach the surface. Something is living, something lives in the tarn, and it is here with me now, and it wants me.

"Madeline, Madeline!" Someone—Roderick—is yelling my name.

I break through the surface, the shore only feet away; it is barren and rocky. The water is too foul for anything to grow near it. It is oily on my skin. I fight toward the shore, but then the thing wrapped around my ankle yanks me back toward the center of the tarn. I try to cry out but choke on a mouthful of bitterness as I'm pulled under.

I feel rather than see the splash as Cassandra jumps in, and I twist toward her, struggling with direction. Everything in the water feels distorted, wrong. But Cassandra finds me; she is warm and strong. I wrap my arms around her as she pulls me to the surface. Even this foulness does not lessen the warmth, the comfort of her body in my arms.

I try to kick, fighting again with my skirts and the thing that still has hold of my ankle. It twines around and around both of my legs, spiraling to my waist. Half immobilized, my only chance is Cassandra. She struggles, yanking me back.

I gasp for one breath before I am pulled under again. Whatever has hold of me is soft and pliable. My hands move through it, yet it is alive . . . it wants to devour me.

It slithers over my skin, and I know this is what fouls the water.

I try to keep my eyes open, but the water burns, and I

can't see anything, and I'm choking.

And then Cassandra is pressed against me again. She can't bite the creature, because it is so gelatinous. She twists away from me and dives directly into the mass of the creature.

For a moment the pressure eases and I'm able to kick again, and I lash out with my arms and legs, trying to disengage, trying to find my way. Where is the surface?

There's one more slither over my torso, one more attempt by the creature to hold me, and then I'm free and doing my best to swim.

I fight my way back to sunlight and heave myself onto the side of the tarn. Roderick is there, grabbing me, holding me.

"Madeline, Madeline, Madeline," he says over and over. I dry my eyes on his tunic and turn back to the tarn.

Cassandra surges up out of the water once, and I dive toward her, but Roderick won't let me go.

"You aren't going back in there," he says.

I turn on him, hitting him with my fists, twisting away from him, but my dress is soaked and heavy with water and slime, and he's too strong.

Cassandra doesn't come to the surface again.

The servants watch us through the windows.

Roderick takes off his coat and wraps it around my shoulders.

"I saw you falling," I whisper, because my throat is on fire. Will I die from all the foul water I swallowed? My lips are swollen and bleeding.

"I fell from my horse, an accident. If I'd gotten here earlier—" His voice breaks. He rubs my shoulders, strokes my hair.

"Cassandra?"

"She's gone, Madeline."

I shudder. "She saved me. I should have saved her, at least tried . . ."

"You were in no shape to save anything. Cassandra . . . she sacrificed herself to save you."

Sacrifice.

I taste the word. It is as terrible as the stinking water that is running down my back.

68
MADELINE IS SEVENTEEN

They serve our birthday dinner in the dining room. Roderick complains the beef is too rare. I take a few sips of broth to appease him.

"I'm only here for three nights," he says. "As always, I had to get special permission to leave school for your birthday."

Our birthday. I sit across from him, wearing my black dress and the ruby necklace. It was his birthday gift, after all. One of the smaller rubies is missing. My neck is raw and scraped to bleeding from a jagged place, a bit of gold that has come loose. Roderick doesn't notice.

An evil thought occurs to me, creeps into my mind and won't go away. How long did Roderick stand at the edge of the tarn, watching me? Was he too afraid to intervene? Could he have done more?

I try to force the questions away, but they creep back in.
I can't cry.

Everywhere, my skin is red and raw, with raised red bumps. As I dressed for dinner, a clump of my hair fell out. The penalty for letting the water of the tarn touch my skin. Roderick's hands are blistered where he pulled me from the water. And held me against my will.

"I am sorry, Madeline. I know you loved that dog," Roderick says, but he does not sound sorry enough.

He was jealous of my love for Cassandra, and now she is gone. But his friend, the one who he cares about so deeply, is still very much alive. Luring Roderick away from the house, and keeping him from truly seeing what is happening here.

69
MADELINE IS SEVENTEEN

Roderick wants some sort of fanfare because he's here. But I don't have the energy. He only spent one night, instead of the three he had planned, and now he's saddling his horse, as if he can't wait to get away. He mutters something about spending some time out of doors, shooting and riding, and that he'll return to see that I'm well before he goes back to school, but I'm not sure what he means. With Cassandra gone, how could I ever be well? And by the time I turn to ask him, he's already gone.

I had hoped for so many things with this visit, and this birthday. Not least of all, I wanted to try to make him understand how dangerous the situation is, here in the house.

I thought that we would find the right time together, that he would be focused on me for once, and he would really listen, perhaps find it in his heart to believe a bit. . . . But he saw what happened in the tarn. He had to see something, but he won't accept it.

The hooves of Roderick's horse clatter as he crosses the causeway. I am alone.

The house is isolating me.

I pace beside the tarn. I throw stones into it. I walk the entire periphery of that sullen, motionless body of water. Someone, perhaps Father, once told me that the depth of the tarn is exactly the same as the height of the house. Things like that used to interest me.

The water is serene and still. Unruffled. There is no indication that anything lives beneath the surface. And there has been no sign of a dog's drowned body. Cassandra is gone. Her absence is ever-present, doubling me over with the agony of loss.

A part of me wants to fight, but then the hopelessness takes over. Standing beside the tarn, the house looms over me. The great trees surrounding the property cast twisted shadows. I am so small, one Usher in an unending line, all captives of the house. How can I fight? I've lost Cassandra. The young doctor stepped away from me, after the kiss in my bedchamber when the house made its intentions clear. He's afraid, and I don't blame him.

The only thing the house didn't take was Roderick. He just left. He turned and rode away.

70
MADELINE IS SEVENTEEN

Roderick is on the property. I saw him through the window, prowling along the distant tree line. It could have been anyone, except for the silvery-blond hair. And of course I'd know him anywhere. So he must be riding and shooting on the nearby moors. I take a dark cloak from his closet, one that belonged to Father.

I only go outside to walk the grounds and work in my garden, and I have only rarely left the shadow of the house, even with Cassandra at my side. At the edge of the Usher land is a platform where the coach stops once a day. The servants use it when they visit their families or go to the nearest village, and the doctors have equipment delivered by coach. I've been there once before, or else dreamed that I was there.

Roderick was walking in that direction, though I'm not

sure why he was walking. When he left, he was riding, so he has his horse somewhere on the property.

I stop in the hallway, not afraid, just gathering my strength.

The chambermaids are in the left parlor talking about me, and I let their gossip distract me from my uneasiness.

"Poor girl," one of them says.

"It's creepy, if you ask me." The other girl sneezes from the dust. "Whenever I see her, I think she's a ghost."

"The doctors scare me worse than hearing ghosts."

"Not me. Nothing scares me worse than ghosts. And this house is full of spooks. Look at that, have you ever seen paneling just crumble away like that?"

"Termites?"

"Nah, they won't come here, any more than mice. Just spiders and rats in the House of Usher."

I wrap Father's dark cloak around my shoulders and stare down the hall, past the room where they are chattering. Their voices fade. The doorway is a frame. The sun is shining on the other side. I can step through to a different world.

I put one foot gingerly in front of the other, as I travel from the shadow of the house to the edge of the trees.

A river of sludge runs through the forest, not quite a stream, more seeping mud with a bit of flowing water. I step over it carefully and keep going. I can see the sunlight through the trees up ahead. A forest of saplings has grown up in the space between the lawn and the mighty trees that line the periphery of the Usher estate.

The air feels different here; it is more difficult for me to breathe.

This is what it was like when Father took me away. I think. The memories are jumbled. Sometimes it seems that we were gone for weeks, living in a rented room by the sea. That Father hired a lady to care for me.

Looking back, I am far enough to see the entirety of the house, the multilayered roof, the additions, the tower that should be lovely to the eyes but only serves to highlight the ungainliness of the rest of the house, crouching over the tarn. I'm too numb for the horror of it to have much effect on me. This way leads to Roderick, I tell myself—but suddenly I am afraid.

I pick my way through the trees, though the saplings and other undergrowth make going slow. A natural barrier hemming in the Usher land. I'm surprised when I get through the trees and feel the warmth of the sun. Ahead of me is the long platform where servants and visitors meet the carriage.

Roderick and his hateful friend are standing on the platform. I study them from the shadow of the forest.

The other boy is perhaps a year older than us. He is tall, but not so tall as my brother, and he looks sturdy and strong. It is Roderick's roommate. Roderick has spoken of him so often that I dreamed of him once, and I've seen him through Roderick's eyes. I have despised this unknown boy for years. But as he laughs, my hatred evaporates.

I admire his easy demeanor and his smile that is not tainted by ghosts and mystery. He is . . . refreshing, like a summer wind that blows away cobwebs and disease. With an unexpected burst of emotion, I discover that I would like to be the one whose company he enjoys. I feel as if an abyss is opening at my feet. Of course Roderick chose this strange boy over me.

The sickly spring sun bounces off Roderick's dark glasses. He wears them to avoid headaches from the sun. Before he disappeared from our lives, Father could not even endure candlelight.

Roderick's horse neighs and stamps, and Roderick soothes it. I realize that the one he's brought isn't the horse he usually takes to school. His friend is obviously waiting for the coach, and Roderick must be going back to the house, at least to swap out horses, perhaps to rest a night before he officially goes back to school.

Walking back across the platform, Roderick trips over a loose board. He catches himself, awkwardly, and his friend throws back his head, and I see his white teeth flash and his eyes crinkle.

If it had been me mocking his clumsiness, Roderick would have turned surly, but not so with this friend. They clasp hands, in the way that boys do, and clap each other on the back. For a moment I think that they are going to embrace.

Then, unexpectedly enough to make me gasp, Roderick claps his friend on the back once again, and swings up into the saddle.

He's riding back toward the house and will expect me to be there. If I ran . . . I could take the more direct path through the woods and beat him. But I don't.

Roderick's friend paces across the platform, full of energy. His vitality is mesmerizing. I take a step toward him, pulled in by something that I can't explain, and he sees me.

"Hello?" he calls.

My heart stops. I edge closer to the platform.

"Hello," he says. "Are you waiting for the coach?"

I shake my head. "I'm just walking," I say. The sun, usually so reticent in these parts, comes out.

He's looking at me too intently for politeness. Does he recognize me?

I feel myself blushing at his attention.

"There isn't anything around here for miles, you know," he says. And then he blushes in return. "Or . . . I guess there must be something. You live here, I suppose?"

I nod.

"Would you like to sit with me and rest for a moment?"

He reaches out to help me up the steps. The tips of my boots are muddy. I try to hide them under my skirts.

What temerity I have, to sit beside this magnificent creature in the afternoon sunlight. Am I mad?

"They say this area is inhabited by enchanted creatures. Are you a pixie?" His eyes are bright and curious. His tone is light. Flirtatious, perhaps?

I laugh. "I wish I were magical, but I'm just a girl taking a walk."

His forehead creases. "A young lady shouldn't walk alone. What if someone came along . . ."

I nearly laugh again. No one in these parts would harm me. There is safety in being cursed. But his concern makes my heart feel odd, like it's beating in circles.

"It's safe," I say. "For me."

"Speaking of young women who are alone in the world," he says quickly, "I'm concerned about the reputation of a local family. A kinswoman of mine is on her way to the House of Usher. She plans to offer her services as a governess. . . ."

A governess? At the House of Usher?

"My friend lives there. Roderick Usher."

I shrug. "No one knows much about the Ushers."

"That's what I'm given to understand. Roderick says

they haven't hired a governess, so I suspect she's going there on a fool's errand, to confront a young man she's fallen in love with."

My heart stops for a moment. Does he mean Roderick? Is that why Roderick is always visiting his friend's home, wanting to stay the summer with him? Not for him, but for this kinswoman?

"It's a doctor who cares for the young lady of the house. An unsavory character."

I'm not sure if this is better or worse. He must mean Dr. Winston. But the doctor's regard is for the house, with a bit left over for me. Where does another girl fit into this? And what does he mean by unsavory?

"It's good of you to keep me company. I've never been to this part of the country. My friend left school to visit his sister, and I followed him. He'd invited me to the house, to meet her, but when my coach arrived yesterday, he said the visit was impossible, so we fished in one of the lakes and then camped here on the moor. We slept under the stars. It was glorious, except for the smell."

He means the smell from the tarn. On clear nights it carries. Sometimes, when there is fog, the moisture settles on your skin, and so does the heavy scent of it.

He is still speaking. I watch the way his mouth moves. Repeating himself, he says, "It's kind of you to keep me company."

"You'll miss your friend." I find it hard to say the word "friend." It chokes me.

"I always do," he says.

"He'll be saying good-bye to his family," I say.

"I suppose so. He doesn't speak of them."

This does not surprise me. Roderick can be extremely focused, thinking primarily on what is in front of him. It can be as unnerving to be the recipient of his complete attention as it is to have him walk away and completely forget that you exist. "Except his sister, he always talks about her. He was quite distressed, said she lost a friend, some sort of tragedy. That's why I couldn't stay at the house."

A friend. Not a dog. I thaw toward Roderick a bit.

"He should be distressed." He turns toward me too quickly, his brows raised. "If she lost a friend," I finish in a rush. "If he loves her."

"Oh, he loves her. More than anything. It makes me ashamed for how little I think of my own family. Except my family is safe, and I feel Roderick's may be in some sort of peril."

He loves me more than anything. Perhaps he understands more than I believed.

"What makes you think they're in peril?" I ask.

"Roderick is troubled by nightmares. I would help him, if I could. He knows that I would move heaven and earth to help him."

I stare at him, rapt. To have a friend like him . . . I cannot imagine how wonderful it would be.

"I don't know what to think," he continues. "When the nightmares come, he wakes the entire dormitory with his screams, and there are times when he is . . . dark. But you are from this area; you must be familiar with the family."

"Yes."

"And are my fears for my dear friend unfounded?"

"No one goes to the House of Usher, unless they must."

"But he speaks of it with great pride, has plans to renovate the rooms, bring the house back to its former glory."

"It is a stately home," I admit.

"Roderick does not feel he can invite me to stay, though he has visited my home many times."

I want him to speak of his home. For his voice to soothe me and create pictures that I can cherish, of a faraway world of sunshine and blooming flowers that border green lawns.

But in the distance, we hear the pounding of hooves. The coach is coming, and he will leave.

I imagine climbing on the coach and going with him. What would Roderick think? Colors swim before my eyes.

What if I fall into a fit? If something terrible happens, how could I bear it, in this boy's company?

Looking down, I see that a tiny little vine, a bit of ivy, has curled around my ankle.

Panic washes over me, along with memories of another coach, long ago. I cannot go. Not now, not yet. Not with Roderick back at the house. Who knows what it would do to him?

The coach rushes up.

"This is good-bye, I suppose." He takes my hand, raises it to his lips, and kisses it.

71
MADELINE IS SEVENTEEN

I watch the coach roll away, moving much more slowly than it arrived, and then I lean down to remove the bit of ivy from my ankle. It's a strain similar to what I've planted all around the base of the house. I feel faint. This is not good. I'm too far from home to have one of my spells.

I stand and take a few steps. It isn't so far, the moors are fairly flat, and then there's the forest of saplings. Maybe some of the servants will be coming along this way. They've never had to carry me from beyond the grounds, but I've collapsed in the house, on the grounds.

I force myself to keep walking as far as I can, watching for a glimpse of the house, until my strength fades away. I force one foot in front of the other, and then I fall.

"Madeline, dearest Madeline . . ." I look up into an expanse of blue sky and the even bluer eyes of Dr.

Winston. "I've been looking for you everywhere."

I try to speak, but my mouth feels like it's stuffed with cotton. My dress is wet, and so is my skin.

"Can you stand?"

I cannot find the strength to shake my head. Or speak.

"Of course you can't. I will carry you. Everyone is searching for you. The servants, the doctors."

And my brother? Surely Roderick is searching for me as well.

I close my eyes, and Dr. Winston lifts me. As we trek back to safety, with his strong arms cradling me, I am uncomfortably aware of each movement of his body.

"I've found her," he calls. I feel shadow on my face and dare to open my eyes. The shadow of the house moves over my skin like something alive.

He carries me over the causeway. I imagine the tarn parting as we pass, like the Red Sea.

The servants line the entranceway, like they do when Roderick makes one of his dashing returns. They watch me solemnly. I cannot tell if they are happy or sad that I have been returned. As we cross the threshold, I find it easier to breathe. Dr. Winston carries me up the stairs, and everything goes dark.

I wake up in bed, listening to the sound of voices. I stare at them, light head and dark head, bent together, talking quietly. Roderick curses and glares at Dr. Winston.

"Dr. Peridue says she must have a keeper," Dr. Winston says. "With that dog gone, she can't be allowed to wander freely, not with the chance that one of the fits will take her. It's too dangerous."

"I cannot leave school. I cannot come home to be a caretaker for Madeline," Roderick tells him.

"Of course not. Dr. Paul has already asked me to do it."

72
MADELINE IS SEVENTEEN

"Madeline?" Dr. Winston is behind me.

I want to tell him I don't need to be followed; I'm fine. But I can't find the words, because a story is hovering at the edge of my consciousness. He's trying to be kind, isn't he? I see so little kindness, I should cherish his, and yet . . .

"Come with me," he says. I hear a slight ticking and realize that he has gotten himself a pocket watch from somewhere. Does that mean he's trying to avoid the notice of the house?

He leads me into Roderick's bedroom.

"Tell me," he says.

Does he know that a story is hovering near? Or just guess? I can't tell from looking in his eyes. Can't tell from the way his mouth turns down.

"Once there was a girl," I begin. "An Usher girl, with long blond hair. Her father took her away from the house. He said that he had to. He said that if he didn't, she would die. The house would consume her. That it loved her like it had never loved another, at least in his lifetime, and he had seen the house go through love after love.

"He said that he'd listened to the house, done all that it asked of him, and still it had taken his mother, his sister, his fiancé. So many losses, the women in his life, consumed.

"He put a needle in her arm, and the girl had gone to sleep. He carried her through the woods, past the platform where the coach stopped.

"A hired black coach was waiting, a coach with a stoop-backed horse. He hurried, limping slightly, balancing the girl in her long nightgown and a small bag.

"Climbing into the coach, he thrust the same syringe into his own arm, expelling the rest of the sedative, and fell back against the upholstered seat, closing his eyes.

"With his daughter, he arrived in a village by the sea, and rented a cottage. But neither of them was well. Wealthy invalids passed the cottage on the path to the healing waters, escorted by caretakers and keepers. But the girl and her father remained inside, sleeping, mostly. The ceiling of the cottage was whitewashed, with beams made of driftwood like some enormous beast had swallowed them whole and they were living in the skeleton.

"She tried to be content with her father. Tried not to cry when he wouldn't wake. But in the end, she betrayed them both.

"She dreamed of the house, and thought of it, and somehow it found her and comforted her. She chose that comfort over her own father, over her freedom."

My voice breaks, and then even the echo of it fades into the silence of this room.

"Go to sleep," Dr. Winston says gently.

It isn't what I want him to say. I don't know what I want. Comfort? Absolution? Not this. Not to be told to rest.

"I don't think I'm going to have a fit. My head is clear," I tell him.

"It doesn't matter, Madeline. I'll sit here while you sleep. I never mind sitting with you."

Neither of us mentions that he's taken me to Roderick's room, that I'm lying in Roderick's bed.

"Why did you want to become a doctor?" I ask. "Was it because you are fascinated with blood?" What I wanted to ask was if it's because he is fascinated with suffering. But I want to stay on his good side. Despite myself, his regard means something to me.

He laughs.

"I became a doctor for the mystery. That's why we're

all here. We want to discover what it is that's wrong with you."

"What if nothing is wrong with me?" I sit up a little and try to look him in the eye, and that's when I catch sight of a sheaf of papers. They seem oddly familiar, even by the light of the single candle. I don't want Dr. Winston to note my curiosity, so I look at him, stare into his eyes. "What if there's no illness, and therefore no cure?"

He starts. Unlike the other doctors, he knows this is true. I'm not ill, I'm cursed.

"Either way, it isn't fair. Why should you bear so much pain? If I were in charge of the world, you would never feel any."

He reaches out and touches my forehead, ever so gently. My head is throbbing, but I'm sure that no spell is coming on. Almost sure.

I close my eyes and force myself to relax. I must not have a fit. Must keep control—even if it's just to sleep.

"The house is speaking to you, isn't it?" he asks. "Saying that it loves you most of all." Is there jealousy in his voice?

I keep my eyes pressed shut and wonder what the voices are saying in his head, and whether he believes that I am asleep.

73
MADELINE IS SEVENTEEN

Yesterday there was a letter from Roderick, and when I tried to read it the words and letters shifted so violently that I could not read at all.

Weeds are growing in my garden, and I let them, because at least there is something, something green, something that wants to grow. The fits are growing stronger, closer together. My head is constantly throbbing.

The books are disappearing from the library. Furniture keeps moving, or being moved. I am always bewildered, always on the edge of collapse.

I slip through the haunted corridors, a shadow of my former self, and my shadow, when I notice it, is long and impossibly thin. Cassandra wouldn't want this, but the grief and loneliness overwhelm me. Will the doctors force me to eat, or let me keep wasting away?

The portraits stare down at me, tiny supercilious smiles twisting thin Usher lips.

They all died young, I remind myself. It doesn't lessen my grief.

I pass by the painting of the house, averting my eyes. The second painting stops me in my tracks.

My pitiful little garden is still there.

And . . . splotches of grey and black shadowy oils . . . a wolfhound romps in the verdant green grass.

I collapse onto the black floor.

And I weep.

74
MADELINE IS SEVENTEEN

When I open my eyes, it is dark. Something is on the bed. Am I dreaming? No, when I shift, there is a thump, and I cower under the quilt as whatever it is scurries away. This is an ancient house, and it would be ridiculous to presume that the walls were not filled with rats. But the rats have never before been bold enough to climb onto my bed. Cassandra protected me from them.

I'm wide awake now, and though the hour may be late, I fear I will not sleep soon.

I light a candle and stare at myself in the mirror. My hair is dirty, and the skin beneath my eyes looks bruised.

"Miss Usher?"

Dr. Winston is in the doorway, holding a steaming mug. He is being very formal with me, calling me Miss Usher, when he usually makes a point of using my first name.

But he doesn't sound unfriendly.

"Is it late?" I ask. Disorientation overwhelms me.

"This will help you sleep," he says without answering my question. I take the cup but don't drink.

Dr. Winston's footsteps echo as he walks away, down the hall to Roderick's room. I wonder what my brother would think if he knew how often the doctor sleeps in his bedchamber. I slip past Roderick's door, gliding through the corridors, up and up, until I reach the trapdoor that leads to the widow's walk.

Resting my hand on the railing, I look out over the trees. Tonight I don't see any ghosts, but there was someone named Honoria who jumped from here. I try to think how I know this. Was it in one of Roderick's books? A story? Some family legend?

The curiosity presses at me, and I feel ashamed that I have been ruled by despondency. I've lost Cassandra, but I'm still here. I tap my foot against the slate tiles, listening to the wind blow through the dead leaves below. I can't count on Roderick or Dr. Winston. I must be brave and clever; otherwise, the house will never let me live. Not truly.

75
MADELINE IS SEVENTEEN

At last I am back to my garden. Though when I see the burrows Cassandra dug, or a dog-shaped indention in the leaves, tears well up in my eyes. Black roses have grown over everything, strangling the weaker flowers—everything but the vines I planted at the base of the house. They need a framework, a trellis. I look up at the house. It's perfect.

Dr. Winston approaches, illuminated by a sudden burst of sunlight. He is carrying a hamper filled with small sandwiches and a bottle of wine. I am wearing one of my better dresses, and I put a ribbon in my hair this morning.

He takes my hand to help me up, and we walk to an area a bit away from the house, where grass actually grows. The dead forest is behind us, but here a few brave saplings have put down roots, and springy moss carpets the ground.

He spreads a blanket, decorated with great yellow-and-orange flowers, over the earth and gestures for me to sit. I tell myself not to trust him, that I can't trust anyone, but I will listen to what he has to say.

"I know how you love flowers," he says.

He puts the hamper between us. We are beneath a ridge of earth, a mound, where something might have been buried long ago, but it's been disturbed by the most recent earthquakes.

Above us, the earth juts out, and the roots of one of the saplings are exposed. We are not far from the area where we found Cassandra, when she was stuck within the earth. I don't say anything about it. It hurts to speak of her.

"This place is so odd," he says. "What do you think was buried there? Why do you think the grass only grows here? Fascinating." He is always saying this about every aspect of the house. The house mesmerizes him. He looks at me out of the corner of his eye. In his mind, how completely am I connected to the house? Can he separate the things that fascinate him? In the time that he's been here, he's changed.

He reaches up and touches an exposed root.

The hillside is scarred, a long, jagged line, raised above

the earth, partially hidden by the shadow of the house.

"The servants say that this crack is a fissure between the land of the living and the land of the dead," he says.

The Usher land is prone to earthquakes. Sometimes, at night, mist rises all about the house, from fissures in the earth. But at this moment, the sunlight is warm and soothing.

"The servants are overly superstitious," I reply.

He hands me a goblet filled with wine and gestures for me to drink. I am supposed to drink red wine every day, to fortify me for the weekly blood-letting sessions.

Before I lost Cassandra, before our ill-fated kiss, he whispered about understanding me. About hearing the house. Can I trust him, even a tiny bit?

76
MADELINE IS SEVENTEEN

There is a commotion at the front of the house, and for a brief moment I hope that Roderick has returned, but it is not him. It is a hired carriage with a distraught young woman.

The servants step back, allowing me to approach her.

"Oh, thank goodness," she says. "I thought this house was abandoned. I thought . . . well, it was silly." She puts her hand on my arm and says in a conspiratorial whisper, "I thought it was a haunted house."

A shiver passes through me.

Dr. Winston comes out the door, and we share a look across the courtyard. Then he frowns as the girl sees him. "Victor!" she cries, and throws herself into his arms. He looks, for a moment, as if he will drop her. But instead he stands holding her awkwardly, as if he doesn't know what to do as she laughs and cries in his arms.

I take two steps back up the staircase.

"Miss Usher." He looks up at me. "This is Miss Emily Burnett, a friend of mine. I hope you won't mind if she stays the night. It's getting dark. . . ."

"Of course not," I say.

The girl regards me with a half smile, as if reconsidering her friendliness. But I liked her smile and her openness when she put her hand on my arm. No one here is open. We guard our thoughts and feelings as if they are treasure, precious and likely to be stolen away at any time.

She looks like the city, with her black-heeled boots and her red coat with black trim. She wears a small black hat at a jaunty angle, accenting her sharp blue eyes, and a fur muff that hangs from a string around her neck. What life does she live? What cold does she hide her hands from?

The older doctors shake their heads from the top of the stairs.

They have the power to send Dr. Winston away. Even the servants defer to Dr. Peridue, as if he is master of the house. He has an aristocratic manner, bossy and self-assured, and he has lived here the longest, though he is in such poor health. His hair is coming out in clumps, and his teeth are yellow. Dr. Paul will probably take control soon.

But I am mistress of this house, whatever they think.

I sweep over to the stairs and nod to one of the maids. "Tell the cook to be sure supper is sent up to our guest. Put her in one of the guest rooms on the main floor." I'd rather she sleep closer to me than to the young, handsome doctor.

I retire upstairs, and then try one of my childhood tricks, slipping down a back stairway to listen to them talk.

"You've been here for an eternity, Victor. Isn't it time to move on?" she says to him. "You could set up your own practice," she suggests. "We could get married."

Married, move on? I grip the bannister. And leave me with just the old doctors, with no one who understands my plight? Though perhaps it would be best for him to leave. The house has been affecting him.

"I'm living with no expenses here. I will force these old fools to publish their findings. People love to read about ancient families, about curses and eccentricities. The others won't live long enough to enjoy the profit, but I will. We will."

"It's so dismal here. I can't believe you want to stay."

"It's no darker than a country house in January."

"This is September, Victor. It isn't supposed to be this dark in September."

I don't like the way she says his name.

"Once I'm rich, we can leave here, and I can pay my

debts and live the way I wish to live."

"I was happy when you said you wanted to be a country doctor."

Her voice is full of longing. She loves him.

"I will never get a chance like this again, to study such a strange illness, an ancient family. I can't leave."

"But this place—"

"Did you see her? She's so fascinating, and the house. No, I can't leave. Not yet."

But perhaps he can be talked into leaving, particularly if his patient is prepared to go with him.

77
FROM THE DIARY OF LISBETH USHER

I cannot leave her. Mr. Usher's sister. I can walk away from my own sister, giddy with plans to usurp me and marry the master of the house, intent on ignoring the horror of the curse.

I visit her every day but only just learned her name. Madeline. My sister laughed; he told her the name when he wouldn't tell me. As if this is some sort of victory. "Perhaps I'll name my first child after her," she said through her laughter.

I have failed. My younger sister has become a monster. And the girl who is called a monster, the one chained in the attics? I cannot leave her behind.

Tonight. I've packed a small bag and stolen the key from the gold chain. We will go tonight.

78
MADELINE IS SEVENTEEN

Miss Burnett sits with me in the parlor. She didn't come down for breakfast, so the servants have brought a selection of tea cakes and desserts, which she is nibbling upon. The maids huddle in the doorway, watching us, until I wave my hand and they disperse back to their duties.

"It must be odd to have three physicians watching over you night and day," Miss Burnett says. "It must make you feel very special."

Or very sick, I think. But I don't say it. I have never had a female friend, and it's nice that she seems so genuinely interested in me and my life.

"If Victor is determined to stay here, then maybe I will too. He says . . . he has suggested . . ." She looks down at her boots. For a girl who barged into an old mansion, she seems hesitant. "That you might like to learn, like your brother. Victor says you didn't go to school, and since I have no offers of marriage, I'm going to have to earn my way. Teaching children. I could practice. You could tell me if you already know what I'm teaching, and if I'm doing a good job."

I want very much to be intelligent and educated like she is, like Roderick. But what I must learn about is this place, and myself. Father couldn't take me away, but Roderick comes and goes at will. What is the difference? Why do I hear the house, why have I always heard it, when Roderick does not?

"Miss Usher could only have very short lessons," Dr. Winston says from the doorway. "I don't want her to be overtired."

"You can stay as long as you want," I say, ignoring Dr. Winston's sudden bossiness. Still, the offer makes me feel shy. I'm not used to making decisions that affect other people. "And I would be happy for you to practice teaching, Miss Burnett. There are so many things that I don't know."

"That's wonderful," she says. "But please call me Emily."

We smile at each other. Sunlight streams through the window behind me. She reaches out to touch my hair.

"It's so beautiful," she comments. "I don't think I've ever seen hair exactly that color. Maybe on a very young child." She picks up a tea cake and nibbles on it. "This is a very interesting house. We must be friends, I insist on it."

She smiles easily, and I envy her worldly manner. Perhaps we could be friends. Perhaps.

79
MADELINE IS SIXTEEN

Two maids stand together at the base of the stairway, whispering. When I enter the room, one of them giggles loudly, covering her mouth with her hand. Arm in arm, they scamper away. I turn to Emily. Is that how friends behave?

She seems to think so, because she steps near, wanting me to share confidences.

"It must be so delightful to have a brother," she muses. "Are any of his friends handsome?"

"Oh, yes," I say, but of course she knows. She's teasing me. Roderick's friend is her relative, a cousin. She knows him much better than I do.

"Who are you thinking of?" Her voice goes low, and her eyes are bright and inquisitive.

I'm too surprised by her curiosity to answer.

"Tell me! Your eyes went soft and your cheeks so pink . . . you're in love!"

"No," I say. "No." I don't even know what love feels like. But she won't leave it alone.

"This is so exciting!"

"What's exciting?"

We both jump. Dr. Winston has crept up behind us. Emily pours him a cup of tea. He's still waiting for an answer, but she doesn't tell him. Maybe I was right to trust her with this.

She puts her hand on his arm and smiles up into his eyes.

"I think Madeline is in love."

"That can't be true," he says. Then he gives me an evil smile. "I won't believe that Madeline is in love."

"Look at her, she's blushing."

I sit stiffly. She keeps touching him, drawing his attention to her. I could never be so flirtatious.

"I've found that when you are in love, you cannot stop thinking about the other person. You can't live without them. You believe their happiness is more important than your own. Is that how you feel, Madeline?" Dr. Winston asks.

I consider this carefully and then shake my head.

"Then perhaps you should find someone else. Maybe he isn't worthy of your devotion."

"There isn't anyone else," I say. "But just because you love someone, it doesn't mean you can't say no to them."

"Or yes to someone else."

The way he's looking at me makes me nervous.

"You two are so serious all of a sudden." Emily laughs. I turn back to her, this girl who has offered me something I've never had before. Friendship.

Deep within the house, I feel something rumble.

80
MADELINE IS TWELVE

I'm exploring, looking for something interesting to show
Roderick when he returns from school. A suit of armor
stands beside the stairway that leads directly upstairs
from the corridor where our bedrooms are located.
There's a groove in the balustrade. I run my fingers over
it, and then look up at the battle-ax that the armor is
holding. The size of the indention looks to be the same
size as the blade, as if it might have slipped from the
metal gauntlets. A frightening thought.

I consider pushing the armor back, to allow for a safer
space, but something keeps me from touching it. My gold
pocket watch ticks away the time, hanging from a ribbon
that I threaded around my wrist.

A dark rug runs up the center of the stairway. Some
steps are more worn than others. Maybe the last Ushers

who used this staircase regularly skipped certain steps, the way Roderick and I always do on the stairs leading to our chambers. This thought makes me feel less afraid, closer to Roderick.

I peer around the corner and see that this hallway is not so much different than my own. Dark woodwork, brooding oil paintings, a few tattered curtains covering the windows at the far end of the passage. I'm only one floor above my parents' rooms, but it feels very far away. Isolated.

The first room is empty. Was it a bedchamber? A sitting room? Impossible to tell. There is a door within the room, so I leave the hallway and open it, peering through the gloom.

Another room and another inner door. Five rooms into the labyrinth of interconnected rooms, fear seeps into me through the bare floor, and I come to a door that is closed. The light from the few windows is nothing more than a memory, and I'm glad I have a candle.

My explorations have already taken me far from my usual path, and I am getting tired. Almost certainly one of the servants has left a platter in my room, broth, perhaps. My stomach rumbles.

I push myself forward. One more room. Maybe there will be something interesting inside that I can show Roderick when he returns.

The door creaks open a few inches and then stops. It's gray inside, rather than pitch black, so there must be a window. I push aside a stack of books and walk over the threshold, into a room filled with books.

It isn't a library, exactly. In the Usher library, the shelves are so high that a ladder is required to reach the ones on the top. This room has no shelves.

This is just a room filled with heaps and heaps of books.

I walk through, coughing a bit, running my hands over the covers.

The only piece of furniture in the room is a dainty writing desk with carved legs, roses and serpents carved onto every surface. In some places, the books are stacked from floor to ceiling. The desk stands before the window, and light from outside illumines the thickness of the air in here. My lungs feel like they've been roasted.

The surface of the desk is covered with scraps of parchment. I read the first. *I love you.* I've seen one exactly like this before, down to the ornate L in love. I pick up another. *I know you.* A third slip of paper also says *I love you.* The next one: *I watch you.* Dozens of scraps of parchment are scattered over the desk. *I love you, I know you, I need you.* Out of all of the scraps, only one says *I watch you.*

81
MADELINE IS SEVENTEEN

"What should we do today?" Emily asks. I sit on her trunk and watch while she arranges her hair with pins. "The days here tend to run together, don't they? It's because the sun never really comes out from behind the clouds, I think."

I'm not sure what to suggest to entertain her. What would she find amusing?

"What do you usually do for fun?" I ask.

"We went visiting, mostly. Where I grew up, there were several families that had manors. Victor, Dr. Winston, lived a few miles from my cousin's house, where I grew up. We would visit for tea parties, picnics, things like that."

A spider runs across the vanity table, and she grimaces. "My cousin goes to school with your brother. In fact, that's where Victor heard about you."

"Heard about me?"

"Your brother was visiting my cousin on one of their school holidays, and he mentioned this house and the doctors who lived here. After that, Victor wanted to do his apprenticeship here. He's very interested in this sort of thing; he wants so much to cure you. And he loves old houses."

She shares the same vitality as Roderick's friend. His friendliness. As though she is a small ray of sunshine breaking through the house's gloom.

"This is a very unique house, isn't it?" She pats her hair one last time and turns away from the mirror.

"Oh, yes." It is so strange for a new person to be here. "Would you like a tour?"

"A tour of the house?" she asks breathlessly. "I would adore that. I've been exploring a bit on my own." She takes a final look at her reflection in the mirror, then picks up her white gloves and puts them on. It upsets her when patches of dust appear on her clothing, or when the lace at the cuffs of her dresses deteriorates during the night.

"Yesterday I went to the chapel. It's quite lovely, though the woodwork is simply falling to pieces. The stained-glass windows are glorious. I was walking around to the back, and I found what appeared to be a priest's hole. Only, as far as I know, the house is altogether too new, built too recently for that sort of thing. And priests were never persecuted here."

I smooth my skirts and stand up, unwilling to show my ignorance by asking what she means.

"And there was a drawbridge at one time, wasn't there? Is it possible that this house was moved here, from some-place else? Someplace older?"

Yes. Roderick and I read about it in one of the old books. The books that she could read. I could ask for her help. Would she want to read about the house? To help me dis-cover the secrets. How long would we have until the house realizes what we are doing and tries to stop us?

I think of my mad grandmother, abandoning Father and his sister, writing all those messages. *I love you. I need you. I watch you.* I don't believe the house loves any of us, but I know it watches.

82
MADELINE IS TWELVE

Father finds me lying on the book-covered floor, crying. I don't know how long I've been here. He picks me up, murmurs my name.

"Didn't your mother tell you not to come up here?" he asks.

There are so many places that I'm not allowed to go.

The pain is terrible. I want him to put me to bed. Why does my head throb so violently?

"Madeline?"

"Why won't the letters stay still?" I ask him in a whisper. "I look at them, and they move . . ."

"Do they? Were you trying to read? Ah, my poor little girl. It's part of the Usher curse. My mother also had difficulty reading. This was her room."

He holds me in his lap, on the floor in front of the desk.

I show him the piece of paper that says *I watch you*.

"My mother, your grandmother, brought all these books up here, made us send away for them, but she couldn't read them. She was convinced that the truth was in one of these books, and the tragedy was, she couldn't even look for it. She left me and my twin sister alone. We were only children. Maybe the truth is here. We'll never know."

Father sees the pocket watch, which had dropped to a dreary-hued rug.

"What's this?"

"I like the way it sounds."

I can read his face well enough to see that he knows why I took it. A smile hovers at his lips.

"You really are clever. I almost believe that you could get away from all of this." He takes the parchment that I'm holding between my fingers. *I watch you*. "My mother wrote those. Over and over, for days on end. Hundreds of them. I still find them all through the house. It was terrifying. I think she forgot she had children. I was afraid for her and afraid of her. I suppose you know how that feels."

Father never speaks this much. My head throbs, and I am afraid that tomorrow I will not remember anything he has said, though I know his words are important. If only I could write them down.

"The house is cruel to our daughters, especially the

twins. As long as I live, I will never forgive the house for what it did to my sister."

He bows his head, and his shoulders shake a little, as if he is holding back sobs. I never knew my father had a sister.

I reach up to the desk and grab a handful of the scraps. The ink flakes off and sticks to my fingers.

"I need to tell you this now, Madeline, before I get sick again, before I forget. I've been thinking for so long, but it is very difficult for me to figure out the patterns, for me to understand the intent of the house. My mother was a favorite of the house, like you. She was one of the rare Usher children whose cradle rocked of its own accord, and who never ever left the safety of the house. It drove her mad, of course.

"My mother isolated herself, stopped speaking to anyone, and wrote these messages all day. When we took her ink away, she wrote all of these . . . in her own blood."

I consider my fingertips, stained with what I believed was ink.

"If you don't fight the house, it will take you, more so than it has the rest of us. The house will never let you go." A story flashes before my eyes. First, murdered children lying heaped on a great flat stone. Then an Usher girl with long blond hair, shackled to a wall. I blink, and the images are gone, erased by the house.

245

Is Father trying to frighten me? The house protects us. Why would I want it to let me go? I try to understand his words, even as the world goes hazy around me.

Father carries me downstairs and puts me in bed. I am surprised that he is strong enough to carry me. As he tucks me into bed, I reach up and kiss his cheek.

83
MADELINE IS SEVENTEEN

Dr. Winston joins us as I guide Emily down the crumbling stone stairs, as if he had been invited on the tour. He keeps trying to take the lead, but I push past him. Emily is so entranced by the house that she doesn't notice.

"The stone in this older wing seems so solid, and yet it's webbed with cracks." She pulls back a tapestry, an artful depiction of a knight mounted on a horse, holding his own severed head. She runs her hand over the wall behind the tapestry, and tiny bits of stone rain down.

"Can you take us to the crypt?" Dr. Winston asks. "Even I haven't seen it yet. Only family members have access." There is yearning in his tone, but what could be the harm in showing them? Emily will marvel at it. "Wait here." I hurry to fetch the keys from Roderick's room, and return to them.

"The vault is through here." I gesture toward a stair-case, cut into stone, leading down.

All three of us light torches at the bottom. There are no windows, of course, not this far underground. The walls glitter, reflecting the tongues of flame with a ghastly and inappropriate splendor.

The door is thick, made of iron and sheathed in copper. The screech as it opens is the stuff of nightmares. The world shimmers for a moment, and I have to remind myself that I am stronger than my pain, that a pin dropping on a summer afternoon is only agony because I let myself succumb to it. I take deep, shuddering breaths. Emily squeezes my hand and takes one step forward. The floor is also covered with copper.

The weight of a thousand Usher crimes presses down on me in this place.

"The copper indicates that powder was once held here—combustible powder, as if for a cannon. That makes no sense." Emily wrinkles her brow. "This house shows all evidence having once been a medieval fortress." Her tone is accusatory, as if we are somehow tricking her, as if we have magically transported her to some other world where it's historically appropriate for a medieval fortress to stand. She will make an excellent governess, and I have to suppress the urge to laugh.

The young doctor holds up his torch. His eyes dart here

and there, lingering on the slabs where the bodies were laid out, where bodies will be laid out in the future. Empty stone sarcophagi line the walls; some made for women, some men. A few are small.

"The bodies are placed here for a few days, and then taken to the family's burial ground," he tells Emily.

It is important that they think this is true. At least, it is important that the servants believe this, so as not to terrorize them. If the servants knew how many Ushers were buried under their feet, in the foundations of the house, they would be horrified.

"Is this a gate?" he asks. "A door?"

"There is another room past this one, but it has fallen into disrepair. The roof is caving." I do not want them to go any farther. Don't want *him* to go any farther. This is the heart of the house, and he is already far enough in its thrall.

"Come." I gesture for them to follow me back to the stairs.

84
MADELINE IS TWELVE

"The spirit of the house—the consciousness of it—gets inside our heads. It sees through our eyes and feels what we feel, especially moments of extreme emotion, moments of passion. Or grief. It loves grief."

Father's voice is feverish and high-pitched. He's leaning close, mumbling. I listen closely. We are sitting beneath the large grandfather clock. Father says that repetitive noises distract the house, but I'm not sure we should be distracting it. Not sure I want to hear what Father is whispering.

"The house never had a strong affinity with your mother. It loved her cruelty, but tired of her quickly. She came from far away and usurped another's place. But you are everything the house wants, and that scares me. It should scare you as well. Mother sent Roderick away. If I can, I will do the same for you."

Terror washes over me.

"I don't want to leave," I whisper. This is my home, this is where Roderick will return to me. I'm safe here.

Father wraps his arms around me, pulling me close, but his arms don't feel as safe as they should because he's trembling so.

"It wants to keep you close, to see what you see and feel what you feel. You've always had a sensitivity that Roderick lacks. You see the ghosts, hear the whispers. You are the love of the house. But ultimately, it wants you to bear a child. To continue the line. Since you and Roderick were born, it has mostly abandoned me, and it goads your mother to madness."

Is Father jealous? Is that what I hear in his voice?

"I'll take you away, Madeline. I promise," he says.

85
MADELINE IS SEVENTEEN

"I told the servants to bring us tea, and that it should be hot. Also, that the cakes should be fresh. I hope you don't mind," Emily says.

I shake my head, charmed by the unfamiliar feminine routine, and sit across from her while she pours steaming tea into a delicate bone-china cup.

"I thought we could chat."

The delicate cup wobbles as I consider. What do people chat about? The weather? The weather is gloomy, gray, relentlessly melancholy.

"Victor tells me that you and your brother are very close."

I choke on the tea.

"We were, as children. Now . . . he's so far away." This feels like a betrayal of Roderick, and yet it's true.

"I don't have any brothers or sisters. I envy you that relationship. It must be very special."

I take a bite of one of the little cakes. It's too sweet.

She puts her hand over mine. "Madeline, are you happy here?"

If I wasn't already on alert, I'd probably drop my teacup. Am I happy here? Am I happy? The teacup rattles against the saucer. It's a somewhat rhythmic noise, enough to distract the house—or is it listening to our chat? Watching us through the eyes of birds embroidered on the wall hangings?

"I would like to live my life in peace," I say. "I would like to be happy."

She leans forward, as if ready to confide in me, but then lifts her teacup and takes a sip. Collecting her courage?

"Why are you looking at me like that?" I ask.

She cocks her head to the side and takes a deep breath.

"Since Victor has not proposed marriage and doesn't seem likely to, I have to find a job, to pay my way. And I thought . . . we could live together, Madeline, find a tiny place in the city. It wouldn't be like this place, but . . . it wouldn't be haunted."

Is she sincere? Or is she just distracting herself from dreams of Dr. Winston? But she is watching me eagerly, waiting for my answer.

"Unhaunted sounds perfect," I say in a quiet voice.

86
MADELINE IS TWELVE

My eyes burn. I am being blinded.

"It's too bright," I cry, surprised by my voice. It is high-pitched, afraid.

"Hush, Madeline."

Father is holding me, cradling me like a baby. Blinding light streams through an open window. The walls in this room are white. Where are we? I reach out my hand to touch the unfamiliar wall. It's a sort of plaster.

Allowing my fingers to rest against the wall, I feel . . . nothing. No emotion, no warmth. We are not in the House of Usher.

"Where are we?"

"I'm going to write to Roderick, at school," Father says. "I'm going to tell him to meet us here."

I pull away from Father's arms, put my feet on the floor.

I'm wearing shiny black shoes. I click them, *tap tap tap*, against the unfamiliar floor.

When I try to stand, my legs are wobbly.

"I gave you some of your mother's medicine," Father says. "It was the only way I could take you away."

I look around, fearful, suddenly, that Mother is here.

"She stayed at the house," Father says. "She loves you, but she wanted to remain under the care of Dr. Paul." I know that at least part of what he has just said was a lie.

Hours pass. Father falls asleep while I sit in the corner, wrapped in all the blankets from the bed. Through the window I can hear the rhythmic sound of the sea. I do not find it soothing.

87
MADELINE IS SEVENTEEN

It is a bright cold day, and I study us in the mirror. Emily is dark, and I am light. Her hair is dark and curly, and her eyes are lively. I am very still and solemn compared to her. My hair is so fair it is nearly silver. My eyes are violet. All of my winter wear, my coat, my hat, my gloves, are white. If it wasn't for the red of my lips and the brightness of my eyes, I could blend right in with the snow and never be seen again.

"Put on your hat," she says. "Victor will never forgive me if I allow you to catch cold."

"No, he wouldn't," I agree.

The snow is deep. It hides the blighted earth around the house as we wait for the grooms to bring the horses from the stable and attach them to the sleigh. There are four white horses with bells on their harness.

The sleigh has two bench seats, one in the front and one in the back. I start to climb into the back, but Dr. Winston stops me.

"There's enough room for all of us on one bench, Madeline."

"Yes, sit between us," Emily says. "We can keep one another warm."

The doctor shakes the reigns, and the horses pull us out into the snow.

"Your brother should be home soon for Christmas, shouldn't he? I long to meet him again," Emily says.

The sleigh glides over the snow, up and down hills. Emily squeals and holds on to my arm. I understand the urge to scream, as we rise and fall, so quickly. My heart quickens, but I don't want to cheapen this moment. The land looks so clean and fresh under the blanket of snow. So beautiful. And I am here with friends. Tonight, perhaps, we will drink cocoa, and they will tell me about their childhoods, about places they have visited, lives that are different than anything I've ever imagined.

I wish this sleigh ride could last forever.

"Victor!" Emily screams as we begin the descent down a rather sharp incline. "What is that?"

It's one of the white trees, fallen from where a forest once stood. Dr. Winston is already turning the sleigh,

forcing the horses around the fallen log. But he's not fast enough. The sleigh tips to the side, and I slide, falling into the snow. For a moment I lie stunned, but then I laugh, because the snow is soft, and nothing hurts.

The young doctor is calling out and the horses are spooked, still running, dragging the overturned sleigh behind them.

A figure on a black horse appears at the top of a hill. I've never seen the horse before, but there is no chance that I would not recognize the rider. He is holding a riding crop, though I don't remember Roderick ever carrying one before. His face is so very, very white, but his cheeks are pink with the cold—and with rage.

He rides down the hill, straight at Dr. Winston.

"What are you doing?" he shouts. "Those horses haven't been exercised in months, and they aren't trained to pull a sleigh."

"I know how to handle horses." Dr. Winston stares into Roderick's face.

"You are a fool, and if you had hurt Madeline, I would have killed you where you stand," Roderick says in a low voice.

There is a whimper behind us, oh, no—Emily! I turn toward her and gasp. She's lying on the ground, and blood is staining the snow red.

Dr. Winston rushes to her side.

"You'd best be glad that isn't Madeline," Roderick says through gritted teeth. Yet even before he's done saying it, he's kneeling beside the girl, lifting her onto his black horse to take her back to the house.

88
MADELINE IS SEVENTEEN

It is time for dinner, so all enmity must be forgotten. I dress carefully and go downstairs to stand in the great hall under the shriveled mistletoe. Roderick joins me.

"When the sleigh tipped, I was terrified," he admits. "If you'd been hurt . . ." His face is still pale, and I can feel his anguish. I struggle to understand why this experience was more traumatic for him than when I nearly drowned in the tarn.

Emily comes downstairs, followed by Dr. Winston. Her bandage is only a shade paler than her forehead. She looks from Roderick to me. Her brows come together for a moment before she smiles a dazzling smile.

"It's amazing how alike you are," she says.

Roderick returns her smile. He obviously approves of her, even though he has always despised Dr. Winston.

"How is your head?" he asks her politely.

Since Roderick is talking to Emily, I take Dr. Winston by the arm as the servants usher us into the dining room.

"And how are you feeling, Madeline?" he asks. His emphasis is upon the word "you." Both Dr. Winston and Roderick somehow caring more about my well-being than Emily's makes me uncomfortable.

"Quite well," I say, because I don't want him fussing over me too much, not in front of Roderick.

"You look well," he says. "But maybe we should take a blood sample to be sure." He stares across the room at my brother, who is taking his seat as we cross the room.

Dr. Paul and Dr. Peridue come into the room. They look uncomfortable; their formal clothing is dusty and ill-fitting, remnants of the lives that they lived before they ended up here.

The servants fill our goblets with wine.

Dr. Paul rubs his hands together, eager for the first course. I lift my fork, examining a chunk of roasted meat in a heavy sauce. It tastes like sawdust. I rearrange the food on my plate so that it looks like I've eaten some of it. Dr. Winston watches me, but for once he's not taking inventory of what I am eating.

"Something is going to happen," he whispers. "Can you feel it?"

I pretend not to hear him and turn to Roderick. He is

dressed all in black, we both are, and he looks particularly handsome. Emily has been admiring him all evening. I hope he has not turned her head enough that she will abandon me so she doesn't have to become a governess. Roderick is the heir to the Usher fortune, after all, even if I am the favorite of the house.

The servants parade into the room with platters of food. As they put the next course on the table, every clock in the place begins to strike. It is an awful, discordant racket that echoes through the house and through my head.

Dr. Peridue struggles to bring his watch from his pocket so that he can check the time. Twelve strikes sound, but it is certainly not midnight. When I last checked, it was ten past seven, though clocks in this house aren't always accurate.

The candles flicker out, one by one, and a loud creaking sounds from all around us, as if the room is rearranging itself. Roderick grasps my shoulder in the sudden darkness. At the same time, Dr. Winston's hand brushes my side and then falls away.

One of the servants drops a tureen of broth, and it shatters when it hits the floor.

"Well, well," Dr. Peridue begins in his raspy ancient voice, but the creaking continues. Something groans from above us, and with a sudden gust of air against my face, something falls.

Dr. Winston yanks me back, out of my chair and toward him, but Roderick has already thrown himself protectively over me. All three of us topple to the floor.

One candle lights, and then another, and soon we can see Dr. Paul lighting the candles on the sideboard. Emily steps around the three of us on the floor and moves to help him. The servants have disappeared.

An enormous wooden ceiling beam has crushed the table.

Roderick's chair is shattered. If he had not flung himself at me, and if Dr. Winston had not reached for me, both of Roderick's legs would have been broken. And then he would have had to remain here, as an invalid.

The house wants Roderick, wants to keep him here.

Dr. Winston squeezes my arm as he helps me to my feet.

Roderick notes it and turns away.

89
MADELINE IS SEVENTEEN

"But why must you leave now?" I ask Roderick for the fifth or sixth time. I hate that my voice is plaintive. I hate the hurt. We haven't even exchanged presents.

The morning sun streams into his bedchamber, and I sit by his window, enjoying its warmth. A magazine lies beside his bed, the *Southern Literary Messenger*, with stories and articles and a few illustrations. In my hands the crisp paper feels like something foreign and precious.

"Because I must," Roderick says stiffly. And I hear something, the same desperation that I heard a year ago, when he told me he was haunted. He's desperate to get away from the house. From the unknown. From me.

"I'll return sooner than you think. I'm not dependent on the coach now that I have my own horses."

Since Roderick is the master of the Usher fortune,

he enjoys buying things for himself, like horses that he rarely rides. The one he takes to school and the others that wait for him to return, neglected and unexercised. Horses untrained to pull a sleigh through the snow.

"We should discuss what happened last night," I say flatly.

He sees that I am shaken, and for a moment I think that he will hug me, like he did when we were children. But instead he says, "Don't be afraid, Madeline."

"Of course I'm afraid. The house was trying to maim you."

He shakes his head. "It is a coincidence that ceiling beam came down right over my chair. I wish it would have crushed a few of the doctors." He means Dr. Winston. For a moment I thought he was beginning to believe, but he's only making a poor joke.

"Roderick!"

"I'm sorry. I know this is upsetting to you, but I wasn't hurt."

"You could be. If you don't believe. If you don't take precautions."

"Oh, Madeline, you know I—" He pauses. "You know I believe that you are the most creative . . . that you can come up with the best stories in the world."

His face registers disdain. No belief, not even the ability to listen.

"Stay away from that doctor," he says. "The young one. I don't like the way he watches you."

Should I tell him that I am no longer fond of Dr. Winston? But then he would know that I was, for a time.

"I love you, Roderick," I say, but instead of answering, he hunches his shoulders and turns away.

90
FROM THE DIARY OF LISBETH USHER

I have crept up to the attic, and as I write this, I watch Mr. Usher's mad sister. She ignores me most of the time, staring at the wallpaper or tracing the cracks in the walls. She seems to be looking for something. As her finger follows the cracks and the designs in the wallpaper, I begin to see a design. Like a language I can't read.

She escaped from her keepers this morning.

I would have missed the excitement, but I was in the nursery minding my younger sister. The attic rooms don't have doors, and even though Mr. Usher insists we stay away from his sister, the maids don't care, so I was half watching from the other side of the arched doorway.

The maid with broad shoulders, who helps carry barrels from the wine cellar, brought a wooden tub up the stairs. Another servant brought hot water, and washcloths, and then they unlocked the manacles with a key kept on a long silver chain.

The maids forced her to sit in the tub of water, and I wondered if it was too hot, because tears were running down her face. I wondered if I should tell Mr. Usher. After the bath, while they were drying her, she pushed the skinny maid into the big one and ran.

I didn't want to get in the way, but I followed the maids. The poor girl made it all the way from the top of the house to the crypt.

The maids were frightened and didn't follow. But I wasn't afraid. Her wet footprints were clear as day against the dark floors.

I followed her down the dark stairway, past the place where the floor is copper, to the big metal gate, which is locked with a key that Mr. Usher keeps on his own private key ring.

She had her back pressed to the gate, and when I came down the stairs, she crouched down and bared her teeth at me. I paused, trying to find a way to communicate with her, but she just growled— and before I thought of anything useful, Mr. Usher was behind me on the stairs. The maids must have gone straight to him.

"Here she is," he called. Servants came down the stairs, timidly, carrying white sheets. He held out his hand to me.

"Come here, Elisabeth."

The light was behind him, and he looked sinister for a moment.

While I was staring at him, the servants wrapped the girl in the sheets, twisting them around and around her so that when they carried her past us, she was unable to fight.

"She always goes to the crypt," he says.

Such sadness in his voice.

"Why?"

I stared through the gate, wondering what lay beyond. He could have unlocked it and walked through with me, but I didn't know whether I wanted him to.

"She had a little baby. It ended up in the crypt," he said sadly.

I wanted to ask him whether she had the baby before or after she went mad, but his face was turned away from me, toward the past, and the shadows from the torch made him look frightening again, despite the tears on his cheeks.

91
MADELINE IS SEVENTEEN

"I'm ready to confide in you," I say to Emily. I lead her up the stairs, past the suit of armor that always gives me chills.

"Where are you taking me?" she asks.

"It's secret." I shush her. I don't want Dr. Winston finding this place. This room.

We pass through the labyrinth of interconnected rooms. "Light the candles," I say, and she uses the one she was carrying to light the others that we've brought.

As before, the single window allows some light into the room, but for the first time I realize that the decorative latticework at the window is actually a series of delicate bars, thin, but made of steel. Designed to either keep someone out, or in.

I gesture to the heaps of books that hide the floor, the furniture.

"I can't just leave," I say. "And it isn't just because of money. Or because it will be difficult, as a girl. My family is cursed. My father tried to take me away years ago, but it was terrible. We both nearly died. Long before that, my grandmother sent away for these." I gesture to the books. "She was trying to discover something about the curse, about how to defeat the house, but I can't read them, and if she discovered anything, she left no records. I did have a kinswoman who escaped," I say, thinking of Lisbeth. "It must be possible."

"There are so many books," she breathes, her eyes big. "What sort of knowledge was she searching for? The curse is a family illness?"

"Yes. We are tied to this land. To the house."

"It would have taken years to read all of these books," says Emily, the future governess. "So the house is haunted, and the inhabitants are cursed? How is it all connected? The house, it watches you—that's what you, and even Victor, have suggested."

"Yes," I say simply.

She shudders, glancing at the curtains, which are moving slightly, though I don't feel enough of a breeze to cause the disturbance.

"If you all believe that, no wonder you go crazy in the end." And so many of us do. I think of the girl Lisbeth wrote of, chained in the attics. At least father surrounded grandmother with comforts, here in this room. "Tell me about this grandmother who loved to read." She stares at the heaps of books, her eyes round and slightly frightened.

"They thought she was mad. Even her son, my father, thought so." I glance back to the window, at the elegant cage they had created for my grandmother. "But I believe she discovered something important. A way to fight the curse."

"And did she succeed?"

"She died. Here in this room."

Emily taps her foot against the faded carpet. I cross the room and push back the curtains, releasing decades' worth of dust into the already dense air.

"Let me see what I can discover." She squares her shoulders and begins sorting through the volumes. "This one is about furniture making," she says. "And this one is ancient." Emily touches the pages reverently. "Look, Madeline, it's handwritten." The book falls open to an illustration of a girl hanging from a rowan tree. She closes it with a snap.

An hour later, we are no closer to finding anything useful.

"It's as if they were chosen at random," she says. "Or by a madwoman."

92
MADELINE IS TWELVE

They have restrained Father; he is strapped to a stretcher.

"It isn't your fault, Madeline," he says over and over. But I know it is.

I don't want to ride in the conveyance—it isn't quite a coach, isn't quite a wagon—but being by Father is somewhat better than being alone. There are no windows. This is a conveyance for sick people. For the dead.

"Don't come near me," he says. I think he's talking in his sleep. What does he mean? "Madeline?" He squeezes my hand. "If I look at you without recognition, if I'm gone, if I'm mad, stay away. Don't trust whatever the house leaves. It won't be me."

They gave Father an injection. He opened his eyes once, but he didn't seem to recognize me. Because of the medicine. It's the sedative talking, not my father.

I don't like the rocking movement, or the jolting way the windowless coach passes over uneven places in the road. Through the window, I watch the trees pass. Healthy, strong trees with great branches bearing vibrant green leaves. I long for the white trunks and dead leaves that surround my home. And even if I hadn't been homesick, Father was not well. He could not take care of me. I hold his hand but then realize that he isn't aware of me, and drop it.

93
Madeline Is Seventeen

The doctor's huge machine pulses and stutters. I've stolen into their tower, and I sit on the floor beneath the window, trying to read by the light of the moon. The old doctors don't know I'm here, and neither does Dr. Winston. In this room, where the house can't spy on me, I find it a bit easier to make sense of the words in the books.

What is the difference? I ask myself. Between me and Roderick. How are we different? I've always heard the house. Roderick never has. Or has never admitted to it. The house made my cradle rock of its own volition, made me swing without moving my legs.

Roderick would close his eyes, put his hands over his ears, pretend he saw nothing, heard nothing, but I listened.

That's the difference.

My curiosity.

My need for love.

I've brought this curse down on my own head. I've damned myself.

Beside me are two books from my grandmother's collection that Emily thought might be relevant—one about ghosts, and the one with the picture of the girl hanging from a noose. It turns out that book is filled with illustrations of dead girls.

I hold Lisbeth Usher's diary close. As I read the pages, they are crumbling. I place the scraps in a box with a lacquered lid—but I doubt I could ever piece the entries back together. It's hard enough for me to read when the pages are whole.

I showed some of the intact pages to Emily, in a tentative effort to introduce her to the realities of my life. Ancient journals. Ancient curses. She gasped and said the journal must be ancient.

I agree. And yet part of me feels that there is something more sinister to the fact that it's disintegrating as I read it. Like it was waiting for me. Unfortunately, my fits wreak havoc on my memory. I don't always remember what I have read for more than a few days.

Still, I feel that there are other forces at work besides the house's will. I've fought the house in small ways, and succeeded. It is not all-powerful, or all-knowing. Lisbeth escaped the curse, and left this journal, forging a bond between us.

Perhaps I can escape too.

94
MADELINE IS SEVENTEEN

Resting my hand against the rough stone at the side of the house, I examine my vines. Wooziness tries to overwhelm me, but I push it back, holding a window ledge to brace myself. My vision clears. I push myself away from the support of the wall, even as a bit of vine caresses my hand. The pain subsides.

I look up, marveling at the faint warmth of the sun, at the breath of a nearly icy breeze reminding me that winter is fast approaching. Marveling because I am still upright.

It's the first time in my life that I have truly overcome one of the fits. Not just held it off, but made it go away. I stand, a silly smile on my face, my hand pressed against a thick vine that twines up the side of the house, nestling into a crack and then out again. Butterflies flutter here and there, and I marvel at my own strength, to do this thing, to overcome a fit. Even the doctors think it is impossible.

95
MADELINE IS SEVENTEEN

I sit in the garden with my feet in the winter snow, planning where I will plant flowers when spring arrives. In my hands I hold envelopes, carefully labeled with ink illustrations. Roderick gave me these packets of seeds, a Christmas gift—though he spends so little time here, even in the summer, who knows if he will even enjoy my plantings.

Dr. Winston is nearby, sitting on a different bench. He was writing in his journal, but now he has kicked the snow aside and is staring into the dark soil beneath. "Everything is interconnected, isn't it, Madeline?" he asks.

It is the house speaking, really. It is greedy and wants us all to be a part of it. Not separate people with contradictory desires. Dr. Winston's eyes are so dark, they nearly burn with unspoken emotion.

Before he can speak to me again, Emily leaves the house in a bustle of coats and scarves.

"Good afternoon," she says, adjusting her fur-lined hat.

Dr. Winston starts at her voice, and stands. "I'm sorry, I have to write a letter for Dr. Peridue. His eyesight is failing him." He stumbles toward the house, veering away as he passes her, as if he doesn't want to get too near.

Emily pretends not to care. She's trying to get past her desire to marry him, but I know it isn't easy. She's good at pretending. She pretends that she likes living here. Pretends not to be dismayed by the spiderwebs, or upset that she sees eyes whenever she looks into the depths of a mirror.

"Oh, no, Madeline, Victor left his journal. . . ."

For a moment she appears ready to follow him. It's an excuse to be near him, after all. But then she considers the journal and sits down on the stone bench he vacated. She gives me a conspiratorial look, opens the book, and begins to read.

"Look, Madeline, look what he wrote." Emily has jumped to her feet, casting a long shadow over me.

The words slither and I want to ask her to read it to me, but having to ask is so hateful. I hold up my filthy hands as an excuse.

She gives a nervous laugh.

"It says 'Her skin is like alabaster.' I don't think my skin is like alabaster, do you?"

An odd emotion prickles in the pit of my stomach. The severed stone head of an ancient statue stares up at us from the undergrowth at the side of the house. I lean forward. I'd investigate it further, as I've not noticed it, or the decapitated statue it must have originally been part of. Emily looks up, thinking I've moved because I'm shocked by what Dr. Winston wrote. Then she's back to the journal.

"His handwriting is hard to read. This next line says 'I'll never be attracted to a healthy woman again.'" Her brow creases.

She stares into the journal.

"I need to go back inside, out of the sun," she says. Though she just got here, and there is precious little sun.

She drops the journal as if it is poisonous, and hurries along the path, back to the house.

I dust my hands on my skirts and pick up the book. It's easy to find where she stopped reading; it's still open to the page.

I can't wait to watch her die.

His handwriting is not that difficult to read, even for me.

96
FROM THE JOURNAL OF LISBETH USHER

Today I witnessed something truly terrible, proving that I must escape. I was following Mr. Usher, who goes to the attic once or twice a month. Those are the only times he can force himself to see his mad sister. He whispers in her ear that all will be well and that he'll take her away from here. Afterward, she seems calmer. She stares out the window. Hopeful. Her escape attempts occur when he has been gone for long periods of time.

Is she truly mad? Wouldn't anyone be if they were chained in the attic?

What was she like before they imprisoned her?

I watch her through the doorway. She fights with the manacles and, in a fit of desperation, bit off one of her fingers. Slick with blood, the manacle fit over that hand. I wanted to cry out, to stop her, but even as she lifted the other hand to her mouth, I choked.

She was stopped by a cry of anguish from the doorway. Her

brother. *My betrothed. He held her in his arms and cried over her maimed hand, wrapping bandages around the stump where the finger used to be. But before he left her, he twisted the manacle tighter, rendering her act of self-mutilation useless.*

He picked up the finger and wrapped it in his handkerchief, putting it in his pocket.

And he gave me a look through the doorway. He knows that I witnessed everything.

97
Madeline Is Seventeen

We've come back to my grandmother's room. It's a good place to hide from Dr. Winston, and I'm stubbornly convinced that there may be some answers here. I don't want to believe that the madness of all these Usher women was in vain. They would want to leave some legacy, to help me escape the curse. I'm not sure Emily believes that I'm cursed, though she's seen my illness. She tries to focus on more practical matters that she can understand. Money.

"You could take some things with you to sell, in the city," Emily suggests. "When we leave."

I laugh. "It would fall to dust." At least that's what happens when maids steal our candlesticks. "Roderick says that we can buy things, but that our wealth is tied to the house, somehow."

"Still, there must be some way. The Usher family

supports a good many charities," Emily says. "You are quite well known for extravagant generosity. Your family gives money to various orchestras. They pay the upkeep on an entire cemetery. A hospital. Why can't their philanthropy support us?"

I wonder if she's asking because she doesn't want to become a governess. It is a precarious way to live.

"I don't want to leave you here," she says. "It doesn't seem . . . safe. But I don't have the means to find a place for us to live. The world can be unkind to young women on their own."

She is completely sincere, but I fear if Dr. Winston stops fussing over me and beckons to her, she'll return to him.

"Since you believe so completely that you must be sedated, I think that would be best. But first we must set up the accounts. . . ."

She believes more than Roderick. She at least thinks the house is haunted, that it affects me and makes me strange.

"But what about the consciousness?" She keeps coming back to that. "It must *want* something."

"It wants to control us. And for the family line to continue." I don't explain how far that control goes, how the two are linked. She doesn't need to know everything.

"But why? Why would a house want that?"

"Because we've lived here all these years?"

"Still, it isn't like it's grown fond of you; it isn't gentle or kind to you. It uses the Ushers like a nasty old grandfather trying to preserve his family's preeminence. Pulling strings and forcing miserable progeny into situations to prosper the family."

A nasty old grandfather? I would laugh at her choice of words, except that they ring true. If I wasn't remembering a story, an image that haunts my dreams. Dead children laid out on a flat stone, like the one in the room beyond the vault.

Emily shakes her head and goes back to flipping through her books. Making her plans. But all of a sudden, I'm afraid. She seems to believe the curse, but does she understand how deep it goes? How much a part of me it is?

Does she believe that once we're away from the House of Usher that I will behave like a normal girl? That I will be a normal girl? Do I believe it? I let her set up the fake charity so that we will have money. I let her collect gold and silver from throughout the house; I don't care if she converts it to cash in the city.

I ignore my fear. With her help, the key to leaving may well be within my grasp. . . .

98
MADELINE IS SEVENTEEN

All I ever do is watch people leave.

We watch Emily ride away from the window at the front of the house. It's snowing, so I'm glad she has the fur muff to keep her hands warm, but I'm sorry to see her go, even if I will be joining her soon.

She carries several letters with my signature, others that I've forged with Roderick's name. A small fortune. She will rent a cottage and send for me. Before that happens, I have to find a way to leave. I have to harness the power that allowed me to fight down that fit, and use it. To remember how Father managed to take me away. Or perhaps the hint I need can be found in the last pages of Lisbeth's journal. Hope wells up—what I think might be optimism. Perhaps its own form of madness.

It's nearly spring, and this is perhaps the last of the snow.

"It'll be better now," Dr. Winston says from behind me. "Now that she's gone. We can spend more time together. In the room upstairs, with the machines . . ."

I put my hands against the window, feeling the cold seep through the glass. The house wants me to step away from him, and for once I agree. He's standing too close.

"It'll be better with her gone," he repeats.

"She reminded me of other places, of cities and places far away."

"You don't need to think of other places," he says.

He puts his arms around me.

I step back, away from him, out of his arms.

"Madeline?"

It would be so easy to pretend to love him, even if he does want to watch me die. We are here alone. He is the only one who shows any interest in me. He offers a sort of companionship. A secondary plan, if Emily fails me. And I am still intrigued by kissing. It would be easy to pretend. He doesn't ever look into my eyes. He would never know.

But I would know.

"That isn't what I want."

"No?"

"No."

His jaw clenches. He is not accustomed to rejection.

"Emily is very fortunate, that you care for her so much."
He puts his hands on my shoulders. His hands are strong,
and he's gripping so tightly that my shoulders feel small.

Through the window we can barely see Emily, riding
through the light snow. She's wearing a red coat over her
white dress.

99
FROM THE JOURNAL OF LISBETH USHER

Yesterday I died.

Or at least that's what everyone believed. I fell into a deep trance, and the servants, believing me dead, put me in my best gown and brought me downstairs. They lit candles around me and put coins on my eyes.

It was like my other trances, but different, more complete. I lost consciousness, and the servants couldn't tell that I was still breathing.

Mr. Usher was away, though he returned as soon as he could, perhaps ready to celebrate his release from our marriage. I ask too many questions, am too inconvenient.

Now I sit in my bed, weak, shaking.

He wishes he hadn't married me. He loves my sister. I knew

when it happened, when the curse passed.

While I was lying there, I forced the presence of the house out of my mind. I have not heard it since.

I will not stay here. I cannot. I am no longer a part of this thing.

100
MADELINE IS SEVENTEEN

I place the last pages of Lisbeth Usher carefully in the lacquered box. The lid is made of mosaic tiles. Looking at it confuses my eyes, and I know that such things confound the house.

A piece of paper falls to the floor. I pick it up. Unfold it slowly. What message is Lisbeth imparting to me?

My heart sinks; it is nothing but scribbling. She has written her name over and over. *Elisabeth Rose Usher.* My middle name is Rose. And then I see something odd. Elisabeth Rose Usher. Daughter of Emmaline, sister of Honoria and Annabel.

My mother's name was Annabel. That doesn't mean anything; it's a common name. This is nearly too much reading for me. My mind whirls round and round, like water swirling downward. At the bottom of the page it says *Elisabeth Rose Usher, beloved of Charles Usher.*

Charles was my father's name.

All this time I've been imagining that Lisbeth lived decades ago, perhaps a hundred years before me—when all along, she was just one generation away. She was my aunt, my mother's older sister. She isn't here. She must have escaped, and she could still be alive.

I think about my parents. My mother's bitterness. Lisbeth didn't save her, as she promised. Mother was always so bitter, hating the house, and her life, and the malady that came on her when she was only six years old. Hating me for being the first child, the cursed one. There is no point loving the one who is cursed, is there?

And Father, he was always the gentle one. Poor Father, who disappeared . . .

I remember him taking me to the widow's walk, warning me never to consider jumping. Like his Honoria, I am somber.

101
MADELINE IS SEVENTEEN

I read by the light of the window, though the bars cast narrow shadows across my book. When I opened it, hundreds of slips of paper fell to the floor. *I love you. I watch you. I need you.* Messages from the house? To the house? They are written in her blood, and so many of them must mean something. That she sat with this book in front of her for many hours?

It's a volume about ghosts and curses. Perhaps, out of everything my grandmother collected, this might be the most useful. The accounts of hauntings are vague, and I skim them, since our ghosts are so feeble and useless. But an entire chapter is devoted to curse origins.

I remember the story of our ancestor, the slaughter. When I close my eyes, I can feel his maliciousness. Archibald Usher. His consciousness is the consciousness of the house, the nastiness that watches and seeps in through the cracks.

And I remember something that Emily said. "The house isn't exactly proud, is it? It doesn't seem to maintain itself." We were in my garden, looking up at one of the many smaller cracks. "Doesn't care about beauty or dignity, though it could have both. What does the house value? What does it protect?"

And I think of the depths below the house. The vault, and the room with the wide flat stone. Only Ushers are supposed to go there. I remember how Roderick and I found the hidden door and made our way there when we were quite small. We were distracted by the crypt, by the horror of the sarcophagi, but that wasn't what the house was trying to show us.

The house is so huge, and has held its secrets for so long. I need Emily to write, to say that she's found a place and that I can join her. I need to get away from here. Away from these horrors. The carefully wound clock in my pocket ticks as the minutes pass. I feel, suddenly, as if time is running out for me.

102
MADELINE IS SEVENTEEN

She isn't coming back. Emily. It has been weeks. She hasn't written, like she promised. Hasn't contacted me with an address, hasn't sent a coach.

I will not let this latest abandonment destroy me. And I won't stay here with Dr. Winston.

I make my plans carefully. It would be better if I could be sedated. But that isn't possible, because I have no one to help me. Since I will be alone, I must not collapse. I must be strong. I must push the house out of my mind. If Lisbeth Usher accomplished it long ago, then I can too.

I am leaving.

I write a note in bold black letters. It says:

My name is Madeline Usher. If I am incapacitated, please take me to an inn or an officer of the law. I beg of you, do not take me back to the House of Usher.

I will pin it to my coat as I walk away from the house.

I collect gold coins and pieces of jewelry. Emily took an entire suitcase full, but plenty of riches are lying around, and I never showed her the treasure trove of jewels in Mother's room. I destroy Mother's necklaces, rip out the gemstones, and put them in a little bag with a drawstring, which I hang around my neck.

I place as much gold as I can reasonably lift into a bag and fold a spare dress over the coins. Then I wrap some bread in a cloth napkin and place it in the bag as well.

Whenever the house tries to invade my thoughts, I push it away. Grandmother's books say you must invite spirits in. The house has been with me since I was born, but I did not invite it. I listened, but I won't anymore.

My preparations are made, and the house has not responded.

Nothing. I feel nothing. It makes me nervous.

This morning I have an examination with the doctors. I must go; otherwise they will know the moment I go missing. If I leave later, then no one will notice my absence for hours. I leave my bag just inside the door of my bedroom.

When I reach the doctors' rooms, Dr. Winston tells me to undress, but I refuse.

"Today should just be a quick examination," I tell him, holding my chin high.

He scowls. "I'll take blood," he says.

I need all my energy today, but I give him my arm obediently.

He lays the needle on a table and picks up a small knife.

"This will be faster," he says. "More efficient." He caresses me gently with the blade behind my ear, then on my cheek before finally placing it against my forearm. The blade is cold against my skin.

"This blade is perfect for you, Madeline."

So, he is no longer content to wait to see me die.

"The house is telling me to do things. I don't want to kill you. I never wanted to kill you. I want you to love me. It's not the same knife I used on Emily."

I freeze. I am always still when the doctors are poking at me, but now I might as well be dead. I've forgotten how to breathe.

That he used on Emily? She didn't abandon me. . . .

I rear back away from him, but he knows what he's doing. The knife opens my flesh, but the cut is so shallow, there's barely any blood.

I throw back my head and scream for Dr. Paul and Dr. Peridue. Footsteps pound in the hall.

"What are you doing?" Dr. Paul is yelling. Dr. Winston drops his knife and dives after me, but I'm too quick; I dart out into the hallway.

I don't have my missive, or my suitcase, or my bread, and blood trails in uneven paths down my arm.

What I do have is a certain inner strength. Resolve. I'm not even sure where it's coming from. But I am neither confused nor afraid.

I run through the hall of portraits. Surely all of the Usher ancestors are frowning at me. Or maybe they want me to escape. Maybe they hated the house as surely as I do.

Down the staircase. I duck past the suit of armor, but it doesn't drop the ax today. Through the dark-paneled hall with all the weapons adorning the walls. Another staircase, ruined rooms at the front of the house . . . I'm charging through the front door. Not sneaking out the back.

Roderick's horses stamp in their stone stalls, and I feel sorry for them in their confinement.

I pause on the edge of the causeway. I could go back inside right now; no one would know that I had planned to escape. They would assume that I was running through the house because the young doctor was threatening me with a knife.

The bag of jewels is heavy around my neck. At least I have that.

I take the first step forward. The water of the tarn boils and churns. But I will not let it stop me. Two steps forward, three . . . the water is moving all around me, on both sides of the causeway. How big is the creature that dwells there?

I try to walk steadily, focusing on stepping carefully. Step four, step five, step six. The activity in the water stops abruptly. What is the creature preparing for? To grab me? To trip me with a slimy tentacle around my ankle?

With one more step, I will reach the shore. I don't look back at the House of Usher, because I know it will unnerve me too completely.

I walk toward the forest of dead trees.

It is not far now. If the servants are looking out the windows, they will see me, but there's no avoiding that. My boot is unlaced, but I wait until I'm hidden by the trees to tie it.

The forest is very dark. A thick layer of dead leaves covers the ground, leaving no visible path forward. Perhaps I should have followed the road, but I was afraid of being caught.

Something rustles in the underbrush, so without stopping, I carefully choose a stick; it is white as bone, and not very heavy. I grip it tightly and hold it before me as I go.

I walk through spiderwebs that cling to my hair, and mud so deep it coats my white boots and the hem of my dress. The trees here are deteriorating, rotting away. The part of me that loves plants hates this forest, because it is a slow graveyard for trees. Nothing else grows here, unless you count slimy green moss.

The farther I walk, the better I feel. According to my

silver pocket watch, it's been two hours. I'm getting farther and farther from the house, and I feel fine. It is growing darker, but soon I will be through. Soon I will see the lights of the town.

I trudge into the dark night. There is no moon. Sometimes I see yellow eyes in the underbrush. A cacophony of crickets and frogs rises up all around. I can no longer tell what time it is, as it is too dark to see the face of my timepiece, and the night seems endless. In the distance is a tiny bit of light. The trees are getting thinner. Surely I am coming now to the edge of the forest. I will see homes, cottages, on the other side. I hurry toward it.

I trip over a decaying log, and skin my hand, but I barely stop, just dust it on my skirts and keep going. The sun is rising as I walk out onto a plain. My heart nearly stops. The House of Usher looms before me.

I stand, staring up at the house, sickened by the sight of it. Then I turn again to the forest. Which way did I go when I left the grounds before? I plan my route and walk back into the woods. Straight line.

Sometimes from my window I can see the distant lights of the village. It can't be that far.

Naked squirrels with distended bellies watch me with big eyes, dragging themselves along the branches of malevolent trees.

Everything on our land is sick and dying.

But I feel fine. I have twigs in my hair and my boots are caked with mud, and I'm tired, so tired, but I feel alive for the first time in ages.

Away from the house, I could grow old, read books. Maybe, if I had a house that was my own, I could have a puppy or a kitten.

I could be content.

Eventually a sort of bog stretches out in front of me. Fetid, green. I'm not sure how deep the water is and don't want to arrive in town stinking and covered with slime. I skirt the water, following a line of willows, testing the ground in front of me before I take each step.

Twice my boots disappear into the mud. The trees thin up ahead, and I hurry forward. Only to find myself standing in the shadow of the House of Usher.

I sink to the ground.

103
MADELINE IS SEVENTEEN

Dr. Peridue finds me sitting with my back against the house. Tiny pointed leaves from the vines I planted caress my cheeks.

He sees the mud caking my boots. His skeletal face changes for a moment, but I don't know how to interpret the expression. Sadness? Suppressed laughter? Disdain?

"Why would you try to leave the house, silly girl? The house is everything, and you are the key. I've spent my life keeping you safe. For the house."

I would ask him what he means, but exhaustion is settling over me, and perhaps a fit that I'm no longer strong enough to fight off.

He asks something about bleeding, but I can't answer him. He wavers before my eyes.

When I wake, I am hooked to the doctors' machine.

My arms are tied down with bandages made from ripped bedsheets. Red roses are embroidered among thorns. I can move my arms, but only a little.

The machine is pumping pumping pumping. The bellows puff air in and out. Something moves through miles of tubing, slow and sluggardly. It is my blood. I look down at my wrist. It is dripping; one drop after another falls into a wide pan below me, and then funnels into more tubing. It's all made from sheep's guts, I know, because I asked Dr. Winston once.

I dream that a rat is sitting on my chest, gnawing at the torn sheets that I'm tied with, but when I wake I am still bound. A crow watches me from the window. But I don't remember this room ever having a window.

I drift in and out of consciousness. Dr. Winston is a shadow slumped in the corner. Does he know I'm awake? What are they doing to me? Is it the will of the house, or some other diabolical plan?

The pulsating sound of the machinery is a lullaby, but I don't want to sleep. Rage overwhelms me. I want to be aware, to see, to understand. And still the pumping, the slow drip of my blood, lull me into some sort of trance.

104
MADELINE IS SEVENTEEN

Still in the doctors' lair, I struggle, and manage to sit up. The bandages are gone and the machinery is quiet. How long have I been trapped here?

"You mustn't try to leave again," Dr. Peridue admonishes me.

"Is that why you confined me here?"

He laughs. "Child, we did no such thing."

I gesture to the machine. It sits, a cold, metallic monstrosity at odds with the simple flowered wallpaper of this room. "I was tied down. You pumped out my blood," I accuse.

His eyes caress the mechanism. "It's a thing of beauty, isn't it? I've been testing your blood since you were an infant."

"To see what's wrong with me?" I ask. Or to break my will so that I don't try to escape again?

"To see how you are different. The Usher line is long and aristocratic. My own family has some Usher connections from long ago, distant relations, I believe. It draws us all, in the end. How could you ever want to abandon your heritage?"

This is the most the oldest doctor has ever spoken to me, and I wonder, seeing how frail he looks, if he is garrulous because he is dying, if he wants to impart something of his life to me, his last victim.

"So you were here for the house all along," I say coldly. "Not for me, or my mother. Not to try to cure us."

"It is all the same," he says softly. "She shouldn't have sent your brother away. That must be what put such mad ideas into your head. That, and your father's foolishness. Leaving the house. We'll see that you stay here. Dr. Winston is feeling much more himself. We've spoken to him at length and he's been under pressure, but I've determined that he is stable. He will act as your keeper. And once a week, he will bring you back to this room."

It is Dr. Peridue's turn to gesture to the machine. He reaches up to caress a nozzle. Though the movement is gentle, the gesture is a threat. He is threatening me with his machine, which even the house cannot control.

105
MADELINE IS SEVENTEEN

"The other doctors have assigned me the task of keeping track of you; therefore I am your keeper, Madeline. You are mine."

They assigned this to him months ago, when I fainted at the edge of the property. Still, they seem to have left me with him.

Did I ever think that he was young and vibrant and attractive? He has aged in the last months. His eyes are ancient, and vacant as the windows of this house, and he wants to be with me every second of the day.

"I'm going for a walk," I tell him.

He stands to go with me.

"You don't have to come," I say.

But he moves to follow me.

"You can watch me from the windows," I interrupt

quickly, to stop him from telling me, once more, that he is my keeper. It is hateful, hearing it from him in his gloating voice. I must find a way to discover what happened to Emily. To get him to lose control again, in front of the other doctors. Not when we are alone. Never when we are alone.

"I always watch you from the windows," he says. "Of course I do. I'm your keeper."

Something falls from a shelf. A book of poetry that was a gift from Roderick. I can't tell if the house is displeased with me, or with Dr. Winston. Lately, when I place my hand on the woodwork, the emotions that seep into me are confusing. Inconsistent. As if the house is going mad, and where does that leave me?

I walk slowly across the room to get my cape and my scarf. It is chilly outside. Dr. Winston can't let anything go. "The old doctors want me with you every moment of the day. If you try to leave again, they will blame me."

I wrap the cape tightly around my shoulders, more as protection against him than against any wind or chill in the air.

"Roderick will be coming home soon," I tell him. We walk into the corridor. He puts his hand through my arm.

"Who is Roderick?" he asks.

I study him. He is walking carefully, as though trying to keep me from falling. But his odd question seems genuine enough. . . .

"Roderick," I repeat, thinking he hasn't heard me clearly. He raises his eyebrows askance. "My brother."

"You have no brother. You are an only child."

He's toying with me, testing me. Trying to make me believe I'm mad, because only a mad girl would love him. He's the one who is crazy, I tell myself. But this strange taunting bothers me.

I try to turn the corner, but he pulls back, stopping me.

"This is my house," I tell him. "You have to let me go."

Why am I arguing with him? Why should I have to?

A dismal throbbing begins behind my eyes. I miss silence. I can't navigate my world with him constantly beside me, whispering lies.

"I need some fresh air."

I walk away from him. The side door thumps closed behind me, and for a few moments, I am alone.

106
MADELINE IS SEVENTEEN

I wake up in the dead of night, and I am alone. No matter how hard I try, I can't sense Roderick.

Dr. Winston's words echo in my head. "Dr. Peridue told me you were an only child."

He said it with such conviction.

I know he was trying to push me over the edge, that he's constantly taunting me with madness, but knowing doesn't keep my heart from beating faster and faster.

Is Roderick pushing me out of his mind?

Spots dance before my eyes, no matter if they are opened or closed.

The world wavers.

Dr. Winston has been drugging me.

107
MADELINE IS SEVENTEEN

I tell myself that I must have heard Dr. Winston wrong. Or that he was taunting me when he said he hurt Emily, like when he pretended that Roderick didn't exist. It must all be lies, designed to confuse me. Dr. Winston was with me when she rode away. She and I had plans together. She wouldn't have come back to meet with him. Would she?

When Dr. Peridue comes to my room to ask how I'm feeling, I begin to question Dr. Winston loudly, about Emily. If he loses control again, I want the other doctors near. I want them to see that they are wrong; he isn't better. He might stab me again, or worse. Unfortunately, he is in control of himself today.

"Have you heard from Emily?"

Dr. Winston smiles. "As if the house would let you leave with her now, to live in the city. How foolish."

I go completely cold. How much does he really know? Every detail? How?

"She was your friend," I insist. "Has she written to you? Contacted you?"

"No. She wasn't a true friend, though, was she? She took a set of silver candlesticks when she left. Put them in her bag, all wrapped up with her brown dress, the one that made her look exactly like a governess. And she hated this house. Thought it was haunted. And creepy, and dirty. She didn't see what we see."

Dr. Peridue makes no comment of his own but holds out a cup. Something within bubbles and fizzes. I take it from him. The porcelain warms my hands. He nods to Dr. Winston and leaves the room.

I stare out the window, hoping Dr. Winston will go, either to consult with the other doctors, or to do whatever it is he does in the few moments of the day when he isn't by my side. When he leaves, I will empty the contents of this mug into a vase or urn. But he sits and smiles, too patient. Far too patient.

108
MADELINE IS SEVENTEEN

Despite some successes at fighting off fits, I fell into a catatonic trance in the hall of portraits today. The portraits themselves, the formal paintings of unsmiling Ushers, don't interest me much anymore, as they always stay the same, except when the servants move them. I'm more intrigued by the dark oil paintings, which sometimes show the future.

My feet scraped across the floor as I walked to the miniature of the house. I had avoided it since I saw Cassandra in it . . . but today I found the nerve to look.

In the forefront of the painting, there was a perfect red rose, untouched by rot or taint.

And in the back, as always, was the House of Usher. But this time the crack, the one that I had seen through the mist with Cassandra, was like a shadow snaking its way up the side of the house and marring the odd symmetry of the many different parts.

There is something here of importance, I told myself. And then I fell.

109
MADELINE IS SEVENTEEN

Tonight is moonless, and it is late. My dressing table is covered with candles of all sizes. I have collected them from throughout the house. Now I have light; my room is ablaze with it.

I take off my dress slowly. Being naked, for me, has always been for the doctors—part of their curiosity, and their cruelty. It has always meant chilly discomfort.

But my room is warm. And I am alone.

It has been months since Roderick left. Weeks in which my only human touch was to have my pulse taken, my temperature gauged, or my blood stolen away. Or Dr. Winston's grasping hands.

I run my hand over my skin. It is amazingly soft, despite the scars. Scars from injuries I don't recall.

Shadows move in the hallway. Someone is standing outside my locked door.

I button my dress quickly. Forgotten scars don't matter as much as avoiding future ones. I turn back to my grandmother's books. Wind pummels the house, howling in through the cracks and crevices. Cracks and crevices. The house is not invulnerable.

110
MADELINE IS SEVENTEEN

I am cursed. I've always known this, but never been quite so aware.

Dr. Winston insists that I lie in bed. I must speak to no one, not even the servants. I must not read. He tells the maids to remove any books they find in my room. For my own good. He forces me to drink the contents of the cups that he brings night after night, and sometimes in the middle of the day.

He claims I am too feeble to get out of bed, advises me to stare at the wall, to think of nothing. I think of ways to kill him.

When I destroy the house, he will be inside and he will die.

When I destroy the house.

This is a new and frightening thought.

Yes, the house is malignant . . . but destroying it?

Lisbeth never made plans on this scale, or if she did, did not record it in her journal. My mother did not think of it, though she at least loved one of her children enough to defy the house and send him away.

I know now that getting away is useless. My life has been spent learning about the house. Father tried to take me away, and I tried to walk away on my own. But now I realize I will never escape, as long as the house is standing. Fleeing takes precious energy. I must find a better way to use the little power I have.

I will bring down the house.

The question is . . . how will I do it?

I've put together things that none of the rest of them did, collected tidbits from Lisbeth's journal, from the books in Grandmother's room. From the library. I've watched the stories play out, night after night, whether I wanted to see them or not.

I pace back and forth across my room. They've taken all the books, even the ones I might use to hold my door in place. Instead I fold the rug.

Long ago, Roderick and I found a book, the one that said the house used to sit beside the sea. The author believed that there was a chalice, and that object was connected to the consciousness of the house.

But they were all wrong. The house was distracting

them. Why would it give anyone a key to its destruction?

There are no magical objects in the house. There is the house itself, conscious and evil, the ineffective ghosts, and me.

And my oldest ancestor, buried in the dungeon. The great foundation stone is his tombstone, moved here from wherever the house was before. The entire house crouches around it, protecting it, so it must be important. The root of everything that the House of Usher is.

The house has forged me. Dr. Winston sees me as his victim, but he is wrong. I do not fear pain. I live through pain every day.

There is nothing that truly frightens me. Not anymore.

If the original Usher's gravestone is destroyed, will the house be able to stand?

A great vicious crack is rending the House of Usher, slowly destroying it. It might take a hundred years. Perhaps fifty, with my tenacious vines speeding the destruction. Or I could bring the house down much, much faster.

If only I can find the proper tools.

111
Madeline Is Seventeen

The gardener's shed sits behind the house, hidden by trees.

I heave the rotted door open and look inside. The shed holds rusted shears, a few spades, a long-handled shovel, and other rusting tools. In the corner I find a great mallet, a sledgehammer, with a head of steel. The wood handle is slimy, but the steel is bright.

It is too heavy for me to carry more than a short distance, and I have to devise some way of getting it into the house without the house realizing what I am doing.

I need pocket watches. Every pocket watch I've ever acquired over the years . . . and even then, will they be enough to distract the house from my intentions?

112
MADELINE IS SEVENTEEN

Carrying a brightly patterned picnic blanket, I walk outside. When did it become spring? I thought winter would go on forever, austere and unrelenting, but green shoots are bursting out of the earth. I wander into the dead forest. Five paces in, ten. At twenty paces, the air changes. The air here is lighter. Mushrooms peer out from between the exposed roots of the trees. Worms slither in and out of the dark earth.

A tombstone stands in what used to be a clearing; weeds and saplings have grown up over the years. I clear it with my hand. LISBETH USHER, BELOVED SISTER OF ANNABEL, it says. I feel myself swaying. She didn't get away. She didn't escape. It makes my own course of action clearer. The house won't release any of us. Not while it stands.

Lisbeth Usher. She looked in the wrong places. She

put her hope in the library. The secret is not there; I've looked. She put her faith in Charles Usher. My father. But I will not put my faith in anyone.

Dr. Winston finds me. I try to look surprised and a little upset, as if I wasn't waiting for him.

I spread the picnic blanket quickly. His mad eyes pass over the bright, busy pattern and focus on my drab gray.

We are, both of us, trying to find something. He thinks we are searching for the same thing. For a moment, my surety wavers. The house wouldn't send him on a useless search . . . but then I remember Grandmother's books, filled with hints about ancient artifacts. She's the one who has sent him chasing through the rooms. The house doesn't care.

"Madeline." He takes a seat beside me in the grass, as if we are great friends. "Do you remember when I came to the house, and you were in the garden?"

I fake a smile for him, waiting for the question.

"You had an urn, Madeline. I said that I thought it was some sort of burial urn, and it glittered oddly. I have been thinking about it, and I suspect some sort of metal—gold, perhaps—was melted down and mixed with whatever pottery clay was used, before it was fired."

He thinks the urn was recast from the lost Usher goblet. It's a good enough guess and will occupy at least a little of his time.

"I remember," I say. "It was useful for carrying water from the well, as the water from the spring is black."

"Yes," he says. So very impatient, always moving, agitated, as if he no longer feels comfortable in his own skin. "Yes. Where is it? In the gardener's shed, perhaps?"

Fear washes over me. Not the gardener's shed, which is my destination. Why would he think it was there?

"The servants took it," I say in a soft voice, as if this is a secret. He leans close, eager to hear. "They said it was a relic of the house. They polished it and put it in one of the front rooms. I saw it there just recently." Just enough detail to make him believe.

He squeezes my hand. "Are you feeling well? I need to go inside for just a few moments, but only if you feel well enough for me to leave you."

"I feel well," I reassure him.

It will take him hours to search through the front rooms. Still, it will be best if I hurry, just in case he returns.

I rush to the gardener's shed. In my arms I carry the picnic blanket, brightly patterned and garish as ever. I have a pocket watch in each of my pockets. Wrapping the sledgehammer in fabric, I heave it into the house. Cook sees me and stops working to stare, so instead of taking it down the endless stairs to the vault, I stow it in an alcove. My arms tremble from the exertion. It is heavier than I expected. Heavy enough to smash stone, if I am strong enough to wield it.

Somehow I must get the servants out of the house and collect my strength.

113
MADELINE IS SEVENTEEN

A magistrate has come to call. He is looking for Emily.

So, she is truly gone. I had hoped the doctor's confession was a lie, even if it meant she had abandoned me.

The servants shake their heads and keep working. After Dr. Peridue bragged to me about his Usher ancestry, I've taken to studying the servants' faces. I've come to suspect that most of them were drawn in by the house. They all have Usher blood. They are stoic with the magistrate. Silent.

Dr. Winston is also silent, but sweat glistens on his brow.

"What about you, Mr. Usher?" the magistrate asks.

It takes a moment for me to realize that the magistrate is talking to the doctor. Dr. Winston also seems perplexed.

"I'm not an Usher." Dr. Winston chuckles to himself. "I'm a physician employed by the family to care for Miss Usher."

"I beg your pardon, sir. You had a look about you. As if you had a bit of Usher blood." The magistrate looks from Dr. Winston to me and back again. "We have a good bit of Usher blood in these parts. It always results in a bit of . . ." He shakes his head. "Strangeness."

"I understand," Dr. Winston says, as if this is a compliment.

The magistrate shuffles his feet, obviously uncomfortable. The floor in this room is wood, dark, and without depth—there is no shine to it, or reflection. As if it absorbs the light of the candles.

"Have you seen anything unusual?" the magistrate asks, turning to me.

Words race through my mind. How much to tell him? What will he believe?

"I—" I begin, but Dr. Winston interrupts.

"I'm afraid that questions tax her too much. She shouldn't even be downstairs. She shouldn't have to hear about that poor unfortunate girl."

"I knew her!" I blurt out, but instead of listening, the magistrate nods and then ignores my words. He thinks I'm unhinged.

Like me, Dr. Winston never leaves the property. If he killed Emily, her body must be near. If I can find it, maybe they'll arrest Dr. Winston for her murder. I walk to the door, hoping the magistrate will stop me, will try once more to ask a question. But again Dr. Winston distracts him.

"Would you like some refreshment?" Dr. Winston offers. A distraction, but also foolish. He should encourage the man to leave. Even if the magistrate isn't suspicious, there's always the chance that a battle-ax or a chandelier will fall on him, leaving us with one more extraneous body.

"Thank you," he says.

I slip out of the room but watch them from the hall.

Dr. Winston sits and calmly sips his tea. He's guilty, and he's gloating, but only I can tell, because he keeps smiling at the magistrate and offering more tea.

He taps his fingers nervously, a staccato rhythm. To me, it sounds like a heartbeat.

Finally the magistrate stands and thanks Dr. Winston. He takes his leave, saying that perhaps he'll be back next week.

By then I must have something to show him.

114
MADELINE IS SEVENTEEN

My arm is speckled with purple bruises. My keeper has a penchant for pinching.

This morning, an odd little hairless squirrel dragged itself onto the ledge outside my window. I was startled for a moment, surprised by the intelligence in its beady eyes. It crept forward, and I saw how awkwardly it moved its body.

I took the bread from my tray and crumbled it in my fist. As I watched, the stunted creature scurried away, hiding in the greenery that grows now on this side of the house.

I scattered the crumbs on the ledge in case it returned and was hungry, before going upstairs for an examination. Dr. Winston passes me on the stairs. He'll wait for me in my room. He doesn't want them to see the way he looks at me.

They have me stand while they whisper together.

Dr. Paul sees the bruises.

"Unsuitable," he says.

"It's difficult to find a trained physician who will come to this sort of place," Dr. Peridue says.

"Better someone untrained than someone vicious," Dr. Paul says.

For the first time in my life, I feel a flush of warmth toward Dr. Paul. At least he sees that something is wrong, even if he won't do anything more than mention it to Dr. Peridue.

115
Madeline Is Seventeen

I write a letter to Roderick. I tell him how much better I've been feeling, that I look forward to our eighteenth birthday. I try to keep track of the days, to count them down, but my calendar keeps disappearing. I do not tell Roderick the things that I truly want to say. If he wants to know how I feel, all he has to do is heed that constant connection between us.

Dr. Winston watches me, shaking his head because he doesn't want me to tax myself by writing. He smiles slyly to himself.

I don't expect Roderick to ever get any letter that I write with Dr. Winston watching, so it doesn't matter what words I put on the paper, and I won't beg him to return. I won't make myself pathetic. I'm the brave twin, after all.

Sometime later, I find a letter on my bureau. How long it's been there, I couldn't say. The tone is distant. He says that he's sorry, but he won't be home for our birthday. What else was I to expect? Darkness closes in.

116
MADELINE IS SEVENTEEN

Again the doctors whisper to one another, as I stand, vulnerable, before them.

"Did you expect her to stay a child forever?" Dr. Peridue asks. His voice is gentle, and he might seem grandfatherly if he weren't so gaunt and ghoulish.

They aren't watching Dr. Winston, but I see his face flush.

He meets my eyes, and there is a sort of anger in his gaze, as if he truly hates me.

I raise my eyebrows, challenging him, but his response isn't what I expected. His eyes dart away. I see that he's been biting at his fingernails and that he's lost some hair.

When I shiver, Dr. Paul wraps a blanket around my shoulders.

"There, there. This old house is drafty," he says. But he

isn't covering me because of the cold. He's never cared about that before. He's shielding me from Dr. Winston, all the while watching, trying to remember everything so he can write it in his ledger later.

"Give me your arm," Dr. Paul says, and he sticks the needle into my flesh.

"She's so white, it's as if she has no pigmentation at all," Dr. Peridue remarks.

I can't tear my eyes away as the blood wells up. It is so very red, dark and luscious, the color of a rose. Spots dance before my eyes. I'm their prisoner as well as the house's. Anger wells up, much like the blood from my arm. Not for much longer. When it all comes down, I'll try to find a way to get the servants out of the house, but the doctors can die, for all I care.

117
MADELINE IS EIGHTEEN

Today, we are eighteen years old.

I sit alone at the window. It's covered with a curtain of ivy, which I planted at the base of the house with my own hands. It's grown more quickly than I would have thought possible. Thriving, as each arm takes root in the cracks of the walls. A breath of wind caresses me.

The clatter of hooves wakes me from my reverie. It could be the post, but we received a packet of letters only a week ago. It could be a wanderer, a beggar, or a holy man, though they tend to avoid this place unless they are truly insane.

I brush the ivy away from the window gently. The clattering hooves belong to a white horse. The rider is wearing a hat, pulled down and covering his hair. It doesn't matter; I know him. My heart soars. Roderick didn't abandon me—his letter must have been a ruse, to try to trick me. To surprise me.

I consider running downstairs to meet him, but that might disappoint him. He craves this surprise, so difficult to achieve with a bond like ours.

The white horse charges across the causeway.

Still, it worries me how our bond has been strained lately. Like my inability to sense the moods of the house. Is Roderick pushing me out of his head, or am I somehow pushing him from mine—or is this an unexpected byproduct of growing up?

"Madeline," he calls from the great hall. "Madeline!" How undignified for the lord of the manor. I smile.

I descend the staircase, carefully.

He picks me up and spins me around.

"You knew," he says, guessing.

"Only just a moment ago." Before that, his abandonment had plunged me into near despair, but I don't tell him that. Not now.

"I have a gift for you."

"A ring?" I ask, because suddenly our exchange seems familiar, tinged with déjà vu.

"A ring," he agrees, "and a promise. I'm home to stay."

Can it be true? Will he really stay? And how will I destroy the house if Roderick is here?

"Happy birthday," he says, and kisses my forehead.

118
MADELINE IS EIGHTEEN

Roderick and I are lying on the floor of the drawing room. We are reflected in the great baroque mirror that covers the interior wall. The top of my head meets the top of his head, and we create a straight line. He has let his hair grow out a little, and our hair, twined together against the black rug, sparkles. It's impossible to tell which is his and which is mine.

Roderick points up, re-creating a childhood game in which we find shapes amid the wreckage of the once-beautiful plaster ceiling. A great crack like a bolt of lightning runs from one side to the other. Others run outward from that one, and more from each crack. The plaster hangs in strips. Roderick generally avoids looking at such things; he hates the dilapidation of the house. Will he really stay here?

"I won't be going back to school," he says.

A year ago, I would have been rejoicing, but even if I didn't have dangerous plans, his voice is thick with pain. I touch him lightly, and he sighs.

"I am in disgrace. They are sending a letter to our parents." He gives a strangled laugh.

"Why?" I whisper the question. Because even though I see bits and pieces of his life, I still want him to tell me. To explain.

In the great mirror, I see his brow furrow.

"My friend and I . . . there were rumors that caused the other boys to turn against us. And then someone saw something that they misinterpreted. I am taking the blame for everything, Madeline. My future is here, and his future is out in the world, where this sort of accusation can ruin a person."

Despite our bond, he believes he is guarding his secrets, just giving me enough to understand his pain, but pictures slide in front of my eyes. Visions. I see everything. I grip his hands tighter. He is my brother and I will love him, regardless.

"It is difficult. My old acquaintances scorn me. I cannot even write to him. He has to pretend to hate me."

"I'm sorry, Roderick." I truly am, because even though he will be staying home, he is heartbroken.

"Look, to the left of the crack that looks like a lightning

bolt, what does that resemble?" he asks.

"A horse," I lie. It looks like a puppy, and that reminds me of Cassandra, and my chest tightens, as if this is a new grief.

"No, over a little, does that look like a clock? Under the holes that are like eyes . . ."

Holes through which the house watches us.

Something falls, drips down from a crack in the ceiling and lands on my face. I wrench my hands away from Roderick's grasp. The liquid runs from my cheekbone to my ear, and at the same time, toward my mouth. I twist my head to divert it.

"Madeline!" Roderick pulls off his shirt and uses it to wipe the substance away. I stumble to my feet and across the room to a basin of water, scrubbing, tearing at my skin. It's a brownish substance, like old blood, or infection. The smell is enough to start one of my fits.

"It's on your dress," he says. I feel his fingers, his long, slender, clever fingers, unbuttoning the back of my dress. I am rubbing desperately at my face, and I don't stop him from undressing me. Whatever fell from the ceiling filled me with such horror that I want even the smallest droplet removed. I will burn this dress.

Roderick's shirt lies abandoned on the floor. My dress falls from my shoulders.

At the same time, I look up to see Dr. Winston's reflection in the mirror . He is watching us from the open door.

"I heard the good news that Mr. Roderick is home to stay," he says.

119
MADELINE IS EIGHTEEN

I've slowly been searching the house. Today I will comb through the attic. Looking for my dead friend. It doesn't seem real. And yet where better to hide a dead body than a place where a live man was lost for weeks, or perhaps longer.

I stand amid the discards of long-dead children, touching things with my too-sensitive fingertips. The dolls with their glass eyes; the drum, which is too far gone, too deteriorated to use to distract the house. A tiny broken tea set that reminds me of summers in the sun, sitting in my garden, and Emily insisting the servants bring hot, fresh tea.

In a chest large enough to fit a body, I find wooden blocks and an army of wooden soldiers. Moving a rectangular building block, I catch sight of a bit of lace. Oh, no. Reaching out curious fingers, I touch it. Perhaps it is a doll, or a doll's dress. Perhaps. It is white, like a wedding dress.

During the winter I had white coats made, white dresses, to imitate Emily, who was so stylish. I thought she was so worldly, with her fur-lined caps over her dark hair and the muff that kept her hands warm. And she reached out to me in friendship. I should have found some way to save her.

Gingerly, I shift another block. For a moment, I fear that I might see her face staring up at me. But no, there is only the dress, complete with pearl buttons on the sleeves. Blocks rain down on the wood floor as I pull the dress from the chest.

It is pristine, and untouched by the thick dust that covers everything else in these quiet, haunted rooms.

"Madeline?" Dr. Winston has crept up behind me.

I turn, clutching the dress to my chest. There is no way to hide what I have found.

"Yes?"

"What do you have?"

He is standing in the doorway of the room with the manacles. And I fear, for a moment, that he will strap me down, that he will say it is for my own good, and that when Roderick returns to the house, that he will shake his head sadly and agree.

He's blocking the stairway, and if I run, he will catch me. The way he watches, I feel like prey, and my blood runs cold. Or maybe that's the mood of the house, seeping through the very boards beneath my feet.

I am so afraid that I nearly collapse onto the floor. Where is Roderick?

I cannot see Dr. Winston's eyes, but I know that they are turning purplish, a purple film over his dark eyes, like a cataract.

"It's my dress," I stammer. "My favorite. I've been looking for it everywhere."

He takes three steps forward. Three steps too close. Why didn't I at least try to run? I'm frozen now.

"It's beautiful," he says.

"I know. That's why I was searching for it." How small my voice sounds. Good. He'll think I'm weak and unsure.

"You should put it on." A smile plays at the corner of his mouth.

"Yes. Tomorrow. I'll wear it tomorrow." I take a step back, measuring the distance from where I'm standing to the stairs.

"Why not now?" We stare at each other. "If you treasure the dress so, and you just found it, you should be excited to put it on. To wear it. We'll have tea."

He's taunting me, but at the same time his eyes are completely mad. How can I tell him no?

"Of course," I say. "You bring the tea. I will put on the dress."

"You may need my help," he says. "It has many pearl

buttons down the back, does it not? Twenty-four of them."

"Yes," I whisper. "Please help me." Where is Roderick?

I let my colorless dress fall down around my ankles. I do not move to cover myself, but he responds as if I had. Laughing.

"You don't have to cover yourself. I've seen you too many times to count."

And it's true. All of the doctors have. But his eyes, moving over me now, make my skin crawl. Twenty-four pearl buttons. Tears run down my cheeks. I'm terrified, but also calculating. Let him see me as helpless

I pull it on quickly. The fabric is beautiful, heavy, with a silk sheen. The pearls at the sleeves are cool against my skin. He fastens the bottom button, just above the small of my back, and then leans in, taking forever to button each one. I hold myself impossibly still.

When I destroy the house, I'll be sure he's inside.

The dress fits perfectly, but the collar is stiff and starchy. It chokes me.

"You are beautiful," Dr. Winston says. He stands looking at me for a long time, his smile stretching across his face. "Sit down," he says. "We are going to have tea. You and me," he adds. "No Roderick." As if Roderick would ever agree to have tea with him.

And that's when the nurseries begin to waver around me.

120
MADELINE IS EIGHTEEN

I'm drowning. I can see the surface . . . but it's so far away. My brain feels wrong, woozy and unsure. I've been ill again. I need to wake up, but I can't quite . . .

The doctor's white face is above me. Dr. Winston. I try to focus on him, to let his presence lead me back to consciousness, but his expression is so odd. So sad. Am I dying? Is he mourning my death?

I try to move my arms. Sometimes, when I can't come out of a fit, the struggle helps me to wake up. Something is weighing me down. The blankets? It's completely dark in my room. As it should be. When the fits come, any light, the tiniest flicker from a candle, intensifies the pain.

"I'm going to put this dark cloth over your eyes to protect you from the light, my dear, my Madeline," he says. I try to say no, because I'm afraid that somehow the cloth will smother me, but I cannot speak to tell him so. Perhaps he knows.

The bed creaks, he must've been sitting beside me, and I hear him moving about. I hope he isn't going to take blood. With as much as the doctors have collected, it surprises me that I am still alive.

I find that I am able to move my fingers, just a bit. I stretch them forward, and back. I breathe in and out, and in and out. I wish I could move my head to dislodge this cloth. The spell has passed, my eyes do not burn, and the side of my head is not on fire. The smell of the cloth is gagging me.

The heat in this unlit room is unbearable.

If my hearing were still heightened, as it becomes during my spells, I could hear a spider spinning its web or the cook drop a slice of crusty bread in the kitchen far below.

I can move my elbow a little. My arm will be next. My body is coming back to life. I remember him coming upon me in the attics. His madness.

I realize that I'm still wearing Emily's dress. The lace inserts at the sleeves bruise my inner arms.

Footsteps sound in the hallway. Can the doctor hear them? The door flies open, and the cloth covering my eyes slides away. Roderick stands framed by the doorway. He is wearing his boots, and his breeches are muddy.

Always, when he returns to the house, he comes straight to me. I want to say something to him, but I can't.

"Get out," he says to Dr. Winston.

His lavender eyes are all ablaze. He is so tall, and even though he is too slight to take up the entire doorway, he seems to fill the space with his anger and his energy.

"Get out," he says again. I am surprised that Dr. Winston doesn't argue. I've seen the way he and Roderick size each other up. The barely veiled hatred.

I expect violence from Dr. Winston, my keeper. Instead he shuffles out the door. I cannot turn my head enough to see him, but my eyes are trained on my brother.

He kicks the door closed behind him, and we are alone.

121
MADELINE IS EIGHTEEN

When I wake, I'm alone in my room. The slant of the light says that it's morning. Emily's white dress hangs over a chair. I pick it up, nearly recoiling, and put it far back in the recesses of my wardrobe, where at least I don't have to look upon the hateful thing.

I walk to my window and look outside. I can see Roderick's shadow, and I know that he is standing in the garden, and he is not alone.

Roderick doesn't know about Emily. Doesn't know that Dr. Winston is a murderer. I must get to them as quickly as possible.

"Madeline!" Dr. Winston calls in his friendliest voice as I rush out the side door, and I remember, with a sense of sorrow, when hearing his voice excited me. "Your garden looks better than ever. Have you done something different?"

There is little to change, he knows that. I walk through my flowers, nudging the stones with the toe of my white boots, imagining what might grow if the soil on our land wasn't so dead. I would rather wait to recount Dr. Winston's crimes to Roderick when we are alone.

"You've done amazing things," Roderick says.

"Amazing," Dr. Winston repeats. The house casts a huge shadow over all of us.

"What are those white flowers?" Roderick asks. "Are they new?"

I turn to see what he is referring to, and a finger pokes up from under the soil beside my newly planted rosebush. I think for a moment that I must be dreaming. It happened too easily—a little pressure from my foot, and there it is. The doctor put her in my garden. I nudge the finger with my toe, and the rest of the hand is exposed, palm up and open. I shudder. Her hand is crusted with thick dark mud, and I imagine the rain hitting it.

I scream once, my brother's name, and then the world wavers. But I cannot let it. Not now, not again. I focus on the flowers, on my garden, pulling my strength from outside the House of Usher.

Then something hits me in the back of the head, and I'm falling to the soft earth beside Emily's body.

122
Madeline Is Eighteen

When I come to, I'm in the parlor. I raise my hand to the bandage on the back of my head. It comes away with just a slight residue of blood. The pain is sharp, but better than a fit, because I have control of my limbs. Through the gloom I can make out the candle on the small table where Roderick puts books after he reads them, but everything else blurs as I turn my head too quickly. My stomach lurches.

Something odd catches my eye, and I go cold. Dr. Winston sits, very still, on a chair in front of the window. Not so different than all the other mornings I woke, watched over by my keeper. Except I'm lying in the parlor, my head is bleeding, and Dr. Winston's posture is very unnatural.

Has he defeated Roderick somehow? Has he brought me here to kill me?

He realizes that I am awake.

"I'm leaving," he says. It sounds practiced, like a speech.

Something isn't right about this. He's completely still, like he's been entranced or is trying to entrance me with the intensity of his eyes.

"Then why are you sitting there?" I ask, wondering what he's done to Roderick.

"I'm going to leave in just a moment. In just a . . . Madeline, do you think you could untie me? So I can go?"

I sit up slowly. Dr. Winston is tied to a chair. He is facing away from me, toward the window.

There is a piece of paper on the table behind Dr. Winston, where he cannot see it.

Madeline, I have gone for the magistrate. The villain is tied securely, and I gave him a sleeping draught of his own devising. Be safe, I love you. R.

I sit on the side of the sofa, collecting my strength, and then I stand slowly, testing my balance. He strains to turn his head toward me. The sleeping draught does not appear to be working.

Roderick did tie him well, using a lot of rope. Still, it won't hold Dr. Winston. Not in this house. Not long enough.

"I'll go get a knife from the kitchen," I say, "so I can cut you free." I make my voice subservient, scared.

This won't convince him for long. Once I'm out of his line of sight, I grab my skirts, take a deep breath, and run. My head throbs and I'm still wobbly, but I have to bring down the house before Roderick returns. I have to be strong enough.

The key ring is in the bottom of Roderick's trunk. He's kept it there since he became master of the house, years ago. My hand is shaking, but I grasp it as securely as I can and stumble down to the heavy copper-sheathed door. Behind it is the crypt. There's no time for thought. No time for fear or doubt.

The sledgehammer is where I left it, in a dark alcove where the servants are unlikely to venture. Wrapped in the flowered blanket, it's avoided the house's notice, as well as Dr. Winston's house-mad eyes.

Lifting it awkwardly, still in the blanket, I lurch down the stairs, bumping against both sides of the passageway. They are so narrow. The metal head of the sledgehammer swings and makes contact with the stone wall, jarring my entire body. The blanket makes carrying this too difficult, so I let it fall away. My shoe catches on a wide crack in the stone that wasn't there a moment ago, and my arm scrapes the rough stone wall. The stonework is icy, and bits of debris rain down on me from someplace above. Oh, the house is not pleased with me.

Soon it will free Dr. Winston, using him to stop me. Roderick does not understand this; if he did, he would not have left the doctor in this house, not even drugged and tied up. I should have killed him while he was tied. The thought occurs to me even as I hurry, dragging the sledgehammer behind me.

I fumble with the key, imagining that the doctor is untying himself right now. The keyhole has been warped by long years and seeping water. At first I think the key isn't going to turn. Is he still in the parlor, or is he searching for me already? I reposition the key, pushing as hard as I can. Finally the lock clicks.

It's open. The air from within is hostile and foul, a mix of warm and cold that is thicker than normal air.

My hands shake. I push the door slightly and turn sideways to slip through. When Dr. Winston comes for me, the screech of rusted hinges will give warning that he is close.

The rows of empty sarcophagi hold no fascination for me now. I hurry past them and into the room dominated by the square stone. It squats in the center, malignant, ugly, pitted. This is what I must destroy.

The stone is the gravestone of my ancestor, the one who built the house. The one whose consciousness is the consciousness of the house, which laps at me, even now. It is the heart of everything.

A movement attracts my attention to one of the holes in the earth, a burrow leading somewhere. What creatures hide down here, under the house?

Footsteps creak above me. Dr. Winston. I know his every movement, from long afternoons in trances. So he is free. A knife would have fallen into his hands, or the ropes that tied him would have disintegrated, rotted. The house is on his side. Whatever has happened, I must succeed before he gets here.

Something slides out of one of the tunnels, and I have to blink the vision away. The house is taunting me. Threatening me. As I turn my head, the bandage falls away and blood seeps down, warm droplets on my shoulder, something thicker in my hair. The injury must have been worse than I imagined.

I wrap my hand around the handle of the sledgehammer, put my foot against the foundation stone, and blow out the candle to keep my position secret as long as possible.

If he has a light, I will see it as soon as he enters the vault.

"Madeline?" His voice echoes all around me. So, he didn't bring a light. "I'd like to see what's inside you. . . ." He's in the room with me. The door didn't screech. The house is on his side.

"I've always wanted to see what's inside you," he says in

a singsong voice. "That's why I became a doctor. To cut people open. I've always wanted to examine the internal organs of an Usher."

I shift the handle of the sledgehammer, wanting to be sure of my grip. Blood drips down from my head wound, but I hold tight to consciousness.

"I could just cut myself open, to see, but dissecting you and Roderick will be much more fun."

"You aren't an Usher." I say it involuntarily. Foolish, foolish. As if I hadn't already determined that everyone in the house has a dash of Usher blood. And if he didn't already know where I am, he does now.

He laughs. "I can see you, Madeline. Your silvery hair gives you away. Even here in absolute darkness, it shimmers."

I square my shoulders. If I can do it correctly, hitting and breaking the stone will take one good hit. There are already cracks in it, fissures from the center leading outward. I raise the sledgehammer.

"Who was your mother?" I ask, to distract him.

He's so close that I can smell him. The wooden handle burns my hand. If I turn, I can hit him, but will I have the strength then, to lift it once more, to bring it down onto the stone?

Someone pounds across the floor above. Roderick is upstairs.

I've never harmed another person, even one as deranged as this doctor. The shadows try to suffocate me. Ghosts weave their way through the miserable atmosphere around me.

"Madeline, Madeline, Madeline!"

It's Roderick. If I bring down the house now, he will die with me. So I turn and swing the sledgehammer at Dr. Winston. He thrusts his arm at me, and there is a searing pain in my shoulder. Then his hands are around my throat, squeezing, even as the sledgehammer makes contact and he screams.

Roderick rushes toward us. His movements are so much louder than the doctor's stealthy entrance just a few moments ago, as if a hundred Rodericks are coming to my rescue.

But I don't need to be rescued. In fact, he just ruined everything.

In the darkness, I can't tell where Dr. Winston went or how badly I hurt him.

"Madeline!" I turn to Roderick, allow him to wrap his arms around me.

With the light of his torch, we search the room. The young doctor is gone, but there is a trail of blood leading to one of the burrows.

123
MADELINE IS EIGHTEEN

The magistrate was away when Roderick reached his home, so we have to deal with this situation on our own, which may be for the best.

My arm hangs uselessly at my side. Roderick carries me upstairs and puts me on a sofa before rebandaging my head. When he's done, he turns on me, angry and shaking.

"Why did you untie him?" he asks, over and over, as if my answer will change if he keeps repeating the question. He's holding a sword that he took from the weapon display in the main hall. The blade is covered with the dust of a century or more.

"I didn't," I say. "Why would you leave me with him? He could have killed me."

"Not if you had left him tied! Did you even read my note?"

"Of course. And I did leave him tied. The house freed him."

He doesn't believe me. I turn away from him, seeing that I won't be able to convince him.

"Did you love him?" he asks quietly. "Did he manipulate your feelings?"

"No!"

"Perhaps just a little bit?" He asks this with such gentle conviction that I do not know how to argue. I've never known how to argue with Roderick. How to convince him of anything.

124
MADELINE IS EIGHTEEN

Roderick has forgiven me, but he still doesn't believe, and in a way, that is worse than his anger. It's early evening, and we're walking together near the edge of the gardens. I search for signs of Dr. Winston, unsure whether any of the burrows under the house tunnel up to the Usher grounds or just go down and down and down.

"I nearly brought you home a puppy." Roderick interrupts my dark thoughts. "I've thought about it for a long time, but I was afraid of your displeasure."

"Good," I say, dropping his arm. "I don't want a puppy." Cassandra can never be replaced. I think of the dark recesses of the house, of hungry eyes watching. Of Cassandra coming from inside the walls. Father was right. No pets. When the house is destroyed, I might consider such a thing.

"You are so often alone."

"You're home now."

He takes my arm again. His hand is reassuring, so I don't pull away.

"It wouldn't necessarily end in tragedy."

It would, but I can't tell him what I'm planning.

"I worry for you." He wraps my cloak tighter around my shoulders. Have I traded Winston for a new keeper? No. It's just that he's finally all mine. I give myself one week to enjoy this victory and to regain my strength.

"Would you like to go back?" I ask. We've avoided my garden; it's tainted now, the burial place of my friend. But we can't stay inside all the time.

"No. I'd like to go all the way to the forest, the cursed bog, the cursed tarn, the cursed house. . . . It's all cursed."

"All save the two of us?" Perhaps I'm testing him, perhaps teasing.

He pushes his hair back from his face. "Oh, we're cursed."

I don't say anything. It's the first time he's acknowledged our looming fate.

He pivots toward me. "Don't you ever think of fighting it?" he asks.

Anger washes over me. What does he think I've been doing all these long years? What does he think I was doing last night? Yes, I was seduced by the house as a child, but I am fighting. I think of the sledgehammer in the vault. Perhaps a week is too long to wait.

125
MADELINE IS EIGHTEEN

The parlor is nearly unrecognizable. Workmen carry in couches, rugs, tapestries, tables, shelves, books. Roderick has decided that we will move into the apartments shared by our parents. He stands in the center of the activity, rubbing his hands together.

I touch the velvet of a new fainting couch. Step lightly across a new rug, something deep and Oriental. Elegant, expensive things. I don't want to touch anything. My fingertips feel tainted, as if the dust of all my fears in the house has accumulated on them, so they are not suited for any of Roderick's new things.

"It's going to be marvelous," he says. "We'll replace the woodwork, and the curtains and even the flooring. This is hideous." He taps his foot against the dark planks. The house responds with a hollow sound. "Oh, yes, new flooring. When this part of the house is finished, we can move on to the other parts. We can make the House of Usher into what it once was. What it was meant to be." Is the house listening? Surely it is pleased by his attention. Distracted from what I tried to do. From my plans.

I touch a bauble that he's bought for one of the end tables. It is so unusual to see something without dust, something fresh and new. What is the house thinking? It is hiding from me, more and more since my threats in the vault.

"This is lovely," I say. I hope against hope that tomorrow he is not disappointed.

His smile is like the sun, brilliant and fierce.

Five workmen struggle under the weight of an enormous candelabra. They climb up on ladders and attach it to the fretted ceiling. Roderick is as proud as if he had designed the room, the ceiling, and the candelabra himself.

"Wait until you see what I have for your new bedroom."

His excitement is infectious, but I'm unsure about leaving the room of my childhood. Unsure about the new bed he has bought for me, the delicate pink bedspread, the silk sheets, and the lovely new dresses.

A loud crash makes both of us jump. I keep looking over my shoulder for Dr. Winston. For a demented suit of armor or a descending ceiling beam. But it was only the workmen dropping a trunk the size of a coffin. I settle closer to Roderick. Dr. Winston knows the house well, but even if he is still alive, he is not our greatest threat. Let the house think that I have been subdued. That I am willing to live here, forever, with Roderick.

He reads aloud a few pages from *The Subterranean Voyage of Nicholas Klimm*, which has always been one of our favorites. The servants bring us dinner, looking around at all the new furnishings, their eyes big as the platters they are serving us from.

"I told them that the tasteless stuff they've been serving is no good. I'll hire a cook from the city to prepare something less bland."

"I asked the cook to leave out the spices," I whisper as Roderick breaks off a piece of bread and hands it to me. It is slightly sweet and dripping butter.

After dinner we sit together, and he reads aloud until it is very late. The clock in the hallway keeps striking. If it doesn't right itself, Roderick will surely replace it with a new one. He's put flowers in a vase on the table. They remind me uncomfortably of Mother, with her imported flowers.

"It's your bedroom now," he reminds me as I glance toward her door.

The last thing I want is to sleep in a room where Mother slept. Still, if Dr. Winston is lurking about, he won't expect to find us here. I can go back to my old rooms and bring whatever I like; it's just that it doesn't seem right to bring the moldering remnants of my childhood into these rooms with shiny new furnishings.

126
Madeline Is Eighteen

I wake to the sound of sobbing. A ghost? Some miserable Usher ghost that is attached to this set of rooms? I ease the door open, fearful of what I will find.

Roderick.

The window he had the servants clean yesterday is still free of grime, and he is bathed by morning light.

The roses have wilted. Black petals lie all around the base of the table. The curtains at the window are tattered and covered with streaks of green mold. A metal spring has pierced the covering of the fine new couch, and the velvet is faded, thin in spots, as if ghosts have sat there all night, every night, for a thousand years, drinking tea and mocking us. The rugs are frayed and worn, faded. The candelabra hangs askew, in need of polishing.

Roderick's hands are pressed to his face. Tears drip

through his delicate fingers, and his shoulders shake.

I reach out to him, but he won't let me touch him.

"Did you know this would happen?" The accusation in his voice freezes me.

"I was afraid," I whisper. "But I thought maybe this time things would be different. Maybe the house would be so pleased to have us both here that it would allow things to be nice for a while."

I hoped the house would let us have this, to try to lull me into submission. I wanted a few nice days before everything fell apart.

127
MADELINE IS EIGHTEEN

Roderick left the house. I nearly followed but thought he could use some time on his own. An hour passed. Then two. Now he's back; his face is flushed from his exertion outside. He slams the door.

"I won't live here," he says.

This could be the answer to the problem of getting him out of the house. Except, from his tone and stance, I don't believe him.

"Where else could you go?" I ask as calmly as I can.

"I have someone . . . there's someone . . ." He has trouble spitting it out. I don't say anything. It is not my responsibility to help him. "I am in love. We could live together in the city."

He starts to say more, but I touch his arm.

"Not here," I whisper.

"What?" He pulls away, determined not to get close enough to hear me.

The lights dim, and the room shimmers around us. The temperature dips. A picture falls from the wall and clatters, and a sharp tile falls, hitting Roderick's forehead. The air in the room grows heavy, like atmospheric dank air that pushes you to the ground and will not let you rise. It's difficult to move, even to raise my head. His hand covers most of his face, and blood flows through his fingers.

I feel a terrible emotion. Pleasure. Finally he will see. His lack of belief has pained me for the last time.

The mirror above the fireplace goes dark. I avert my eyes, struggling to put my sleeve up to his forehead to staunch the blood, standing on my toes. The two of us being this close will appease the house, I hope. I pray.

"Madeline," he whispers, and I can feel his fear. The same fear that crippled him as a boy. And finally I understand that he is not strong enough to withstand the darkness that is the house, the consciousness of it.

"I am driven to the brink of insanity," he whispers.

The warm blood seeps down through my sleeve where I hold it against his head.

The floor ripples under our feet.

"Outside," I whisper. We must get out. Now. But he doesn't move.

"I hear the house now," he says. "It fills my mind." The

way he looks at me reminds me of when we were children. He's vulnerable. But I can't fix this for him. "It fills my mind with you. I should not think of you. I don't want this, Madeline."

"I know," I tell him, looking into his eyes, trying to be calm for both of us.

I start to pull away, but the house groans and the floor shifts sharply beneath us; the air of the room compresses. We stumble. And Roderick's lips touch mine.

The house sighs. My mind opens to his, and I know how my lips feel to him at the same time that I feel his lips against mine.

"No." I push him away. I will not let the house win, let it turn our bond into a curse.

His hand grips my arm above my elbow. We stare at each other. My shock mirrors his. This must never happen again.

I start to say that, but then he screams and falls to the floor, holding his head. The blood is forgotten, a superficial scratch. He has finally come into his Usher heritage.

128
MADELINE IS EIGHTEEN

Every day I search the house for any sign of Dr. Winston. I question the servants and the other doctors. Finally I go to the vault. Everything is as we left it, including the sledgehammer. A chill passes through me as I consider it. I could end the house right now. End all the misery.

From one of the passages above, I hear one of the maids laugh. Not derisive, but a true mirthful laugh. And Roderick is resting upstairs. Other people live in this house besides me. I have to lay my plans carefully, to save the servants—though as Usher descendants, they might try to stop me if they knew.

129
MADELINE IS EIGHTEEN

A week has passed with no sign of Dr. Winston. My shoulder is nearly healed. I must devise a plan to get Roderick and the servants away from the house.

Roderick is painting. At least that's what he calls it. He stares at the palette for hours on end, contemplating slate blue, indigo, perhaps charcoal gray. Only occasionally does he put the brush against the canvas, but when he does, the images he creates are amazing and powerful.

I walk into the studio. He looks up from his current painting and stares at me for a moment.

"I never noticed how beautiful your teeth are," he says.

I don't answer. He doesn't expect me to.

"You should always wear black dresses. Somber colors make your hair glow."

I don't tell him that I found a strand of white this

morning. As always, I avoid telling Roderick anything too serious.

Dust has settled around his slippered feet. He is fading; sometimes I can almost see through him. He stares out the window, into some world that only he can see.

Roderick is here to stay. He fully believes that the house is watching us and that we are cursed.

I have what I wanted.

It is bitter.

130

Dearest Roderick,

I've left school now, officially. Graduated. Father is sending me on tour, to travel for a few months before I take over the family business and estate. I'd hoped to visit you, but you haven't written.

Noah

131
MADELINE IS EIGHTEEN

Whatever reprieve I had, whatever sense of fleeting wellness Roderick returned, is gone. Even the softest fabric exacerbates the sensitivity of my skin. All of my dresses bruise me. I feel raw. This is a new curse, this deep pain. Even if I find the strength to lift the sledgehammer, will I be able to swing it? And the house . . . the house wants a child. Mine and Roderick's. After our kiss, it is hopeful. Waiting. It doesn't care if I die, as long as I have a baby before I succumb, so the Usher line continues.

Roderick has begun painting images of my death. First he painted me broken at the bottom of the staircase, and then dead on the flagstones of the courtyard.

But I won't die that way. No matter how the house threatens me.

Roderick continues to deteriorate.

I lift a spoonful of soup to his mouth. Most of it splashes back, another stain on his white shirt. I keep trying, hopeful that I can get a little nourishment into him. He turns away, muttering. Poor Roderick. The house whispers that this is my fault. That if we accept our fate, the curse will be lifted. At least until the next generation of Usher children are born.

132
MADELINE IS EIGHTEEN

The ivy I planted has grown everywhere, over everything. It covers the base of the house, scrabbling its way upward. Something living and green can survive on the great expanse of ancient rock and mortar. A few stones have finally crumbled. Plants are stronger than they look.

Roderick stands beside me up on the widow's walk, his hand on my elbow. We look out over the grounds and the dead forest without speaking, for what seems like an hour. I enjoy the silence of his companionship.

"Do you ever think of jumping?" Roderick asks.

"I promised Father I wouldn't."

"I sometimes think of ending it. Poison? Not jumping." He won't look at me, ashamed of what he is saying. "You're stronger than me, Madeline. You've had these fits for years. Mine've only just begun, and I don't know how I can bear them. How did Father tolerate this?"

"What about Mother?" He knew her better, after all.

"Mother channeled her pain into cruelty, but she died young. Father was older."

Yes. He would have to be. He waited for Honoria, then Lisbeth, and finally their younger sister. Was she happy with her choice? She seemed to scorn Father, but she loved Roderick. How did Father feel about her? I know he loved me, when he was aware. Did he recognize me as he wandered the house, irrelevant and mad? Did he watch me? Did he remember?

I don't think that Roderick could fade in the same way, but if he does, if I can't muster my strength, will the house win?

"I wish our parents had left us some clues. Some message or record that we could understand. I guess they knew it wouldn't matter. We won't live long enough for it to matter."

"Don't say that."

"I like to face the truth. Maybe we should summon a priest to bless us, or pray for us."

"We are Ushers."

"They won't come?"

"They won't come."

We stand together, hand in hand.

133
MADELINE IS EIGHTEEN

Dearest Roderick,

Still no word from you? Are you unwell? Please write to me. I am very concerned. If I don't hear back from you, I may be compelled to visit your home to check on you.

Noah

I clutch the letter.

Would Roderick's friend really visit us? What if he came through our front door? What if he said hello to me, if he smiled at me? Would he recognize me from when we met before? Would I be able to have a conversation with him?

None of that is important, but Noah could divert Roderick's attention. His company could help Roderick feel better. We could declare a holiday and send the servants away. And he could take Roderick camping on the grounds, like before.

The selfish part of me wonders . . . is there any possibility that he might look upon me with affection?

Does he like girls who are ethereal, fragile? Who are doomed?

134
Madeline Is Eighteen

I sit alone in what's left of my garden, leaving Roderick to his music. He isn't aware of me.

The garden is haunted now. I cannot help but remember Emily's hand, her fingers stretching up through the earth, as if she was trying to reach me.

Faltering footsteps sound behind me. They drag, as if the person who is walking toward me can barely move. A twig snaps. I'm afraid to turn and look. . . . Could it be Emily, back from the dead? Or Dr. Winston?

But when I do, it's only a little girl.

We consider each other.

Her hair is very pale.

She takes another step toward me, and I see that she is lame, that her foot drags behind her. She's an Usher. The house is drawing them in, the bastard lines. Like my father's sister, the one who was chained in the attic, it has found me wanting.

This child is so delicate, with her twisted leg. Tiny and frail. Roderick would kill to protect her. She couldn't replace me, though. Not with Roderick. I wonder if my father's twin, the one I'm named for, had the same thought.

The child watches me and does not smile.

135
MADELINE IS EIGHTEEN

Roderick has not left the house in days, and he rarely leaves the suite of rooms that we share. He keeps painting pictures of the house, writing odes to it. "The Haunted Castle." He plays his guitar and sings to the house. The house is very pleased. So happy to have a new favorite, and one that appreciates it so much.

"Tell me of your school friend," I beg. This is the only subject, besides the house, that he ever wants to speak of.

He is staring into space, strumming his guitar. The sounds that come from it are melancholy and beautiful.

He stops playing and bows his head.

"I cried. Every day. For you, Madeline. I also cried for Mother and Father, and for the house, but mostly I cried for you. The other boys taunted me and teased me. My first roommate complained that he couldn't get any rest because of my crying and asked for me to be moved to another room." Roderick smiles, but it doesn't reach his violet eyes.

"And then *he* came. He was a new student, from a well-known and prosperous family. I knew they were putting him in my room, because his trunks were delivered, and I got nervous; I didn't want my miserable loneliness to be invaded by another bully.

"After lessons, we were allowed to play in the court-yard, and I was sitting alone, reading a book, when he arrived. The other boys crowded around him and vied for his attention, but then he noticed me.

"He stared at me and then looked away. We didn't speak. All through dinner I would find him looking at me. I know that he asked the others who I was, because one of the boys said, 'Oh, that's Roderick Usher. He's crazy.' And another said, 'He's to be your roommate,' and that's when he walked over to me and introduced himself.

"'You don't have to talk to Usher. If you ignore him, he'll fade away. Or cry,' one of the others called.

"The other boys started to chatter about how they could make me cry. But he stood in front of them, pushed them back.

"'Leave him alone,' he said. 'He's going to be my friend.'

"And from that moment, we were. We were always

together, so much so that they whispered about it."

"What is he like?" I ask.

"He's brave," Roderick says. "And heroic."

Yes. That's what we need. That's what Roderick needs.

136
Madeline Is Eighteen

I pace from the fireplace to the grandfather clock and then back again, across the dark floor. I have to summon Roderick's friend, Noah. I must. He's our only hope. Roderick is going mad. He won't leave the house. If I could get him to go outside for just a day, for just an hour, I could do what I must. But I cannot hurt him.

I study Roderick's handwriting. Why must I find this so difficult? Hours upon hours, while my brother sits staring at the mosaic tiles of the floor, crooning to them, screaming at them, I practice forging his hand. At last, though the sinews in my hand and my wrist are tired and stretched, I can do it.

I give one of the maids a gold coin to post the letter for me. And so, it is done. I wait.

137
MADELINE IS EIGHTEEN

I watch his arrival from the widow's walk. His horse is a deep brown, and he rides it well. He comes through the dead forest and stops. I lean forward, intent, willing him to fight off his initial horror. To continue. The horse is skittish. He pats her neck, comforting her. The horse tries to back up, but he won't let her. He dismounts and stands, looking up at the house.

He is too far away, and I cannot tell if he has closed his eyes, but he does not avert his face.

I can barely breathe. If he rides away, will all be lost?

Noah gets back on his horse. His back is stooped, and he looks defeated. He's leaving; he's abandoning friendship.

I twist the fabric of my skirt, too nervous to breathe.

But no, he's riding forward. He doesn't stop again. He

rides through the marshy area before the tarn, across the causeway.

He's entering the house.

I hurry inside, to Roderick.

"We have a visitor," I tell him. "I think it's your friend from school."

Roderick starts. I can tell he's excited, his eyes are shining—but instead of rushing downstairs to greet his friend, he takes a seat in his studio. "The servants will bring him up, Madeline. That's how these things are done."

"But he's come so far. . . ."

"Have the servants bring wine."

I ignore him and hurry down the side stairs. I must watch and see what happens. The groom has taken his horse to stable it next to Roderick's. A servant is leading him up the stairs. Dr. Paul stands in the shadows. Roderick's friend stops to greet the doctor, but Dr. Paul squints at him with an unpleasant expression and then moves on.

Roderick's friend stops several times to admire paintings and tapestries, but he looks overwhelmed, and a bit frightened. Walking into this house took an impressive amount of courage. I will try my hardest to protect him, to be sure he walks away from here alive. With Roderick.

Now they are sitting, fair head and dark head close together. Painting. Perhaps Roderick will be inspired to paint something besides the house. He is pleased to see his friend, but ashamed of his own debilitation. Roderick has become more ethereal, more fragile.

"This is Noah," Roderick says. And then, turning, "And this is my dear sister, Madeline."

He looks up, and a smile lights up his face. Though I meant to be serious and stately, meeting him here for the first time, I find myself returning his magnificent smile.

138
Madeline Is Eighteen

The curtains rustle, silken and sad. Noah stands in front of the window.

"I feel as if I know you, Roderick spoke of you so often. He cried for you in his sleep." He smiles when he says this, so it doesn't seem to have annoyed him. I return his smile. We both care for Roderick. It makes me feel close to him, though we've only just met. "You know, I almost passed right by the house. I kept staring up at it; I could see a sort of blur in the distance, but no house. Then, all of a sudden, I saw all the plants, the lichen and ivy, and under that, the house. Roderick says you nurtured those plants."

"Yes."

"I wouldn't have made it here without them. My first impression of you as a little pixie, some kind of nature spirit, was exactly right."

He means when we met at the coach platform. It seems so long ago.

"You knew me?" My voice sounds breathless. I try to breathe normally, but it's difficult with him so near. The way he inspects our art and exclaims over the antique carpets . . . he makes everything seem more interesting. When his eyes light on some architectural wonder, a part of me is envious of the colonnade, the graciously arched gothic windows. Some part of me wants his gaze to linger on me.

"Of course I did, but I didn't want to frighten you away. You seemed on the verge of running, and I thought anonymity might be comforting."

I sip my wine. So that I don't have to look at him. So he won't see me blush.

"I came because I was worried about Roderick, but I also had another reason," he says. My heart flutters. "My kinswoman, my cousin, who came to this part of the country, has not been heard from."

I picture Emily, with her dark hair and laughing eyes.

He studies my face, my demeanor, and he knows.

"Something happened to her." His voice is sad, but not surprised. "It was that villain she thought she was in love with, wasn't it?"

I nod. "I hit him with a sledgehammer, but he crawled away. For all I know, he's still alive somewhere."

He stares across the room, lost in some dark reverie. "A sledgehammer?" I'm not sure if he believes me. His tone as he asks the question is neutral.

Do I dare confide in him? It would be nice for someone to know the full story. Otherwise, no one will ever know. Not Roderick, who refuses to truly listen, not anyone. It will be lost, like Lisbeth's disintegrating journal.

"I had hoped that there was a chance for Emily. My parents washed their hands of her, scandalized that she would follow Winston across the country. They felt it was desperate and unladylike. But I understood. People do odd things for love."

"And you loved Emily?" My hair falls forward, and I let it conceal my face. It makes speaking candidly easier.

He looks up, his eyes deep and filled with remorse.

"Like a sister. At least that's what I thought, until I heard Roderick's voice change when he spoke of you. Such adoration."

I feel my face flushing.

"I'm sure you loved her dearly," I say at the same time that he reaches forward to gently push back the errant lock of hair that I've been hiding behind. "She was easy to love," I finish—breathless because speaking of her is painful, and because his fingers against my forehead are sure and soothing.

"She was," he agrees. "And I didn't protect her. Didn't even know she needed protecting."

I wait to see if he will speak of vengeance, but he stares off across the room, obviously upset. Still, he doesn't mention her again.

"I am determined to do what I can for Roderick. He is alive, so I can still save him."

Roderick is lucky to have such a friend. I don't want him to think that we sacrificed Emily.

"She was my friend," I tell him.

He wipes away tears with the back of his hand. "We were close as children," he says. "And I wish I could have saved her. It was one of the reasons I came here, to see what I could do, and if she was gone, as I suspected, to try to save Roderick."

"And what do you think, now that you're here? Now that you know?"

"Roderick has changed Melancholia is overwhelming him. Is it the family illness?" he asks.

"Yes. You must get him away from the house. Please. It is killing him. Living here is killing him."

So, there it is. All these years of waiting for Roderick to return to me, and neither of us is happy. He is going mad, and I am mad with worry for him.

"He doesn't want to leave," Noah says slowly. "I've mentioned travel. He says he's finally found his place."

"That's the madness speaking," I tell him. "This was never his place before."

"On the contrary." He's intense now, his eyes boring into me, forcing me to believe him. "He was always aware that his place was here, with you. School was merely an interlude."

Again, the tragedy nearly overwhelms me. I waited so long for Roderick, and here we are. Deteriorating, going mad, at the whim of the house.

I tap my fingers against the side table, remembering that I must distract the house when I can.

"It doesn't matter whether he says he wants to stay. He isn't in his right mind. To save him, you must get him out of the house."

"Even when he says he is dying?"

I've thought about this, considered. Can Roderick survive now without the house? I don't know. But what other options do we have?

"Yes."

This was why I had summoned him. We need a hero. Watching his reflection, framed by the baroque mirror that Roderick introduced to the room, I know that he is exactly what we need. His answer does not disappoint me.

"I will do whatever you ask."

139
MADELINE IS EIGHTEEN

My sleep is disturbed by footsteps pacing up and down the hall through the night. I sit up, terrified. Dr. Winston? Sometimes I am sure that he must have a hiding place beneath the house, or perhaps within. That he will burst through the wall, like Cassandra, except this surprise will be horrible and end with someone dead. I hope, if he was trapped somewhere, he died quickly.

Or maybe he is just waiting someplace, waiting for us to die.

How strange it is, I think, that there are three of us here, now, so near the end, when before it was always me, alone. Having companionship is addicting. Wonderful. The very idea of being alone again strikes fear into me. Despite the circumstances, the odd moments when Roderick is painting and Noah sits across the room, scanning a book, fill me with contentment.

This morning, Roderick sleeps late. Exhausted.

I sit in the parlor and ask the servants to bring me tea. I dilute it with water, since the taste of tea itself is overwhelming, like most foods have become, but the warmth is soothing.

"Good morning, Madeline," Noah says from the doorway. All of the bedrooms in this wing look out into this common area, with couches and rugs and bookshelves and Roderick's musical instruments scattered about.

I offer him tea. He sits next to me, too close, perhaps, on the love seat, and accepts the cup from my hands.

"You keep so much inside," he says. "I can tell. You are so worried, so overwhelmed."

"Yes," I say. His concern unsettles me, and I find myself dangerously close to tears.

"Perhaps it would help to tell someone," he suggests. "I would be honored to listen."

I have been waiting for a very long time to tell someone.

I reveal myself to him, slowly at first, and then in a rush, blurting all of my hopes and my tenuous dreams. He's easy to talk to, with attentive eyes and a manner that doesn't indicate that he thinks I'm lying, even when the things I say must seem difficult to credit, or that he's judging me. Without meaning to, I tell him things that I've never told Roderick. I explain in whispers how I want to destroy the house, how I must destroy it. I beg him to protect my brother so that I can finish this task.

"I cannot do what I have to do, if there is a chance it will hurt my brother. I've always tried to protect him." I've asked him before, to take Roderick out of the house, but I hadn't explained fully, hadn't said the words, until now.

His eyes narrow, but his expression is gentle. Does he know how desperately I wanted Roderick to see the truth? And now the truth is killing him.

"I understand," he says.

I don't know if I believe him. How can anyone understand, really? But it is good for him to at least pretend, to listen and try.

"Thank you," I say.

"But I haven't done anything. Not yet." He holds out his arms. "Come here, Madeline."

We are sitting so close that we are touching, and it seems natural to go into them, to let him hold me. I put my face against his shoulder.

"There, there," he says, holding me tight and comforting me like I could be a child. I think how different this is from embracing Roderick or Dr. Winston, how different he is.

Roderick walks into the room, stopping on the threshold, either to give us a moment of privacy, or to allow me to compose myself and dry my tears.

140
MADELINE IS EIGHTEEN

Noah comes to my room later, stopping in the doorway. I would invite him in, but I don't want to shock him with such impropriety. Instead, I meet him at the threshold. He is on one side of the door frame, and I am on the other.

"Roderick is sleeping," he says. "He needs his rest."

"Did he take something?" I ask. The doctors leave sleeping draughts. I don't take them, but Roderick often does.

"Something from a mug." His brow creases. He's worried. He cares so much about my brother.

Noah leans into my room, close enough to kiss me.

"Do you find me very much like him?"

"In looks. Not in disposition. Roderick is a dreamer. You are more . . . focused. Grounded. I like that."

I have dreams. I told him earlier. But they are not as flimsy or as intellectual as Roderick's dreams.

"If I asked you, would you take me away from here?"

It isn't a fair question, and I would never leave Roderick, but it's pleasant to pretend.

He closes his eyes. "I would never forgive myself for abandoning Roderick. But yes, if you asked, I would take you away from here. I would put you on my horse, and take you tonight."

Possibilities float before me. Futures. He would take me away from here.

I could be happy. I could live. I deserve this future. But I can never claim it.

"Madeline!" It's Roderick, calling my name from his bedchamber.

"I think he's calling in his sleep," I say.

"Yes, he calls for you when he's distressed. Only you can soothe him."

"I won't leave him, of course." I couldn't. We both know this. Still, there is sadness as the possibilities wither away.

I will not abandon my brother. I will see this thing through.

141
Madeline Is Eighteen

The servants have prepared a feast. It is to be their last meal for us, though they don't know it. Tomorrow they will be sent away, to the coach station, or at least to the closest village.

We are seated at the new dining room table that Roderick had built to replace the one that was broken. The wood is imported. The beam that fell from the ceiling was carted away ages ago, and I do not know what holds up the ceiling now.

By the light of dozens of candles, the room is almost elegant. The candles create shadows where the ghosts can hide.

Roderick is smiling.

But our guest senses the ghosts and is frightened. His eyes dart to the shadows, even as he denies his fear. He watches Roderick.

"I dreamed of dying last night," Roderick says. "I don't know when I will die, but I know how it will happen. My fear will be the end of me; I will die of fear."

His hands shake as he relates this bit of madness.

Noah laughs. "You can't die of fear." He doesn't sound certain, though.

It's the right thing to say. The mood lightens. Roderick grins. "Always so literal, so practical."

"What else is there?" his friend asks.

"What about you, Madeline?"

Shyness overcomes me. I don't know how to answer.

"Do you live in a world of reality, or in Roderick's world of the sublime and the supernatural?"

There is nothing I can say that will please him. In my world, the sublime and the supernatural are the only realities.

142
MADELINE IS EIGHTEEN

So, this is my last night in the house. It is well past midnight.

I am in my bedroom, but not alone.

He is so beautiful. I watch the firelight on his face; it makes him glow gold. His eyelashes are dark against his cheeks.

He should not be here in my bedroom, but propriety doesn't really matter; I'm destined to die young.

The fire is warm. I stretch, basking in the warmth, forgetting my fear. We speak in whispers. His hands on my skin are cool and soothing. His sleeve brushes against the velvet of my dressing gown. In the warmth of the candle, our skin is the exact same shade.

I choose this. So few things, in my life, have I had control over.

Still, no matter what experience I've gained, I remain curious about kissing. I suppose that if I die tomorrow, I will continue to wonder about it, and all the other things I've never done.

143
MADELINE IS EIGHTEEN

From the widow's walk, I wait for Roderick and Noah to leave, to cross the causeway. I must be sure they are gone. The servants have left on their holiday.

The trapdoor creaks open. I whirl around.

Dr. Winston.

In a way, I've been expecting him. Listening, waiting.

I'm surprised by how handsome he looks. When I imagined his return from the grave, I expected him to be coated with loathsomeness and dirt. Madness should be apparent, not hidden behind a kindly smile. Of course Roderick only becomes more beautiful as he loses his mind too, so I should not be shocked. They are both Ushers, after all. We are all Ushers.

"Once again, the house has chosen," he says. "Mr. Roderick, who never even cared about any of it." When he moves, I note that he has developed a peculiar twitch.

I watch him warily, unsure what he will do.

"Did you think it would be you?" I ask. My eyes scan the roof, looking for an escape route. Besides the flag-stones below, my only way is back to the trapdoor, and he is blocking my path.

He shakes his head. Dr. Winston has changed. Whatever madness had taken over in the end, when he proclaimed himself my keeper, it seems to be gone. His eyes look clear again, dark, but not mad. He holds out a pocket watch.

"I found this under the house."

I hold out my hand, and he drops it onto my palm. My first pocket watch. The one I took from Dr. Paul's over-coat. The one I lost in the tarn when Cassandra drowned.

"I found this too." He reaches into his coat and brings out a leather collar that belonged to Cassandra. "I thought you should have it. She was the only one who was ever really worthy of your love."

How did this come to be under the house? I reach for the collar. It belonged to her and is precious to me. When he gives it to me, I snatch my hand back, as if his touch might contaminate me. But instead of threatening me, instead of crooning that he yearns to cut me open, he reaches out a hand to me. Unlike the rest of him, it is smeared with grime from beneath the house.

"Come with me," he says. "The house doesn't care. Its

love is fickle. Come with me. We understand each other. None of the rest of them—Roderick, his friend, they won't understand."

"No," I say. I step back, prepared to dash back if he attacks me. He is between me and the trapdoor.

"Madeline?" Tears run down his face. "I don't hear the house anymore. Something happened when I was crawling beneath." His entire body twitches again. "I'm like the pocket watch. The house isn't aware of me. I could help you."

"You killed Emily," I say. He doesn't deny it.

"So many regrets," he says. And I think how Emily loved him, and that she was kind, and he killed her. "I see clearly now that the house has released me. We understand each other. Choose me."

I can't, of course. I can't choose anyone. That is not how this is going to end.

He smiles. The smile from before—a ghost of the young man who came here with hopes of understanding the illness and making me well.

The house is resourceful. Even if he doesn't know it, it is still using him to try to stop me.

"No," I tell him. "No," I repeat, and take another step back.

The house rumbles, and planks shift beneath my feet. Dr. Winston's hand snakes out. He grasps my wrist.

I don't mean to push him, not really. But my hands connect with his chest, and he falls, just as the roof begins to cave in. A platform appears below, ready to catch him, but my vines twine around and around and strangle him.

I spin. I have to get to the crypt before Roderick and Noah return.

But the roof is falling away beneath my feet, even as I grab at splintering planks and slide into the house. I land in an unfamiliar corridor, ceiling tiles raining down around me.

I dash down the corridor. At the end are a staircase and a suit of armor. With all of my momentum, I shove the armor hard, my hand vibrating dully from the impact with the hollow breastplate. It falls into a mirror, which shatters, even as I leap over and keep going.

The house shimmers around me, and a ceiling beam crashes down. Ghosts follow in my wake. Lights flicker and shadows dance as I pass through the great room. Roderick once put a knife to my throat in this room. Hundreds of weapons line the walls. Swords, lances, axes, maces. A thousand blades, dark and dull with age.

The ghosts surround me. Every spirit and haunt that has ever wandered through these halls crowds in, and I stumble to a stop. A great family crest is painted on the floor. No matter how many Usher bastards the house can attract, Roderick and I are the only ones who matter. The line ends with us—or, if we fall under its spell, continues.

"This is the end of the House of Usher," I whisper.

One moment I'm standing, proud and defiant. The next, every weapon, every shield falls from the wall, echoing through the house, and I'm on my knees. Pain overwhelms me, searing spikes in my head, as all my overtaxed senses collide. I throw back my head and scream, and then there is pain and blackness, and the house whispering in my mind that Roderick will find me here when he returns from his ride. That he will know what to do.

144
MADELINE IS EIGHTEEN

W̱hat happens next isn't waking. It's simply a continuation of foul dreams. Except that, gradually, I realize it is real. Roderick's head is bowed. He stands over me, weeping. The image in my mind, and in his, is of the manacles in the attic.

The house tells him that I am mad. Suggests he confine me, as our father confined his own twin sister. The Usher line must continue.

Roderick puts his hand to my throat. The gesture is half caress, half clinical. If the doctors were here, they would tell him that sometimes, during my fits, everything slows, including my heart. They would tell him that even if he doesn't feel my pulse, that I still live. His fingers linger on my cheek. He leans closer, as if he will kiss me.

And then he pulls back, as if the touch of my skin burns him.

"No," he says. "No." He's speaking to himself. "I will be strong. For her."

"Noah," he cries, his voice breaking as he summons his friend. "My sister is dead."

The house is wroth with him, and with me. Darkness takes me again.

145
MADELINE IS EIGHTEEN

Waking is slow, silent, and stiflingly dark. Tenebrous.

I'm disoriented as awareness returns, searching for my blanket, slowly feeling my eyes to make sure they are still there.

Trembling, in the compressed darkness, I realize where I am. Has there ever been any question? Roderick has buried me alive in the vault. I'm in one of the sarcophagi.

He found me, put me in the white dress. Emily's dress with the pearl sleeves, the lace inserts. Someone put up my hair.

I tear at the dress, at the collar that is strangling me. I tear at everything. I tear at my own eyes, frustrated by my pitiful relief that they are still there.

Blood trickles from my ripped fingernails, as I remember that I've been in one of these boxes before. Roderick was locked inside. Is it possible to get out?

I collect all of my strength, force myself to be calm, to ignore my claustrophobia and think.

In the silence, I can hear the wind blowing through the upper floors where the ceiling collapsed. I can hear the restlessness of the house; it feels injured and angry. Vulnerable. And I hear Roderick.

"I'm going mad," he says.

"Roderick, please, let me take you away from here. . . . Come with me." His friend is begging.

They will leave me. They will abandon me. Fear and anger are eclipsed by hope, I've been trying to get him to leave the house for months. Let Roderick leave. Let him live.

"I can't leave Madeline. I will die here, like her, be buried with her," he insists.

Tears of frustration run down my cheeks.

"Madeline wanted you to go. She begged me to take you out of the house. Consider it her final wish."

Does Roderick know that I am not dead? He must have suspected. The house must be whispering to him, even now. Somehow he's ignoring it.

Ever so slowly I begin feeling the walls of my prison, looking for a latch that will open the lid. As my fingers explore, my mind searches for Roderick's. I hear his thoughts.

Madeline. Oh, Madeline. I hear you. His voice is clear in my mind. *I've heard you for days, nonstop. Please, be silent, Madeline. Be still, please.* He's crying. *I left you before, and I'm sorry. Don't let your ghost drive me to madness. Please, be at peace . . .*

I throw back my head and scream my frustration. He thinks our connection is some sort of ghostly visitation.

My scream hurts him. He pleads with me, and I cannot stand it. *Please, if you love me even a little, I would have traded my life for yours. I'll be buried beside you soon.*

"Let me read you a story, Roderick. It will soothe you." Noah is searching for some way to calm him. They are in the oldest part of the house, protected from the damage of the collapsed roof. A storm is blowing in.

"Have you seen it?" Roderick asks. "Have you?"

He means the storm. Noah shakes his head. "I'm so sorry, Roderick," he says. "I can't imagine your pain." And then to himself, "I should have stayed and tried to help her."

He opens a window. A whirlwind outside blows dead leaves and debris about. The clouds are so low that they press against the turrets.

"There are no stars," Roderick croons. "No stars ever again, today is the last night, the last night ever. The stars have all gone away."

He is right. I see through his eyes, and there are no stars. There is no moon. There is thunder, but no flash of lightning. A glowing green light enshrouds the mansion.

"You are being silly, my friend. It's some sort of electrical force, some sort of cloud that's come up from the tarn. We will leave in the morning, after the storm has blown over. Come away from the window."

Roderick paces, his movements feverish and erratic.

"We'll read *The Mad Trist*, by Sir Launcelot Canning. It's the story of a tragic maiden, and a knight, and a hermit who has evil intentions." He clears his throat and begins to read. "'And Ethelred, who was by nature doughty, waited no longer to hold parley with the hermit, who, in truth, was obstinate and malicious, but, feeling the rain on his shoulders, he uplifted his mace and, with blows, made room in the planks of the door for his gauntleted hand, and cracked and ripped and tore it asunder.'"

Roderick cowers. Like the boy he was, afraid. He said once that he would die of his own fear.

I've listened long enough.

I reach up. I am not powerful, but my afflictions have made me able to withstand great pain. Pressing both hands against the lid of the sarcophagus, I push upward. Wood splinters, and cool bits of ceramic crumble and rain down.

They should not have stored these death boxes for so many years in this place of rot and decay.

I stand, letting the crumbling stoneware fall from my

body like water trickling from some drowned artifact that has been brought to the surface.

The wind is blowing, blowing. I hear it in the house above and wish that I could feel it, could feel anything in this stifling vault. My mouth is thick with something that feels like cotton. Emily's white dress clings to me.

Noah is reading, trying to soothe him.

"'But the good champion Ethelred, now entering the door, was enraged, but instead of the malicious hermit, he came upon a dragon. And Ethelred uplifted his mace and struck upon the head of the dragon, and it fell upon him with a shriek so horrid and harsh that Ethelred put up his hands to cover his ears. . . .'"

I stand still, surprised by how even the dry underground air revives me after the horror of the coffin. Usually there is not a hint of moving air in the vault, but tonight something is different. Perhaps it is the force of the wind; perhaps the fissures in the house are opening, like pores, absorbing the violence of the storm.

I do not move toward the stairs. I am not going up. Instead, shuddering and repulsed, I go deeper into the crypt. I haven't the strength to get Roderick out. He'll have to do that on his own.

A sleepwalker is what I am, a reanimated corpse. I am afraid of failing in what I have to do, but I'm not terrified of death.

I push through the last gate, to the hidden place, the deepest chamber under the darkest part of the house. Here is the foundation stone.

I put both hands on the wooden handle of the sledgehammer.

Above, Noah continues to read.

"'And now the champion, having escaped the fury of the dragon, approached the silver shield that hung upon the wall, but as he moved closer, it fell, with a mighty great and terrible ringing sound.'"

I lift the sledgehammer and tremble. It is so heavy. I twist, using every muscle and all of the strength in my body to bring it down, hard on the stone.

Nothing happens.

146
MADELINE IS NINETEEN

My entire body is quivering from the first hit. I lift the sledgehammer again, and bring it down with a crash that reverberates through me.

"Did you hear that?" Noah asks, afraid now.

"I have heard it, and heard it, and heard it, for days on end. We have put her living in her tomb!"

Ignoring Roderick's faraway sobs, I bring the sledge-hammer down for the third time. It takes all of my strength, everything that I have in me, or have ever had.

The house shakes and quivers, pain washes over and through me, and stones crash down. The foundation stone shatters into a million pieces.

I've succeeded. Done the impossible. And all I feel is the need to find my brother.

I don't want to die in this dungeon, not alone. There

may still be time to save Roderick and his friend, but only if I'm very fast. I run away from the secret room and the vault with my coffin, through the copper tunnel, up the steep stairs, following the bond I share with my brother.

The house is hemorrhaging. Cracking. The house is dying.

Can either of us outlive the house?

I don't know, but I must try.

Running as walls collapse around me, I reach the studio. I know they are inside.

I throw the door open, and Roderick is there, gasping my name. We don't have time for an embrace, but still he wraps his arms around me, tightly, like he will never let me go.

"Run," I say over my shoulder to Noah. And then, when he doesn't seem inclined to obey, louder.

All three of us run. As we reach the end of the corridor, the ceiling begins to collapse inward. A lone beam seems to be holding what's left of this passage in place. We have to crouch to enter the stairwell.

"I told you I would die of fear," Roderick gasps. He takes a step down, but I grab his arm.

The smell of burning is all around us. Untended candles must have lit the curtains and rugs. A chandelier crashes and shatters, just as the floor beneath our feet begins to shake, and I feel the house collapsing, feel it as if my very bones are crumbling. But the arm that supports Roderick remains strong and steady. The house is dying, but I'm not.

In the corridor ahead, I see a wide arched window, but no light comes through, only great unnatural darkness. The house is being swallowed by the cavernous earth below. I won't go back underground. I reach out to stop Noah before he goes down the stairs.

"If we go lower, we will be crushed under the weight of the house. We have to go up."

The three of us turn. We must try to reach the doctors' tower. It's the highest point in the house. As we crest the next set of stairs, I see light ahead. Not the burning light of the house afire, but natural light from above. Sunlight? I feel a burst of optimism. It must have been near dawn when I crawled out of the coffin.

As we turn the last corner, a beam crashes down. Roderick falls beneath twisted and trapped.

"Go!" Roderick shouts. "Both of you, go."

"No." I kneel beside him. "If we can get out, we can escape. The curse is broken."

"All the more reason for you to leave me. I left you often enough."

Noah is trying to move the beam, hitting it with his shoulder. It only moves a tiny bit, and when that happens, Roderick screams.

He's broken. Noah hits the beam again, and this time it shifts away from Roderick, freeing him, but at the same time, tiles from the ceiling two floors above rain down, blocking the tunnel. We are on one side, Noah is on the other.

"Go up," I call to him. "To the tower. The house is collapsing inward—at least up there, you won't be crushed. The heights must still be aboveground. . . ."

"What about you?" He's starting to dig through the rubble that's separating us, but it's no use.

"We're going back down, to the vault."

"To bury him alive?"

Like he did to me? I don't acknowledge the shock of the question. The sudden pain. But the doctor hid in the burrows under the house. There is still a chance.

"The vault is reinforced with copper, and there are tunnels there that may lead outside."

He's still digging.

"You've done enough. More than any friend could be expected to do. Go now. Get out. Please, go."

Roderick clings to my hand, but I twist it away and wipe it on my skirt before sitting down and calmly retaking his hand in mine.

"We're Ushers," he says, and his voice sounds stronger than it has in a long time.

147

The earth rumbles, and trees fall, splintering like toothpicks.

A great fissure opens. The house trembles on the edge of the chasm, and the tarn empties itself. Waves crash over the slate tiles of the roof, and two tentacled arms wave in the air before they disappear into the fissure.

Small cracks slither over the surface, and the vines fall away as the stone and mortar disintegrate.

A figure appears, running amid the destruction. He trips when the ground beneath his feet drops; on his hands and knees, he crawls a few paces, desperate, and then picks himself up and begins to run again. Finally he can run no more, and so he walks with his head bowed.

Now there is silence. The fissure disappears, leaving nothing but a long, jagged scar in the dark earth.

He turns and looks, taking off his hat.

A wolfhound chases after him and puts her nose into his hand. She wags her tail and follows him for a few steps, and then she turns. She runs back to the barren earth where the house once stood, as though someone has called her. After a long moment, the young man joins her. The wolfhound shakes the tarn water from her thick fur, and side by side, they begin to dig.

Be swept away by the *Red Death* duology . . .

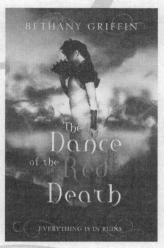

Everything is in ruins.

A devastating plague has decimated the population. And those who survived live in fear of catching it as the city crumbles to pieces around them.

So what does Araby Worth have to live for?

Beautiful dresses, glittery make-up . . . and so many tantalizing ways to escape from it all.

But in the depths of the Debauchery Club Araby may find something – or someone – not just to live for, but to fight for. No matter what it costs her.

Go beyond the pages with the

Newsletter!

Sign up for the

Fierce Fiction Newsletter

to get the inside information about your
favourite authors, your favourite books,
exclusive competitions, early reading
copy giveaways and the hottest book gossip!

fiercefiction.tumblr.com

Follow us 🐦 @fiercefiction
Find us 📘 facebook.com/FierceFiction